PENGUIN BOOKS
THE LOST VICTORY

Khushwant Singh was India's best-known writer and columnist. He was founder-editor of *Yojana* and editor of the *Illustrated Weekly of India*, the *National Herald* and *Hindustan Times*. He authored classics such as *Train to Pakistan*, *I Shall Not Hear the Nightingale* (retitled as *The Lost Victory*) and *Delhi*. His last novel, *The Sunset Club*, written when he was ninety-five, was published by Penguin Books in 2010. His non-fiction includes the classic two-volume *A History of the Sikhs*, a number of translations and works on Sikh religion and culture, Delhi, nature, current affairs and Urdu poetry. His autobiography, *Truth, Love and a Little Malice*, was published by Penguin Books in 2002.

Khushwant Singh was a member of Parliament from 1980 to 1986. He was awarded the Padma Bhushan in 1974 but returned the decoration in 1984 in protest against the storming of the Golden Temple in Amritsar by the Indian Army. In 2007, he was awarded the Padma Vibhushan.

Among the other awards he received were the Punjab Ratan, the Sulabh International award for the most honest Indian of the year, and honorary doctorates from several universities.

Khushwant Singh passed away in 2014 at the age of ninety-nine.

KHUSHWANT SINGH THE LOST VICTORY

RAVI
DAYAL

PENGUIN BOOKS

An imprint of Penguin Random House

PENGUIN BOOKS

USA | Canada | UK | Ireland | Australia
New Zealand | India | South Africa | China | Singapore

Penguin Books is part of the Penguin Random House group of companies
whose addresses can be found at global.penguinrandomhouse.com

Published by Penguin Random House India Pvt. Ltd
4th Floor, Capital Tower 1, MG Road,
Gurugram 122 002, Haryana, India

| Penguin
Random House
India

First published in the US as *I Shall Not Hear the Nightingale* by Grove Press
Inc., USA 1959
Published by Ravi Dayal Publisher 1997
Published in Viking by Ravi Dayal Publisher and Penguin Books India 2004
Published in Penguin Books 2005
This rejacketed and retitled edition published 2016

10 9 8 7 6 5 4 3 2

ISBN 9780143426325

Typeset by Rastrixi, New Delhi

Printed at Manipal Technologies Limited, India

www.penguin.co.in

MIX
Paper | Supporting
responsible forestry
FSC® C043100

This is a legitimate digitally printed version of the book and therefore might not
have certain extra finishing on the cover.

For
Manjushree Khaitan

The narration in this novel is set in 1942–3 from April to April

Chapter I

'There should be a baptism in blood. We have had enough of target practice.'

The trunk of a tree thirty yards away bore imprints of their marksmanship. Its bark was torn; in its centre was a deep, yellow gash oozing a mixture of gum and sap. From one branch dangled a row of metal heads of electric bulbs; their glass was strewn on the ground and shone like a bed of mica. Littered about the tree were tin cans and tattered pieces of cardboard sieved with holes.

'What about it, leader?' asked the smallest boy in the party slapping the butt of his rifle. 'We should sprinkle blood on our guns and say a short prayer to baptize them. Then they will never miss their mark and we can kill as many Englishmen as we like.'

Sher Singh smiled. He tossed his revolver in the air and caught it by the handle. He took careful aim at an empty sardine can and fired another six shots. The bullets went through into the earth kicking up whiffs of dust. His Alsatian dog, Dyer, began to whine with excitement. He leapt up with a growl and ran down the canal embankment. He sniffed at the tin and pawed it gingerly to make sure that it was dead, then picked it up in his mouth and shook it from side to side. He ran back with it and laid it at his master's feet.

'Why waste good bullets on tin cans and trees? What have they done to us?' asked another member of the party.

'That is why I say we should have a baptism in blood,' repeated the little boy.

'We will have our blood baptism when the time comes,' replied Sher Singh pompously. 'Let us be prepared for action. When duty calls, we will not be found wanting.'

'Brother, it is an old Hindu custom to baptize weapons before using them. Our ancient warriors used to dip their swords in a tray of goat's blood and lay them before Durga, Kali or Bhavani or whatever name the goddess of destruction was known by. We should keep up the tradition.'

Sher Singh could not make up his mind. He had never killed anything before. Even the sight of a headless chicken spouting blood as it fluttered about had made him turn cold with horror. He had been full of loathing for the cook who had wrenched off the fowl's head, and had given up eating meat of any kind for some months. But this was different. They were training to become terrorists. They had to learn how to take life — to become tough. He, more than the others, because he was their leader.

'My gun is thirsty,' went on the little boy. 'If it can't get the blood of an Englishman or a toady it must drink that of some animal or bird.'

There was a general murmur of assent. Only Sher Singh was reluctant. 'You don't want to smear the blood of a jackal or a crow on your guns, do you? What else can you find this time of the year? The shooting season closed two months ago.'

'We will find something or other round about the swamp,' assured Madan. 'There may be deer coming to drink. Perhaps a duck or two which could not migrate.'

That decided him finally. Madan was the strong man of the University. He had won his colours in many games and had played cricket for his province. His performance against a visiting English side — he had carried his bat after scoring a century — had made him a local hero. He had brought the other boys with him and would have been the leader of the band except that he knew little of politics. And it was Sher Singh, and not he, who had arranged the smuggling of rifles and hand-grenades from across the frontier. Although Sher Singh had assumed the leadership of the group, Madan was its backbone. He was both Sher Singh's chief supporter and rival: one whose presence was an encouragement and a challenge at the same time.

'O.K., brother, O.K.,' said Sher Singh in English and stood up. 'We must be quick. It will be dark in an hour.' He collected the empty cases lying on the ground and put them in his pocket. The boys also stood up and brushed the dust off their clothes. They put their guns in the jeep. One of them volunteered to stay back.

Sher Singh loaded his rifle and led the party down the canal bank towards the marsh. Dyer ran ahead barking excitedly.

They crossed the stretch of chalky saltpetre and got to the edge of the swamp. There were no birds on the water. On the other side was a peepul tree on which there was a flock of white egrets. Right on the top was a king vulture with its bald red head hunched between its black shoulders. Beneath the tree were bitterns wading in the mud. The birds were over a hundred yards away; well beyond Sher Singh's range of marksmanship.

The party surveyed the scene and considered the pros and cons of taking a shot from that distance. The vulture stuck out its head and the egrets began to show signs of nervousness. Suddenly there came the loud, raucous cry of a Sarus crane followed by another from its mate. They were in a cluster of bulrushes not fifty yards away. The boys sat down on their haunches and stopped talking. The cranes continued calling alternately for a few minutes and then resumed their search for frogs. The vulture and the egrets on the opposite bank went back to sleep.

'Kill one of these. They are as big as any black buck,' whispered the small boy.

'Who kills cranes?' asked Sher Singh. 'They are no use to anyone. And I am told if one of a pair is killed, the other dies of grief.'

'If you are going to funk shooting birds, you will not do much when it comes to shooting Englishmen,' taunted Madan. 'You will say, "Why kill this poor chap, his widow and children will weep," or "His mother will be sad." Sher Singhji, this is what is meant by baptism in blood; get used to the idea of shedding it. Steel your heart against sentiments of kindness and pity. They have been the undoing of our nation. We are too soft.'

That was enough to provoke Sher Singh — particularly as it came from Madan. 'Oh no! nothing soft about me,' he answered defiantly. 'If it is a Sarus crane you want, a Sarus crane you will have. Come along Dyer — and if you bark, I'll shoot you too.'

Sher Singh got down on his knees and crawled up behind the cover of the pampas grass, his dog following warily behind. He stopped after a few yards and parted the stalks with the muzzle of his rifle. One of the birds was busy digging in the mud with his long beak; the other was on guard turning its head in all directions looking out for signs of danger. Sher Singh decided to be patient. He wanted to get a little closer and also get enough time to take aim. Missing a bird of that size would be bad for his reputation.

After a few minutes, he looked through the stalks again. Both the cranes were now busy rummaging in the reeds. He crept up another ten yards, Dyer behind him. He paused for breath and once again parted the pampas stalks with the muzzle of his rifle. One of the birds was again on the lookout. Sher Singh drew the bead on the other — at the easiest spot to hit: the heavy, feathered middle of its body. The sentry crane spotted Sher Singh. It let out a warning cry and rose heavily into the air. Its mate looked up. Before it could move, Sher Singh fired. The bullet hit its mark. A cloud of feathers flew up and the bird fell in the mud. Dyer ran across to seize it. The boys came up from behind, clapping and shouting.

Sher Singh clicked open the catch; the metal case of the bullet flew out and fell on the ground. He picked it up and put it in his pocket. He blew into the barrel and saw the smoke shoot out of the other end. He was a jumble of conflicting emotions of guilt and pride. He had mortally wounded a harmless, inedible bird. But this was his first attempt to take life and it had succeeded. Then his friends came up, slapped him on the back and shook his hand by turn. The feeling of remorse was temporarily smothered.

The shot had not killed the crane. It flapped its wings and dragged itself out of the pool of blood a few feet farther towards the water. When Dyer came up, it turned towards him and pecked away fiercely with its long, powerful beak. The snarling and snapping Alsatian kept a discreet distance. Then the other crane flew back and began to circle overhead, crying loudly. It dived down low over the dog to frighten it away.

'Leader, give the other one its salvation too. Let them be together in heaven or hell.'

'Yes, let's see you take a flying shot,' added Madan.

The argument appealed to Sher Singh. The anguished cry of the flying crane was almost human. If he did not silence it, it would continue to haunt him for a long time. If both of the pair were dead, perhaps they would be together wherever cranes went after death. Sher Singh took out the magazine of his rifle and pressed six bullets in it. He followed the crane's flight with his barrel and fired when the bird was almost above him. The bullet went through one of the wings. The bird wavered badly in its flight and some feathers came floating down. Sher Singh fired the second shot. Then the third and the fourth and emptied the magazine. The crane flew away across the swamp, ducking nervously as the bullets whistled by in quick succession.

Sher Singh blew the smoke out of the barrel once more.

In his excitement he forgot to pick up the empty cases.

'Its time is not up yet,' said Madan to console him. 'Put this one out of its agony.'

Once having embarked on the bloody business, Sher Singh could not stop half way. He walked up to the injured bird and put his right foot on its neck. The crane began to kick violently and gasp for breath. Its beak opened wide showing its thin, long tongue. Sher Singh took out his revolver and fired two shots into its body. The bird's dying gurgle was stifled in its throat. Its legs clawed the air and then slowly came to a stop in an attitude of prayer. Blood started trickling from its beak and a film covered its small black eyes.

'This one is finished. Let us take it to the jeep and baptize our weapons in its blood.'

Two of the boys caught the crane by the wings from either end and dragged it out of the swamp. Dyer sniffed at the dead bird's head dangling between its trailing legs and began to run round in circles yapping deliriously. Sher Singh saw his handiwork and a lump came up in his throat. He did not respond to the backslapping and hilarity of his companions.

Before they got clear of the swamp the other crane flew back and started circling over them. They saw it high above in the deep blue sky catch the light of the

setting sun; then heard its cries piercing the stillness of
the dusk. Sher Singh ignored requests to have another
go at the flying bird; in any case it was too high and the
light was failing fast. When they got to the canal bank,
it became dark. The crane flew lower and lower till they
could see its grey form with its long legs almost above
their heads. They shoo'd it off. The bird disappeared in
the dark only to come back again and again. Its crying
told them it was there all the time, trying to reclaim its
dead mate. Sher Singh wanted to get away from the
place as fast as his jeep could take him. That was not
to be.

When they got to the jeep, they saw a Sikh peasant
talking to the boy they had left behind. He was obviously
waiting for them. When the man saw what the boys had
brought, he spat on the ground: 'Sardarji, why did you
have to take the life of this poor creature? Is anyone
going to eat it?' He spoke to Sher Singh as Sher Singh
was the only one carrying a gun.

'Oi Sardara, what do you know about these things?
Be on your way,' answered the boy holding one end of
the crane's wings.

The peasant spat again; the spittle fell near the foot of
the boy who had spoken rudely. 'The shooting season
closed two months ago and you are still going about
killing birds. Have you a licence?' he asked.

'Oi, who do you think you are?'

The peasant stood up. He was a big man standing
well over six feet. He was also broad and hairy.
Long strands of hair trickled out from all sides of his
clumsily-tied turban. A thick, black beard covered most

of his chest. He carried a bamboo staff shod with iron at either end.

'Keep quiet,' said Sher Singh angrily silencing his companion; then turned calmly to the peasant. 'There is no open or closed season for birds like these; that is only for game.'

'Nevertheless you have to have a gun licence,' continued the other truculently. 'I am the headman of the village beyond the swamp. I heard the firing. It sounded like machine-gun practice. You have to show me all your arms licences.'

'There is only one gun,' said Sher Singh with presence of mind. 'I will show you mine.'

He fished out his father's shotgun licence from his pocket and wrapped a five-rupee note in its folds. He put his arm around the peasant's shoulder and took him aside: 'Come along, Lambardar Sahib, you have got angry for no reason. You can see the licence and anything else you like.'

Madan felt that he was entitled to join them. Before Sher Singh could hand over the licence, Madan spoke to the headman: 'Lambardarji, you know who you are talking to? This is Sher Singh, son of Sardar Buta Singh, Magistrate. You have heard the name of Sardar Buta Singh, I hope.'

The headman turned to Sher Singh. He looked at him for a brief moment and then took Sher Singh's hands in his. The scowl on his face turned to a broad, friendly grin. 'Who doesn't know of Sardar Buta Singh?' he asked. 'But how should I have known! Do forgive me, Sardar Sahib.'

'Not at all,' answered Sher Singh. 'It is you who must forgive us for speaking rudely! You are a lambardar and we should respect you!'

'I am your slave,' said the peasant, touching Sher Singh's knee. 'The slave of your slaves. You must come to my humble home for some water or something.'

'That is very kind of you; we will another day. Do see my licence. And this is for your children.'

'No, no, Sardar Sahib,' protested the headman. 'Do not shame me. I am not short of money. By the Guru's blessing I have plenty to eat and drink. I only need your kindness. If you step into the hut of Jhimma Singh I will ask nothing more. Your slave is named Jhimma Singh.'

They rejoined the party. The headman's mood had changed completely. 'Babuji,' he said, addressing them all, 'if you are fond of shikar, you only have to say the word and I will arrange one for you. I could get the villagers to beat through the fields and you could shoot to your hearts' content. Partridge, hare, deer, wild pig — anything.'

'We will ask you when the shooting season opens,' answered Madan.

'Now you are making fun of me; I was only doing my duty as a headman. Sardar Buta Singh is the king of this district, who dare tell his son when he can or cannot shoot? Isn't that so Babuji . . . Babuji . . . what is our name?'

Before Madan could reply, Sher Singh answered, 'He is Mr Nasir Ali; he is a captain in the army.'

The boys took up the game eagerly and introduced each other to him with false names. The peasant shook hands with all of them. 'What have I to do with names? You are all friends of Sardar Sher Singh, that is enough for me,' he said with a knowing smile.

'If we have your permission,' said Madan taking the peasant's hand again. 'It is getting very late and I have to report at the cantonment by nine.'

'Of course, of course, Captain Sahib. Please forgive me for detaining you. You promise to let me know when you come next time?'

They all promised and parted the best of friends.

The boys threw the dead crane into the canal without the ceremonial baptism and turned back homewards.

It was evident that Sher Singh was still upset. One of the boys tried to draw him out. 'That was a narrow escape!' he said cheerfully. 'You know what these village headmen are! All informers. They would inform against their own parents to please the police. Leader, you were very clever in not letting him know Madan's name. Wasn't he?'

'Very clever. Great presence of mind,' they agreed.

'He knows mine,' said Sher Singh grimly.

Madan felt he had to explain. 'If I had not mentioned your father's name, he would not have let us go. He will never dare to say a word about you to anyone, you take my word for it. I know his type. He will probably come to you with presents of tins of clarified butter or farm produce. Really, you have no need to worry.'

Sher Singh did not answer. They all fell silent.

When they got to the end of the canal road, they found the way barred by the gate meant to keep off general traffic. The gateman heard the car and came out of his hut with his log book. Sher Singh took it from him and entered a name and a car number and handed it back. The gateman took the log book and examined the entry in front of the headlight. He looked at the number plate on the jeep and came back. He spoke politely but firmly: 'Sardar Sahib, I do not know English but I am not illiterate. You have put in a wrong number for the car. I will have to report it to the canal officer.'

'It is not his car, it is mine,' replied Madan promptly. 'He does not know the number. You enter the correct number and report it to anyone you like. Tell them it was the car of Mr Wazir Chand, Magistrate, driven by his son, Madan Lal. Now open the gate.'

The tone of authority did not fail to impress the gateman. He walked quietly to the gate and unlocked it. He salaamed as the jeep went past.

Everyone was convinced that Madan had atoned for his earlier indiscretion — if any. Even Sher Singh felt he had been a little mean in his resentment. 'If we let ourselves be bothered by informers and canal road gatemen, we won't get far with our plans. To hell with them. Revolutions cannot be stopped by vermin,' he proclaimed loudly.

'Indeed not,' added Madan. 'And what has anyone learnt anyhow? That you have a gun. Of course you have a gun — and a licence for it too. And that your father's jeep used the canal road! What more?'

Sher Singh felt very relieved. His fears were purely imaginary. He pulled up the jeep. 'I've had too much tea,' he announced. 'I will dedicate its remains to the lambardar and the gateman.'

They roared with laughter and leapt out of the jeep. They lined up along the deserted road. 'On the headman,' said one.

'On the headman and all informers.'

'On the headman, all informers, and all Englishmen.'

'No,' said the smallest boy, 'mine is for the Englishmen's Memsahibs.' They laughed louder and continued laughing for a long time.

'Quiet!' ordered Sher Singh. 'Listen.'

The laughter died down and they listened. Above the purring of the motor engine they heard the cry of the Sarus crane. They looked up into the black sky studded with stars. A large grey form flew up from the side of the road they had come. It circled over the jeep a couple of times and landed right in front of the glaring headlights. The crane called to its mate.

'It's been following us all the way; thinks we've got the other one in the car,' said the little boy. Even he could not bring himself to repeat the suggestion that Sher Singh should kill the bird. 'Brother Sarus,' he said addressing the crane, 'your dear mate is in heaven. Don't cry. Go and find yourself another wife.'

The crane turned to him without any sign of fear. It spread out its enormous wings and charged. The boy ran round the jeep. Dyer began to growl and bark but even he did not have the courage to attack the angry bird. Other boys came up yelling loudly and the crane retreated. It kept calling all the time.

The boys got back into the jeep and Sher Singh stepped on the accelerator as hard as he could. They heard the crane calling above them for a little distance till they mixed with the traffic going into the city.

After dropping the boys near the main bazaar and Madan at his house, Sher Singh drove home. He took the jeep into the garage which was at the back of the house alongside the servants' quarters. He locked the box containing the rifles and hand-grenades and put it back in the trench in the centre of the garage (meant for the mechanic to examine the car from the bottom) and covered it with greased rags and motor tools. He took his father's shotgun, bolted and locked the garage door and leant back against the wall to spend a few moments with himself before facing his wife and parents. Quite involuntarily he looked up into the sky. The figure of the crane flying in the dark and its crying came back to his mind. Then the picture of the wounded bird kicking its legs, the deafening reports of the pistol shots and the end of its struggle in an attitude of prayer like the effigies of ancient English kings on their tombstones. Now that Madan and the other boys were not there, the sense of assurance also left him and he began to be assailed with doubts. Would the headman report him to the police and the police to the Deputy Commissioner? Mr Taylor had been particularly good to his father whom he trusted more than any other officer in the district; that trust would be lost for ever. His father's career in service and hopes of recognition for what he was doing for the war would be dashed. And what would Buta Singh do if he came to know that his son had been misusing the jeep given by the government to further war work, to take out terrorists training for sabotage and to destroy people like him and Taylor?

It was strange, thought Sher Singh, that he had not really considered these possibilities before committing himself to the venture. He had somehow believed that he would muddle through, getting the best of the two worlds: the one of security provided by his father who was a senior magistrate, and the other full of applause that would come to him as the heroic leader of a band of terrorists. Now for the first time he realized how utterly incompatible the two were and he simply had to make a choice. He began to feel tired and depressed. There was his home with its high walls like those of a fortress. They enclosed the courtyard and the lit up rooms; it looked snug and friendly. From within came reassuring sounds: the voices of his mother and sister welcoming the dog who had gone in and his wife shouting to the servant to go and see why the young master was taking so long in the garage. And there was the world outside — dark and lonely. The gardener had flooded the lawn; it looked like a black sheet. Fireflies flitted about the ghostly forms of orange trees.

The courtyard door opened and the boy servant, Mundoo, came out to look for him. Sher Singh handed the shotgun to the boy and went indoors.

Although he had no appetite, he sat down to dinner to avoid the women nagging him. His wife and sister joined him. His mother, Sabhrai, who never ate before her husband had been served, also sat down with them.

'Did you get anything?' asked Champak.

'No, there is very little game about this time of the year. I thought I might get a pigeon or two, but we didn't come across any.'

'I am glad,' interrupted his mother. 'I don't like this business of killing poor, harmless birds.'

'Where is father?' asked Sher Singh.

'He hasn't come back from the club,' answered his mother. 'He had to ask a friend to give him a lift since you had taken the car. He was cross.'

'How was I to know he wanted it?'

'Son, it is not our car,' remonstrated Sabhrai gently. 'It has been given to your father for war work. He doesn't mind your using it but you must ask him. Also, he said if you are keen on shikar, you should apply for a licence and have the gun transferred to your own name.' She added, after a pause, 'If you ask for my advice, I would say, "Sell the shotgun." It is the cause of sin. To take the life of innocent creatures is sin.'

Sher Singh did not contradict her. Sabhrai tried to make up. 'You did not kill anything, so you don't have to bother.' She changed the subject abruptly. 'Why don't you help your sister with her examinations now you have the time? She has to go out to other people's homes to prepare for them.'

'No, thank you,' interrupted Beena hastily. 'Sita is giving me all the help I need. She is the best in our class.'

Mother and daughter began to argue. It gave Sher Singh the chance to get away. 'This heat has given me a headache,' he complained and stood up. 'I am going to bed.'

'Yes, you must be tired,' agreed his mother. 'Champak, press his head, he will sleep better.'

'I will,' replied Champak standing up. She bent her head to receive her mother-in-law's blessing. 'Sat Sri Akal.'

'Sat Sri Akal,' replied Sabhrai lightly touching Champak's shoulder.

'Sat Sri Akal,' said Sher Singh.

'Live in plenty. Live a long age,' replied Sabhrai taking her son's hand and kissing it. 'Sleep well.'

Sher Singh and Champak retired to their room on the side of the courtyard.

It was one of Sher Singh's grievances that since his marriage he had to give up sleeping in the open because his wife wanted privacy. The rest of the family slept on the roof and the courtyard was visible from it. So they had to be in the room and suffer the hot air churned up by the ceiling fan. They had been married only one year and Champak felt that wasn't asking too much. She forestalled his complaint. 'You have a bath and let the breeze of the fan dry you. That is the advantage of having a room of one's own. I will press your head and legs and you will sleep nicely.'

Sher Singh did as he was told and let his wife press his limbs. The service demanded returns to which he attended with as much enthusiasm as he could muster.

Neither the day's fatigue nor the sex produced the deep sleep they are reputed to produce. For a long time Sher Singh lay awake, staring at the ceiling and the walls. He saw the emblems of strength with which he had surrounded himself. Above the mantelpiece was a shield with the Sikh sabers crossed behind it. On his desk, the porcelain bust of the Mahratta warrior Shivaji; on the wall facing him a colour print of Govind Singh showing the Guru on horseback — his falcon with its wings outspread on his hand. On the other wall was a panel of photographs pinned on a wooden board. They showed him with the Student Volunteer Corps which he had organized the year before at the University. The one in the centre was of him in uniform taking the salute at a march past; another, receiving Mahatma Gandhi when he had come to visit his college; and two more shaking hands with VIPs. He saw these things and felt ashamed that the simple killing of a bird should have upset him. He had shrunk in his own estimation. He tried to recover his faith in his own courage and his future. He tried to seek solace from Madan's assurance that all the headman could tell was that Sher Singh had used his father's jeep and shotgun — nothing more. It was of little avail. He could not sleep. Four figures kept going round and round in his tortured mind. They were those of Madan, the headman, his father, and Mr Taylor. Then he began to dream. He saw himself crossing railway lines. There were four tracks with trains coming towards him from either side. He crossed one track and a train came up from the other direction. He jumped clear of the train on to the third track — only to find yet another train almost on him. He jumped clear of that too but found himself right in front of the engine on the fourth. He woke with a cry of terror and looked round for his wife. His cry had not wakened her. She lay like a nude model posing for an artist: one hand between her thighs covering her nakedness and the other stretched away to expose her bust.

Sher Singh wiped the cold sweat from his forehead. He put on his pyjamas and looked out of the window; it was dark without a trace of grey anywhere. He looked at the clock on the table; it was just after 3 a.m. He went back to bed and tried to sleep. Once more the four figures came back: Madan, the headman, his father, and Taylor. When sleep overtook him again, he found himself crossing the rail tracks once more. This time he kept reminding himself in his dream that this was only a dream. When one of the trains bore upon him he woke up — but without the cry of terror. The sky had turned grey and the morning star shone brilliantly. His mother and Shunno were already up and at work in the kitchen. He sat down in his armchair and tried to calm himself. A drongo started calling. Crows began to caw softly in their morning sleep and sparrows twittered dreamily — uncertain whether or not it was time to get up. Then all the crows began to caw furiously and all the sparrows began to chirrup. The spell was broken. A kite perched itself on the roof of the kitchen and let out its shrill piercing cry for food: *Kreel . . . Kreel . . . Kreel. . . Kreel.*

Sher Singh got up to face another day.

It was New Year's Day by the Hindu calendar. Sabhrai was expecting all the family in the temple for the first-of-the-month ceremony. Shunno, the maidservant, came twice to say the others were waiting. Sher

Singh had a quick bath and hurried to the room set apart for worship. His father and sister sat cross-legged on the floor facing the Granth. Buta Singh wore his magisterial dress of grey turban, black coat, and white trousers. A band of muslin ran round his chin and over his turban (it was meant to press his beard in shape). His grey drooping moustache fell on either side of the band. Both his sister, Beena, and his mother, Sabhrai, wore bright pink headpieces above their white Punjabi dresses. The prayer room also wore a festive appearance. The Holy Granth had been specially draped in silks for the occasion, with roses, marigolds, and jasmines strewn in front of it. From the four points of the velvet canopy above the holy book hung chains of coloured paper. From either side, sticks of incense sent spirals of scented smoke upwards to the canopy till the breeze of the ceiling fan scattered them about the room.

Sabhrai was reading the Granth quietly. She looked up and spoke to her son: 'We have been waiting for you for the last hour. Your father is in a hurry. He has to go to see the Deputy Commissioner.'

'How was I to know this was New Year's Day?' answered Sher Singh. 'Nobody told me.' Everyone knew that Sabhrai's remarks were really meant for her daughter-in-law. Before Champak could make her excuses, Buta Singh intervened. 'Let us get on with the service instead of arguing,' he said.

Sabhrai picked up the fly-whisk lying beneath the cot on which the Granth was placed and began to wave it over her head. She started with the hymn to spring:

It is spring and all is seemly —
The bumble-bee and the butterfly

And the woodlands in flower.
But there is sorrow in my soul,
For the Lord my Master is away.

If the husband comes not home, how can a wife
Find peace of mind?
Sorrows of separation waste away her body.

The koel calls in the mango grove,
Its notes are full of joy.

But O Mother of mine, it's like death to me
For there is sorrow in my soul.

How shall I banish sorrow and find blessed
     peace?

Spake the Guru: Welcome the Lord in your soul
     As a wife welcomes her master when she loves him.

Everyone bowed as the last words trailed off. Buta
Singh invoked the Guru loudly. Sabhrai ran the palms
of her hands along the broad pages of the holy book
and placed them on her eyes.

Shunno came in carrying a steaming tray, placed it
on a low stool in front of the Granth, and sat down in a
corner. On the verandah outside, Mundoo bullied little
children from neighbouring houses into keeping quiet
and sitting in a row. Behind him, whining impatiently,
was Dyer.

Sabhrai closed the massive Granth, holding the
ends reverently in her hands and then let it open as if

it had a will of its own. She scanned the opening lines of the first verse and, having assured herself that they prophesied no misfortunes to her family, read in a calm clear voice:

When I think of myself
Thou art not there;

Now it is Thee alone
And my ego is swept away.

As billows rise and fall
When a storm sweeps across the water;

As waves rise and relapse into the ocean
I will mingle with Thee.

How can I say what Thou art
When that which I believe is not worthy of
    belief?

It is as a king asleep on the royal couch
Dreams he is a beggar and grieves;
Or as a rope mistaken for a serpent causeth
    panic.
Such are delusion and fear.

Why should I grieve?
Why be panic-stricken?

If God is in every heart
And in every soul
He is in mine.

He has many manifestations
Yet is closer to us than our hands or feet.

These passages were always listened to carefully as prophetic announcements on problems which were uppermost in their minds. To Sher Singh the only lines that had significance were those asking him to discount delusions that caused fear and panic. The Guru himself had given him a personal assurance that he had mistaken a rope for a serpent and had really nothing to worry about. He was not religious or superstitious; nevertheless the words had a strange reassuring effect.

The ceremony ended with a short invocation recited by Buta Singh during which everyone remained standing. It was followed by the distribution of the prasad — a hot syrupy batter made of flour, sugar, and clarified butter. There was an awkward silence which made people conscious of the noise they made eating.

Buta Singh took off the beard-band and wiped his greasy hands on his beard and moustache. He looked at his wrist-watch. 'I must be going,' he announced in a tone of finality and stood up. 'A quick cup of tea and I must run.'

Everyone made a last obeisance in front of the Granth and went out into the verandah and put on their shoes. Sabhrai threw Dyer's share of the prasad into the air. The Alsatian leapt up and caught it in his mouth. They all adjourned to the breakfast table.

Buta Singh opened the morning paper. The family sat in silence waiting for him to say something. Sher Singh was particularly nervous. Would his father ask him about taking the government jeep for a private outing?

'The war seems to be going badly for the English,' he said at last, putting down the paper.

'Things are not too good for them,' answered his son, somewhat relieved.

Shunno brought a tray full of fried chapatis and vegetables. Sabhrai poured out the tea. The meal continued to be described as 'tea' although it was the main meal of the day, combining both breakfast and lunch.

'You take a lot of interest in politics,' continued Buta Singh, sipping his cup of tea. 'What do you think will happen to the British? The Japanese have driven them out of Burma. This chap Rommel has defeated them in Africa. German submarines sink British ships in English ports. They seem to be losing on every front.'

Sher Singh was always somewhat non-committal on political topics when talking to his father. 'I think we should be more concerned with what will happen to us,' he replied. 'We are far too concerned with other people. Our Communist friends are only worried about what will happen to Russia; others think only of what will happen to Britain. Very few of us are bothered with our own future.'

Buta Singh noticed the attempt to snub him. He ate a few pieces of chapati and curry before replying. The long pause was meant to convey disapproval of his son's tone of talking. 'You can say what you like,' he said at last, 'but I do believe that in this war our interests and that of the English are identical. If they lose, we lose. If we help them to win, they will certainly give us something more than we have now. We should know who are our friends and who are our enemies. The English have ruled us for over a hundred years, and I don't care what you say, I believe they have treated us better than our own kings did in the past; or the Germans, Italians, or Japanese will do if they win and take over India. We should stand by the English in their hour of trouble.'

'Why don't they let us help them? Gandhi is willing. Nehru is willing,' said Sher a little warmly.

'Don't talk like a child,' replied Buta Singh also warming up. 'What does their willingness amount to? Nothing. Are the British short of recruits? Despite your Gandhis and Nehrus more turn up than are wanted. And what are you to do with your Muslims? They don't want a free India until the country is cut up and they get their Pakistan. One should bargain with knowledge of one's weakness.'

It was only in recent years that Buta Singh had begun to think in terms of bargaining with the British. Before that, loyalty to the Raj had been as much an article of faith with him as it had been with his father and grandfather who had served in the army. He, like them, had mentioned the English king or queen in his evening prayer. 'O, Guru, bless our Sovereign and bless us their subjects so that we remain contented and happy.' Then things had begun to change. Gandhi had made loyalty to the British appear like disloyalty to one's own country and traditions. Larger and larger numbers of Indians had begun to see Gandhi's point of view. People like Buta Singh who had been proud of being servants of His Britannic Majesty were made to feel apologetic and even ashamed of themselves. Loyalty became synonymous with servility, respect for English officers synonymous with sycophancy. What shook the faith of people like Buta Singh was the attitude of the new brand of Englishmen coming out to India. Buta Singh would have withstood the scorn of his countrymen; but he could not withstand the affection of people like Taylor. Other English officers had kept their distance from Indians and set up the pattern of the rulers and the ruled. Taylor, on the other hand, not only met Indians as equals, made friends with his subordinates, but also openly expressed his sympathies with Gandhi and Nehru. At first Buta Singh had looked upon Taylor's professions with suspicion. When he was convinced of the Englishman's sincerity, he began to look upon him as an oddity — an oddity he respected and liked.

Buta Singh could not comprehend why any Englishman would like to see the end of British rule in India. But many besides Taylor had begun to say so. And most of the Indians were actively agitating for its end. In this state of flux Buta Singh had decided on a muddle-headed and somewhat dishonest compromise. When he was with Englishmen he protested his loyalty to the Raj. 'At my age, I cannot change,' he would say. When he was amongst his own countrymen, he would be a little critical of English ways. He let his son cast his lot with the Nationalists and did not object to his organizing the students and making political speeches. He explained his son to Taylor as 'of your way of thinking.' By many people, Buta Singh was described as double-faced; any compromise in a situation like the one in which Buta Singh found himself would appear to unsympathetic people as double-faced.

They ate in silence. Buta Singh finished his meal with a loud belch. 'Oi, water for my hands.'

Mundoo brought a jug of water and basin and handed his master a cake of soap. Buta Singh washed his hands and rinsed his mouth without getting up from his chair. He belched again and dried his hands and mouth with the towel. A bit of curry stuck to his moustache.

'A bulbul on the bough,' said Sabhrai with a smile. Buta Singh wiped his moustache with the towel again.

'Now!'

'Still on the bough,' said Sabhrai giggling. Buta Singh brushed his moustache a third time.

'Now!'

'It has flown,' they all replied in a chorus and burst out laughing. The atmosphere changed to one of hilarity. Sabhrai noticed her husband glance at his watch. She made another attempt. 'Will any of you have the time to go to the temple today?' she asked.

'I have to see the Deputy Commissioner first,' answered her husband. 'On days like these there is always danger of Hindu-Muslim riots; all magistrates have to be on duty. I will go if I have the time.'

'I have to be there,' replied Sher Singh. 'We have organized a meeting outside the temple.'

'You go to the temple before you go to your meeting,' snapped his mother.

'And,' added Buta Singh with indulgent pride, 'don't say anything which may cause trouble. Remember my position. I do not mind your hobnobbing with these Nationalists — as a matter of fact, it is good to keep in with both sides — but one ought to be cautious.'

'O no, no,' answered Sher Singh. 'I know what to say and what not to say.'

It was not customary to consult the girls. Beena was expected to go with her mother unless there were good reasons for not doing so. She knew her only chance of getting away was to bring up the subject while her father was still there. 'There are only a few weeks left for my exams. I had promised to go to Sita's house to work with her. We help each other with the preparation.'

'Why can't she come here? Why do you always have to go to her?' asked Sabhrai. She had been getting more and more difficult about Beena going to Sita's house. Her sharp tone made Buta Singh react adversely. He came to his daughter's rescue.

'Let her go to Sita's. There will be nobody in the house today to give her lunch or tea. I will drop you at Wazir Chand's house.'

That ended the argument. Buta Singh's word was never questioned. The only one left was Champak. Sabhrai was not much concerned with her plans. If she came to the temple, she would not say anything. If she decided to shut herself in her room with her radio at full blast — as she often did — she would still say nothing. Nevertheless Champak felt that the situation demanded some explanation from her. 'I haven't washed my hair for a long time. If it dries in time, I will go in the afternoon — if I can find anyone to go with. Otherwise I'll stay at home and put away the Granth after evening prayers.'

Buta Singh looked at his wrist-watch. 'I must be going,' he announced with a tone of finality and stood up. 'Get your books and things, Beena.'

'Baisakhi Day! All the world is on holiday but we have to work. Others go to their temples, mosques, or gurudwaras; this is our temple and mosque.'

Buta Singh made this comment to his colleagues sitting in a circle in the verandah of the Deputy Commissioner's house. They had all been told the evening before to present themselves at 10 a.m. sharp. 'I would like to know what the Sahib would say if this were Christmas Day,' he added.

His colleagues refused to be provoked.

'They are our rulers,' exclaimed one. 'What they order we obey.'

'I agree with Sardar Buta Singh,' said another. 'But who is to bell the cat?'

'Sardar Sahib, you are the seniormost amongst us. Why don't you tell the Deputy Commissioner not to summon us on religious holidays?' asked Wazir Chand with a smile. He had a way of talking to people which made them feel small or stupid; Buta Singh found his tone particularly irritating. He did not mind the attempt to trip him — that was fair according to the rules of the game — but he objected to being taken to be so simple as to fall into so obvious a trap.

'I am quite willing to tell the Sahib; I don't care,' answered Buta Singh. 'Don't you know that I told the last Deputy Commissioner? He kept sending for me on every religious festival saying, "Duty first, duty first." I told him plainly: "Sahib, duty or no duty, I am going to the gurudwara. If you do not like it, here is my resignation." That made him quiet. Mr Wazir Chand, it is not leadership we lack but unity. I say one thing to the Sahib and another goes behind my back and says something else.'

Wazir Chand knew the last remark was meant for him. 'Sardar Sahib, you are a big man and we are but small radishes from an unknown garden,' he said with mock humility. 'You lead and we follow. Don't you agree?' he asked, turning to the others.

There was a murmur of assent. Buta Singh was angry. Before he could retaliate, the Deputy Commissioner's orderly interrupted them. 'The Sahib sends his salaams,' he said, addressing Buta Singh.

Buta Singh's anger vanished; the Sahib had sent for him first. He rose with deliberate ease to impress the others that he took this sort of thing in his stride. He stopped in front of the hat-rack to adjust his tie and turban. He gave his beard a gentle pat, and went in.

Taylor received him in his dark, air-cooled office. They shook hands and Buta Singh took a chair on the other side of the working table. Taylor helped himself to a cigarette and pushed the box in front of his guest. Buta Singh shook his head.

'Beg your pardon, Buta Singh. I keep forgetting I mustn't offer a cigarette to a Sikh.'

'That is all right, Sahib. Just an old superstition,' explained Buta Singh. His reaction to a similar indiscretion by a fellow Indian would have been a little more emphatic.

Taylor lit his cigarette; a cigarette usually determined the length of the interview.

'Sorry to have sent for you on a holiday; it's something like Christmas for you, isn't it? I hope you don't mind.'

'Mind?' queried Buta Singh in a tone of righteous indignation. 'Mind, Sahib! It is our duty. What impression would the people in Delhi get if they heard that while these Japanese are at our gates, we can't even keep law and order in our towns just because it is Baisakhi Day and the magistrates want a holiday? Sahib must have seen what the American paper, *The New York Times* has said: "India talks —Japan acts!" There is some truth in that. Air raid warnings in Calcutta, bombs dropping on Colombo, and here, our so-called Nationalists and Muslims are quarrelling about little details with the English instead of getting on with the work.'

'I wish other Indians talked like you, Buta Singh! I rely on you to guide them. I do not anticipate any trouble today but one never knows. A small incident may lead to a major riot. There are some politicians looking for trouble. I am told there are many meetings this afternoon.' Taylor paused to drop the ash off his cigarette. As Buta Singh made no comment, he continued, 'The Superintendent of Police informs me that your son has also organized a meeting of students. I told him not to bother about him. "If he is Buta Singh's son," I said, "we can trust him, even if he is a Nationalist or a Communist or anything else." '

'You are most kind, Sahib. He is a young man and you know what youth is! Hot and full of ideas. But he is all right. He is, as you say, Buta Singh's son. And through his hobnobbings with these Gandhi-capped Congress wallahs and Red flag wallahs, Buta Singh knows what is going on in the city and whom to watch.'

Buta Singh's accent and vocabulary changed when he spoke to Englishmen. 'Wallah' figured prominently in his speech.

Taylor stubbed his half-smoked cigarette. Buta Singh understood that the interview was over. 'What are the orders for the day, Sahib?' he asked, standing up.

'No orders, Buta Singh,' answered Taylor, coming up. 'Just tell the magistrates to leave information of their movements so that we can get them quickly at short notice; you can organize that. I will be at the fair. Shall I see you there?'

Buta Singh was not going to lose the opportunity of being seen in Taylor's company by milling crowds. Almost the entire Sikh population of the district turned up to see the procession and the fair outside the walls. 'Yes sir. I will be there in the afternoon and then with the procession.'

'Well, see you later, Buta Singh. Your excellent work in the collection of war funds and in recruiting soldiers will not go unrewarded. I will speak to the Commissioner.'

'Thank you, Sahib. Thank you. You are most kind.' Buta Singh knew that this was a reference to the next Honours list. That sort of thing still mattered although other things mattered more. 'Sir, I have a small request to make.'

'Yes.'

'You know, sir, I do not like to ask for personal favours.'

'Yes, yes, Buta Singh. Anything I can do for you, I will. What is it?'

'Sir, my work in collecting funds and furthering the war effort has caused a lot of envy. I receive letters threatening my life. I am not afraid, but if I could get a police guard at my house for a few days, it would stop evil designs. If it is at all inconvenient . . .'

'No, no. I will speak to the Superintendent of Police; this is a very small matter. Well, goodbye, Buta Singh. And thank you once more.'

'There is nothing to thank me about, sir. I thank you, sir. Goodbye, sir.'

Buta Singh emerged from the meeting wreathed in smiles. 'Chutti!' he announced triumphantly clicking his thumb and middle finger in the air. 'Holiday! Go home or wherever you like.'

'Why, what happened?' asked his brother magistrates getting up from their chairs.

'Why do you want to know? I promised you a holiday and I have got you a holiday. Haven't I been true to my word?'

Buta Singh extended his hand. The magistrates smacked it in turn. 'Can I be of any other service?' he asked with exaggerated politeness when Wazir Chand touched him with his limp hand.

'Long live Sardar Buta Singh!' answered Wazir Chand.

Wazir Chand's home was very much like Buta Singh's except that it was Hindu instead of Sikh and not so concerned with religion and ritual. As a matter of fact the only evidence of religion in the house was a large colour print of Krishna whirling a quoit on the mantelpiece of the sitting-room. Wazir Chand's wife occasionally put a garland of flowers round it and touched the base of its frame as a mark of respect. She did the same to a portrait of Mahatma Gandhi which was kept discreetly away in the bedroom.

The real 'god' in Wazir Chand's home was the son, Madan Lal. He was a tall, handsome boy in his early twenties. Being the only son, he had been married as soon as he had finished school and had become a father in his second year at college. He had not made much progress in his studies, but had more than compensated for that shortcoming by his achievements in sports. His promotion from one class to another had to be arranged by the college authorities. He was doing his sixth year at the college and had not yet taken the degree which normally took four. But the mantelpiece of every room in the house displayed an assortment of silver trophies which he had won in athletics and other team games. He had been captain of the University cricket eleven for three years and had played for his province against a visiting English side. His performance at this match had made him a legend in the Punjab. There were few days in the year when the sporting columns of the papers did not have some reference to his activities. This was a matter of great pride for his parents. They gave into every one of his whims; they practically worshipped him.

The only thing in common between the tall and broad Madan and his slim, small sister, Sita, was their good looks. He was bold and easy with strangers; she almost tongue-tied and shy. His obsession for games was matched by her aversion to any form of sport. He avoided books; she spent all her time with them. He had barely scraped through the exams he had passed; she had won the highest scholarship for girls in the University. The combination of the athletic prowess of one and the academic distinction of the other and the looks of both had made them the most sought after couple in the University circles. It was after several months' abject admiration and hanging around that Beena had succeeded in getting to know Sita.

Beena's anxiety to please Sita made her gushing and enthusiastic about everyone and everything in Wazir Chand's home. She addressed Sita's parents in English as 'uncle' and 'auntie.' Madan and his wife she addressed as 'brother' and 'sister' in Punjabi. She spent hours playing with their son and teaching him to call her 'auntie.' Sita was just Sita; but Beena repeated her name as often as she could in every sentence almost as if she feared losing her if she did not.

Madan had just returned from an early morning practice at the nets when Beena came in. His shirt was drenched with sweat and clung to his body displaying a broad hairy chest. Although it was hot, he carried his white flannel blazer on his shoulder. Its outside pocket bore the insignia of the University with rows of letters in old Roman embossed in gold lace beneath. He was playing with his son who was trying to walk in his father's cricket boots. The scene was too overpowering for Beena. She rushed to the child, picked him up and covered him with kisses.

'Ummm, ummm. Little darling wants to wear Papa's shoes. Namaste Bhraji.'

'Sat Sri Akal,' replied Madan without getting up or removing the cigarette from his lips.

Beena hugged the child and wheeled him round and round; her pigtails flew in the air. The child began to whimper. She thrust him into his father's lap. 'He likes you more than he likes me. Bhraji, where is Sita and Lila sister and Auntie and Uncle?'

'Father has gone to see the Deputy Commissioner. Mother is in the kitchen. Sita is studying. Lila is in her room; she is not feeling too well. And yours sincerely is at your service.' Madan got up and bowed.

Beena ignored his pleasantry. 'Hai! What's wrong with Lila sister?' she asked with exaggerated concern; she frequently used 'hai' to express it. 'Nothing serious, I hope. I must go and see her.'

'No, no, it's nothing, really nothing. Just a little out of condition,' answered Madan. 'She is in her room.'

Beena picked up the child once more and hurried to Lila's room. Lila explained that she was not really ill; the feeling of nausea came on only in the mornings. When Beena persisted in her inquiries, Lila patted the back of her hand and said she would understand better when she was married. Beena understood and blushed with embarrassment. She sat with Lila till Sita came to take her away. 'Madan says he can take us to a matinée show this afternoon. We can work for two or three hours and go with him. Lilaji, you will be all right by the afternoon, won't you?'

'I'd better not go. The stuffy atmosphere of the cinema will make me sick and your brother will get cross with me. You two go with him.'

Beena had a twinge of conscience. Studies were considered sacred enough to excuse going to the temple. But in her home the cinema was still associated vaguely with sin. The only time the family went to the pictures was to see the life of some saint or other or some story with a religious theme. Regular cinema goers were contemptuously described as tamasha-lovers. If her mother learnt that she had spent the afternoon at a cinema instead of the temple, she would use it as an excuse to stop her coming to Sita's house. 'No, I really could not. I haven't asked my mother,' said Beena quickly.

'She would not object if you came with us. I am sure she would not,' assured Sita.

'And yours sincerely is not going to invite you every day,' added Madan in his half-baked stage manner as he came in. 'Besides we won't tell anyone. We will go in when the show has started and you can cover your face during the intermission.' He drew his hand across his face to imitate a woman drawing her veil.

'It's not as bad as that,' answered Beena laughing. 'If I had asked first, it would have been better.' Before she could check herself in her imaginary flight to freedom she heard herself say: 'Of course I'll go with you but we must work first.'

During the time that Beena went over her notes and textbooks in Sita's room she was bothered by what she would say when she got back. If she said nothing and her parents found out it would take many months to re-establish her credit. Perhaps she could mention it casually as something she had been compelled to do. She was seventeen and wasn't going to be bullied by her illiterate mother any more. Pictures could be instructive; maybe this one would have a religious theme and she could persuade her mother to see it too. By the time they left the house, her mind was a muddle of fear and rebellion.

A tonga was sent for the two girls. They took their seats in the rear while Madan rode on his bicycle behind them. He wore a new silk shirt with short sleeves and carried his white flannel blazer on his shoulder; the gold crest and rows of initials glittered in the sun. He kept up a loud conversation with the girls, in between nodding and waving to the many acquaintances he met on the road.

The cinema was crowded. Peasants who had turned up for the Baisakhi festival from neighbouring villages were milling round the cheaper ticket-booths and around the stalls selling soft drinks. The tonga made its way through the crowd and drove up to the porch. Two cinema assistants rushed to take Madan's bicycle. He was a regular visitor and had admirers all over the city. Besides, he was the son of a magistrate; and magistrates, policemen, their friends and families, had privileges which go with power.

The manager of the cinema came out to welcome them and show them to their seats. Madan took out his wallet and pulled out a ten-rupee note. The manager caught his hand and pressed the note and wallet back into Madan's pocket. 'No question of money,' he protested. 'It's on the house.' Madan whispered in his ear that the other girl was Buta Singh's daughter. The manager turned to Beena with an obsequious smile. 'How is your revered father?' he asked, rubbing his hands. Beena replied politely that he was well. 'So glad to hear it. We pray to God he should always remain well. Do convey my respects to him. And any time any of your family want to come to the cinema, please ring me up. It will be an honour for us — a great honour.' Beena promised to convey the information to her father.

The party was conducted to a box reserved for VIPs and pressed to take something to eat or drink. The manager withdrew after extracting a promise that his hospitality would be accepted during the intermission.

Madan took his seat between the two girls. He lit a cigarette and the box was soon full of cigarette smoke and the smell of eau de cologne with which he had daubed himself.

The lights were switched off and the cries of hawkers of betel leaves, sweetmeats, and sherbets, and the roar of hundreds of voices died down. First came a series of coloured slides advertising soaps, hair oils, and films that were to follow. The literate members of the audience read their names loudly in chorus. Then the picture started and the few recalcitrant talkers were silenced by abuses loudly hurled across the hall.

Madan stubbed his cigarette on the floor and lit another one. In the light of the flame he saw his sister completely absorbed in the film. He held his cigarette in his left hand and put his right lightly on the arm of Beena's chair.

Beena's mind was still uneasy about the consequences of the escapade. She tried to drive away unpleasant thoughts by concentrating on the film and enjoying the feeling of being with Sita and her brother. He looked so dashingly handsome in his silk shirt, flannels, and sports blazer; he smoked with such compelling nonchalance and exuded that heavenly, cool, and clean fragrance of good eau de cologne.

Madan's hand slipped down the arm of the chair and came into contact with Beena's elbow. For a moment she held her breath. He seemed to be engrossed in the film and could not have realized how far his hand had travelled. She did not remove her elbow lest the gesture offend him. It was pleasant to have him so close. His hand stayed where it was till the lights came on for the intermission. He casually smoothed his hair and began discussing the film with his sister.

The manager reappeared followed by a relay of bearers carrying trays of soda pop, ice-cream, and fried potatoes. He started talking to Sita. Madan turned to Beena. 'You know, your brother and I have become great friends. For so many years we have been in the same University and it is only now we have got to know each other. He is the most popular man in the students' circles.'

'More popular than you, Bhraji? I don't believe it. We have all seen you play cricket; so has everyone in the world, my God!'

'Cricket is nothing,' said Madan with disdain. 'Our brother, Sher, will go far. He is almost certain to be elected President of the Students' Union. He is the best candidate and I am getting all my friends to vote for him.'

'Your name alone should win him the election. Everyone in the city knows you. We were at the match when you scored your century against the English eleven. I . . . everyone . . . was so proud of you. Sixer after sixer. Oh, it was wonderful!'

'It is nothing. You could be a good cricketer if you tried. You have an athletic figure.'

Beena blushed. That was the first time anyone had paid her a compliment, and it was Madan, *the* Madan. 'Oh Bhraji, I am no good. I couldn't see the cricket ball coming towards me at that speed.'

'Yes you could. With those eyes of yours you could hit anything for six,' said Madan, bending close to her to avoid the manager or his sister overhearing.

'Hai Bhraji, you are really terrible. Making fun of a girl like me!'

The conversation was interrupted by the bearers coming to collect empty glasses and plates. The manager was still rinsing his hands with invisible soap. He took his leave promising to appear again at the end of the show.

As soon as the lights went out, Madan put his hand on the arm of Beena's chair. This time she knew it was not an accident. She could hardly believe that anyone, let alone Madan, would want to make a pass at a plain and simple girl like her. It was unbelievably flattering. But he was married and it was obviously wrong. Beena had no doubt about Madan's intentions as his fingers closed round her elbow. Would he get angry if she withdrew? What would Sita say if she saw? Madan began to caress her arm. Beena did not move. Then his hand brushed against her breast. She shrank away into the farther corner of her chair. Madan calmly lit another cigarette and took no further notice of her.

When they came out of the cinema, the road as far as one could see was a jostling mass of peasants, tongas, bicycles, and hawkers. Around the ticket-booths men were clustered like bees on a hive. Streams of weary, blinking people came out from the many exits; newcomers stood around impatiently for their turn to go in.

A tonga was waiting for them in the porch and a cinema attendant had Madan's bicycle ready. The manager was there bowing, smiling, and still rubbing his hands. He bade them farewell after many reminders that they were to consider the cinema as their own. They went through the crowd with the tonga-driver shouting at the pedestrians loitering on the road. Madan cycled slowly behind. Whenever the tonga stopped, he put his foot on the ground and then cycled on with a slight push. Throughout the journey he did not talk to nor even look up at Beena.

Beena was dropped home first. She said a hurried 'Namaste' and disappeared inside the house. Fortunately for her only Champak was in and she seemed too taken up with the radio programme to bother. Beena went to her room and bolted it from the inside. She flung herself on her bed and lay there in the heat. When it got dark she switched on her table lamp and continued lying on her bed staring blankly at the ceiling.

There is no wine in the world as heady as applause; and it has the same effect. It temporarily subdues anxiety and restores confidence.

Even before Sher Singh arrived on the scene, there was a large crowd to receive him. The uniforms and smartness of the Students' Corps impressed the peasants more than volunteers of the Nationalist and Communist Parties in their slovenly shirts and loose pyjamas. The S.V.C. also used modern techniques to draw the masses. Although they were largely Sikhs (hence Madan and the Hindu boys of the terrorist gang were not present), it was not Sikh religious songs they played over their microphone. They started off with the most popular songs from the films and large numbers of peasants came over from other meetings which had nothing better to offer than political tirades or religious sermons. Thereafter they switched on to martial music. The Volunteers paraded up and down the fair grounds keeping step with the military march which blared from the microphone. Then Sher Singh arrived, like a field marshal coming to inspect his troops. There was much shouting of commands and saluting. He unfurled the S.V.C.'s black flag with silver sabers crossing on it. He took the salute at the march-post and went up to the rostrum to address the throng.

The fear of discovery of the activities of the day before, the sinister figure of the village headman, and the wrath of his father, receded into the dim background.

Sher Singh knew that there were police reporters in the audience and whatever he said would be reported to Mr Taylor by the evening. A war was on and the police were armed with powers to arrest and detain at will. He had to be cautious with his words. There was a limited range of subjects to choose from, but an infinite variety of forms of expression. He started in a tone of humility. He paid homage to the Gurus, repeated the well-known facts of the day they were commemorating, and then switched on to political problems. 'Comrades, we meet at a critical time. The enemy is at our gates.' He paused to let his words seep in; then he lowered his voice to a confidential whisper. 'Comrades, we not only have the enemy at our doorstep, we have enemies within our own house.' He raised his voice: 'Those who sacrifice the interests of the motherland for foreign countries are our enemy No. 1. They have been rightly named as the *Kaum nashts* — destroyers of the race.' He paused for applause. The audience had heard the pun on the word 'Communist' before so there was no response. Sher Singh went on: 'There are also people who want to cut off the limbs of Mother India and make another state of Pakistan. They too are our enemies.' Even this did not arouse any applause. His Volunteers were not doing their duty. Sher Singh worked himself into a fury and let his voice rise to a crescendo. 'But we are Sikhs who do not fear any enemies. We shall destroy all those who stand in our way.' A roar of applause went up. One of the Volunteers ran up to the mike and shouted 'Sher Singh;' the Volunteers in the crowd answered 'Long live.' The crowd joined in. Sher Singh allowed the applause thirty seconds and then raised his hands demanding silence. He started again. 'Comrades . . . ' He could not proceed further because of a clamour from the farther end of the marquee. People shouted to say that they could not hear. The mike was dead. Volunteers rushed up to test it. They tapped it, yelled, 'Hullo, Hullo. One, two, three four. Hullo, hullo, hullo.' But the mike refused to respond. The mechanic fumbled with the battery and it suddenly came to life with a piercing boom. Sher Singh tried again. 'Can you hear me now?' The heads at the far end nodded. 'Comrades,' he started. Once more they waved their hands to say 'No.' The mike was dead again. This time even the mechanic's fumbling with the wires did not bring it back to life. The meeting dispersed.

Sher Singh knew it was no use losing his temper; in nine cases out of ten, meetings ended because of mechanical breakdowns. In any case he had said the two important things he wanted to say and the crowds had seen him and his S.V.C.

Sher Singh spent the morning with his Volunteer friends going round the stalls at the fair and standing them soda pop. In the afternoon he watched the procession pass by. It was over a mile long with brass bands, parties of singers, men demonstrating sword and stick play, more parties of singers on top of motor lorries, in trucks and bullock carts — ending with the flower-bedecked van which carried the Holy Granth guarded by five Sikhs with drawn swords. By then it was late and he was too tired to go to the temple. He decided to look up Madan and tell him about the big turnout at his meeting. He might also get to know Madan's pretty sister whom he had seen but never met.

Sher Singh collected his bicycle from the stand at the fair ground and cycled down to Wazir Chand's house. He put the cycle against the pillar of the porch and went into the verandah. The wire-gauze door leading into the courtyard was bolted from the inside and the house seemed empty. Sher Singh rattled the door and shouted *'Koi Hai.'* He heard Madan's mother shout to the servant to see who was at the door. The servant

came up and without opening the door informed Sher
Singh that no one was at home.

'I have come for Beena. She came over to study with
Sita Bibi.'

'The Bibijis have gone to the cinema,' answered the
boy. They went with our Babu. Will you come in and
wait for them?'

'I will come again.'

'What is your name?'

Sher Singh did not answer. He picked up his bicycle
and rode home.

Absence of privacy is a phenomenon that pervades
all life in India, urban and rural, of the rich and the
poor. It has been so for many centuries and the weight
of tradition is heavy against those who live in society
and still wish to be alone. Rooms of Indian palaces
seldom had any doors and those that did could rarely
be bolted from the inside. There was never any need for
doors because the most intimate of relationships could
apparently be consummated and enjoyed under public
gaze. Examine any old painting depicting a love scene.
There will be the prince and his paramour in different
stages of disarray — one of his hands on her bosom,
the other holding the pipe of his hookah. Standing by
will be female servants fanning away flies, sprinkling
scented water, or serving wine. In the background there
will be a party of musicians and singers.

Amongst the poor, shortage of living space has
always made privacy an expensive luxury.

Things have not changed very much over the centuries. Amongst the Westernized well-to-do class, although separate bedrooms and bathrooms are provided for members of a family, the spirit remains the same: to want to be alone is to be queer. Amongst the middle, lower middle, and the working classes, the joint family system requires large numbers of kinsfolk to live under the same roof. They eat together, sleep together — men in one row, women, in a different part of the house, in another — go and relieve themselves in groups, bathe in rivers or by wells in company and accept the possibility of relations watching sexual intimacies through keyholes.

The cheek by jowl existence in an Indian joint family has many consequences. In the first place, an Indian whose soul yearns to know itself has no option but to take the extreme step of renouncing life and seeking solitude as a hermit. It combines an inner craving with outward respectability. This certainly is one, if not the most important, reason why so many in the country take to the ascetic life of the yogi.

Another consequence of the absence of privacy is that the art of making love, which demands the strictest privacy as well as leisure, is practically unknown. In the land of the *Kama Sutra* and phallus worship, sex is practiced in conditions which provide neither the time nor the opportunity for a man to rouse the passions of his woman to that fever heat which makes her yearn for lusty fulfilment. The institution of the honeymoon where a young married couple can make each other's physical acquaintance is unknown except amongst the anglicized upper middle class. For the rest, a newly married girl's first few experiences follow a soulless pattern. After some days her mother-in-law will persuade her to take a tumbler of milk to her husband before he goes to sleep (other members of the household having been told to be away for the time). More likely, the girl will go to a tryst in the fields after dark on the pretext of answering the call of nature. She will be brutally ravished by her impatient husband equally anxious to hurry back home to keep up the appearance of having gone out to ease himself. That is all most Indian women know of sex — an unpleasant subjection to men's desires — necessary in order to have sons, bearable because of its brevity. To the mass of Indian womanhood, the sixty-five ways of kissing and petting, the thirty-seven postures of the sex act so beautifully portrayed in stone on temple walls make as much sense as a Greek translation of the treatise *Kama Sutra* itself. Unfulfilled sexual impulses result in an obsession with sex and in many perversions which result from frustration: sadism, masochism, and, most common of all, exhibitionism.

People, when they are left alone, find that they cannot help behaving in an odd way. This is strange because one would expect those who do everything under public gaze to be less inhibited, and therefore have less to get out of their systems than those who enjoy privacy. However, the one desire which those who live in crowds have to suppress is that of self-discovery. This is suddenly aroused in momentary solitude and is expressed in acts which appear quite mad. Thus a man, normally sober and steady, who finds himself alone in a railway compartment, may get the urge to sing loudly, expose himself, or even indulge in adolescent pastimes. He will continue to behave oddly till he gets used to the idea of being alone.

Buta Singh's home had made some concessions to Western notions in the matter of privacy. There were separate bedrooms for everyone, with the married couple having a bathroom of their own. Champak spent as much time as she could in her own room with her radio. She was also given to taking a long time at her bath. On religious holidays, because everyone went out, she stayed at home. She could then stroll about the courtyard in her dressing-gown with her hair loose about her shoulders, and she could also sing loudly to herself.

On Baisakhi day Sabhrai had ordered Mundoo to stay at home to scrub kitchen utensils and heat the water for Champak's bath. Champak protested there was no need for hot water, but her mother-in-law had her way. 'Hair washes better with hot water,' she had insisted.

Champak sulked in her room. She switched on the radio and lay on her bed reading her favourite film magazine. After some time, she flung the magazine on the floor and looked out into the courtyard. Mundoo sat on his haunches scrubbing a big brass pitcher with ash. Beside him, on a smoking hearth, was a large tin canister.

'Oi Mundoo, is the water hot or not?'

The boy patted the canister with his dirty hands. 'No, Bibiji, not yet. It will be ready in a few minutes.'

He went down on his hands and knees and blew into the hearth. Smoke and ash whirled round the hearth and into his eyes. He stood up and wiped his tears with the hem of his greasy shirt. All he wore besides the shirt was a red loin cloth which only covered his front. His buttocks were bare except for the string which ran between them.

'Bring it into the bathroom when it is ready.'

Champak got up, opened her wardrobe, fished out a shaving set hidden in the folds of her saris and went into the bathroom. She did not close either the door behind her or the other one which opened into the courtyard. Mundoo was not going to restrict her movements. He was just a servant and a grubby little boy at that. She decided to ignore his presence.

After a few minutes she came back to her bedroom without anything on. She put the shaving set back in its place and stood in front of her full length dressing-table mirror to inspect the results of the operation and admire the contours of her chocolate brown body. She loosened her hair and turned round to see how she looked from behind. Her hair fell to the point at which her buttocks rose like softly rounded water-melons. There were dimples on either side of her rear waist. She turned round once more, inhaled deeply, and lifted her breasts with the palms of her hands and then ran her fingers round her nipples till they became rounded like berries. She clasped her arms above her head and wriggled her hips in the manner of hula-hula dancers. She drew her belly in as much as she could and stroked it with her hand down on either side to her knees. She studied her face and figure in all the postures she had seen in photographs of nude models. She found the reflection in the mirror to her satisfaction.

In the courtyard, Mundoo finished washing the kitchen utensils and was on his hands and knees once more blowing into the hearth. He looked like a frog with the wrong end up.

Champak smiled to herself and went back to the bathroom. She shut the door opening into the courtyard without bolting it and shouted for the bath water. She turned the tap full on into the bucket and began to hum the tune coming over the air.

Mundoo lifted the canister of hot water by the wooden rod which ran through it on the top. It was heavy; he carried it a few paces at a time. When he reached the bathroom door he put it down to regain strength to take it over the threshold. He gripped the handle with both hands, knocked the door open with his forehead, and carried it in. He put the canister beside the bucket and looked up.

'Why don't you knock or call before you come into the bathroom?'

Champak hid her nakedness with her hands between her knees. Her raven black hair fell on either side of her neck. Her breasts looked out from between her arms. Mundoo stared stupidly at her without replying and then started to back out of the door.

'What shall I mix the water in? Both the bucket and the canister are full.'

Mundoo turned off the tap, tilted the bucket a little to let some of the water run out, and began to pour the hot water from the canister with a small copper mug. His eyes never rose above Champak's knees, nor left them. Champak remained as she was, hiding her nakedness with her hands, watching the boy's embarrassment.

'In future, knock before you come in. Sometimes I have no clothes on.'

'I must tell you what happened today. My God! I nearly died of shame.' Champak always added 'my God' or 'by God' whenever she wanted to emphasize something. She also had the habit of turning the conversation to herself. It was either some compliment paid to her, a pass made at her in the street, or someone looking at her lecherously. It invariably ended the same way, 'my God,' or, 'by God,' the embarrassment had nearly killed her. Her husband paid little attention to these anecdotes, and that evening he had matters of greater importance on his mind so he barely heard what she had to say.

'You should not have stayed alone in the house all day; you should have come to the fair. What a turnout at my meeting! First we had a march past of the Student Volunteer Corps. No one had seen such smartness from civilians before. The S.V.C. has come to mean something. Then I addressed the meeting. There was absolute pin-drop silence.' 'Pin-drop silence,' was a favourite among his repertoire and clichés. 'Packed to capacity,' 'sacrifice our all,' 'eschew all differences' were some of the others which figured frequently.

'Accha! Wonderful!' she responded enthusiastically. 'You will become a minister in the Government one day and we will have a flag on the top of our house; we will have an official car and peons in uniform. Then we candismiss this useless Mundoo of yours. Really you've no idea what he is like!'

'Oh, yes, I have,' interrupted Sher Singh impatiently. 'He is just a poor, underpaid boy. The condition of domestic servants is one of the most pressing problems of urban society. We work them twenty-four hours of the day, underpay, underfeed, and underclothe them. Their living quarters are filthy. They are abused and beaten at will. They are dismissed without notice after a disgraceful search of their belongings. It is scandalous. It must stop. I will stop it.' Sher Singh found it hard to switch from oratory to multitudes to talking to individuals.

'I am sure you will. But this Mundoo . . . really.'

'What's wrong with him? He's no different from other servants. The trouble is we never can see our own faults. Whenever I have difficulty with people, I put myself in their shoes and see their point of view. It is a very good principle.'

Sher Singh and his wife were too full of themselves to listen to each other's tales. They both abandoned the attempt.

It was hot. The ceiling fan only churned the air inside the room. Other members of the family slept on the roof in the cool of the moonlight. Even Dyer, who never left his master's side when he was at home, refused to be in the room at night. Sher Singh had to suffer because of his wife. He looked at his watch. 'It's after eleven. I didn't realize it was so late. I've had such a tiring day.' He put up his arms and yawned.

'Your mother hasn't come back from the temple. The procession could not have ended.'

'I don't know about her but I could hear father's snores from the courtyard. And there is a light in Beena's room. She must be studying.'

Sher Singh gave himself a long look in the mirror before taking off his turban and uniform. He went into the bathroom, poured a few mugs of water on his body, and came back dripping to dry himself under the fan. He saw himself in the mirror. His paunch showed no sign of reducing. He pulled it in and thought how much nicer it would be if it always stayed there. He bent down and touched his toes three times and re-examined the effect on his middle. He put on a thin muslin shirt and pyjamas. Before switching off the light he looked round the room to see if everything was in place. Champak had taken off her kimono and lay stark naked on her belly. She had the pillow between her arms, her legs were stretched apart. Sher Singh knew what this meant. 'My God I feel fagged out,' he said wearily and switched off the light.

Champak stretched out her hand and caught her husband's. 'Now it's dark, I can tell you about this Mundoo of yours. He's not all that innocent, you know!'

'Oh? What did he do?' asked Sher Singh yawning at the same time.

'Come over and I'll tell you,' she mumbled, tugging at his hand.

Sher Singh rolled over on to her bed and let her put her hand on his arm. 'When I bathe, he keeps peeping through the crevices of the door.'

'How do you know?'

'I know. And today he burst into the bathroom on the pretence of bringing in the hot water. I didn't have a stitch on me. Not one thing! My God, I nearly died of shame.'

'Why don't you bolt the bathroom door?'

'Never occurred to me; I thought everyone was out. In any case he should have knocked before coming in.'

'I suppose so. He's only a little fellow,' he said. 'Let's go to sleep.' A minute later he began to breathe heavily.

Champak's body twitched. She moaned as if in a nightmare and snuggled closer to her husband. She caught his hand and took it lower down her body. Sher Singh knew there was no way out.

'What have you done?'

'Just to give you a little variety.'

•

When the procession came back to the temple from its round of the city, it was well past midnight. Only a handful of men and women were there to welcome it back. Sabhrai and Shunno were amongst them. They had walked behind the decorated motor-van which carried the Holy Book for the first mile or so till the heat and jostling from the crowd had become too much for them. They came back to the temple to await its return. Shunno went to the open-air kitchen to help other volunteers wash and clear up the mess, over 10,000 people having been fed there that morning. Sabhrai sat beside the platform, on which there was another copy of the Granth, listening to the recitation.

By sunset the mammoth mile-long procession of the afternoon had been reduced by half; an hour later only a few hundred people remained. When it came to the temple there were just the men carrying gas lamps, some volunteers, and the five men who had marched with drawn swords all the way. A last quick prayer was said and the Granth was laid to rest.

Sabhrai and Shunno came out into a deserted street. There were no tongas or taxis at the stand, so they had to walk home; the mistress in front and the maidservant a few paces behind her. One side of the narrow street was whitewashed by the moonlight; a dark shadow slanted down from the other. People slept on platforms in front of their shops. The road was occupied by stray cows placidly chewing the cud and brahminy bulls who roamed about bellowing into the stillness.

Part of their way lay through the prostitutes' quarter, where there was some life. Several tea shops, pán and soda pop stalls were still open. Long-haired pimps sat in groups gossiping. From some balconies came the whining of harmoniums and the tipety-tipety tum-tum of the tabla; from some others the shrill notes of singing and the jingle of bells. Farther down the street were women who did not pretend to combine dancing or singing with their real profession. They sat on their doorsteps under the lights of hurricane lamps to display their heavily made-up faces and artificial jewelry.

Sabhrai and her maidservant aroused no comment; only the pimps stopped talking and turned round to see them. (Vice responds only to vice; it seldom dares to accost virtue.) Shunno drew her veil across her nose, came alongside her mistress, and whispered an angry comment on the profession of street women. Sabhrai ignored her remark and started mumbling her prayers. Shunno dropped back. She cast surreptitious glances at the women and tried to overhear the negotiations between them and their patrons. They came out of the bazaar and its warm smell of stone and sewage to the grassy cool of the municipal garden. It was bathed in silvery moonlight; the fragrance of the lady of the night pervaded the lawns.

The women quickened their pace. Save for the croaking of frogs and the challenging cries of watchmen from the roofs of neighbouring houses, it was still.

When they got home, everyone was asleep. Mundoo lay on the kitchen floor. Shunno kicked him with her bare feet till he woke up and sent him to the servants' quarters. She went up to the roof with her mistress.

Sabhrai said another short prayer sitting cross-legged on her bed. When she lay down, Shunno began massaging her feet and legs.

'Go to sleep. You must be tired.'

'It doesn't matter. You will sleep better if I press you a little.'

Sabhrai knew that the maidservant wanted to say something. She did not openly encourage Shunno to gossip; neither did she discourage her more than to occasionally call her a gossip-monger.

'Everyone is asleep,' said Shunno to reassure her mistress.

'I thought Beena was stirring,' whispered Sabhrai to indicate that she knew what was on Shunno's mind.

'Beena Bibi, are you asleep?'

There was no answer.

'No, she must be asleep. It is long after midnight,' assured Shunno. After a few minutes, she spoke again.

'Bibiji.'

Sabhrai mumbled inaudibly.

'Bibiji, are you feeling sleepy?'

'No.'

'Bibiji,' continued Shunno in low tones, 'one shouldn't say such things, but . . .'

'But what?'

'If you don't take it ill, this house our Bibi Beena has started going to, the one with those hairless Hindus, is not a very good one.'

'Bus, bus, enough! You know nothing about them.'

'I am just telling you what I have heard, it is my duty. If something happens don't blame me for not telling you what people say.'

'What do they say?'

'The son is said to have bad habits. One hears he spends his time playing cricket and going to cinemas. He has other habits too. . . . One hears his wife is very unhappy.'

'Bus bus! You are always slandering people. . . . Who told you?'

'Who told me? All the world knows.'

'Accha, accha! Go to sleep and don't gossip.'

'Whatever I say is gossip,' grumbled Shunno. 'As you wish! Sat Sri Akal.'

'Sat Sri Akal.'

Shunno heaved herself up and went down the stairs praising the Guru.

Sabhrai sat up in the bed once more and repeated the prayer for the night to wipe out the effect of Shunno's words. She too had heard stories of Wazir Chand's son. But Sher had made friends with him and Beena almost worshipped his sister, Sita. And Wazir Chand was a colleague of Buta Singh. Sabhrai did not know what she could do without upsetting the rest of her family. She had infinite faith in the Guru and was sure of His special interest in her husband and children.

He had helped her husband to rise to the position of senior magistrate. He would no doubt get her Sher to settle down to a steady occupation and find Beena a nice husband, not necessarily rich, just well off, but a good Sikh with his hair and beard unshorn. That was not too much to ask or hope for. Sabhrai shut her eyes and invoked His blessings for her family with all the fervour she could command.

•

'These English are funny.'

It was not usual for Buta Singh to be in good temper at breakfast. 'Bhai, yesterday was great fun,' said he, making a second attempt to interest his family. When no one asked him why, he continued of his own accord. 'These English, they don't know anything about our customs. Yesterday the Deputy Commissioner offered me a cigarette. I said, "Sahib, today you have done this and I do not mind because we are old friends, but don't do it again." Then he started apologizing.'

The family took Buta Singh's stories of his candour with English officials with a pinch of salt. 'Did you tell him that Baisakhi is a big day for us and he should not ask people to be on duty?' asked his wife fanning flies away with a hand towel.

'He apologized himself. He said since I was the only one who really knew the people in the city, he had to rely on me. He also tried to bribe me with the promise of a title. I said, "Sahib, you keep your titles. I don't care for such things."'

'Sardarji,' said Shunno chiming in, 'there is a policeman with a bayonet at our gate since the morning.'

'Oh yes, I had almost forgotten that part of Mr Taylor's orders,' said Buta Singh in a lordly way. 'The seniormost official in the district is to have a sort of decorative guard outside his house just like the one outside the Deputy Commissioner's. I don't think the other magistrates will like that.'

'It will hurt their eyes,' commented Sher Singh expanding with filial pride.

Buta Singh suddenly realized that his daughter had spent the whole of the day before at Wazir Chand's. 'How are you getting on with the preparations for your exams?'

'I worked yesterday at Sita's house,' answered Beena. She made one attempt to clear her conscience. 'We worked all morning and got so tired that nothing would stay in our heads. So we decided . . . '

'No, no, it is foolish to force the mind to things it cannot retain,' interrupted her father, trying to make up. 'When I was at college, I never worked more than two hours at a stretch. When I got tired, I used to take a walk in the fresh air; fresh air is best. Some of the boys used to go off to the cinema after working all day. When the eyes are tired, the stuffy atmosphere in a cinema can do them no good.'

Beena did not have the nerve to mention the pictures after that. Sher Singh realized that and decided to keep the knowledge of his sister's escapade to himself and question her when the occasion arose. Buta Singh had not finished talking about himself. 'The Guru was merciful; yesterday went off peacefully. Our Sahib was scared: "There will be a Hindu-Muslim riot. . . . The

Communists will be up to mischief." I said, "Sahib, don't worry, all will be well." He also wanted to know about your meeting.'

'The place was packed to capacity.'

'I hope you didn't say anything indiscreet.'

'O, no! There's no such danger.'

'You have to be careful. Many people would like to create mischief for the family. It is wise to be cautious.' Buta Singh rose from the table. 'I better inquire from Mr Taylor whether he slept well or had nightmares of riots.' The family obliged with a laugh.

Buta Singh left. Sabhrai turned to her brood with maternal aggressiveness. 'Did you go in the gurudwara or just carry on your buk buk nonsense?' she asked her son.

Sher laughed. 'There are so many to say prayers for me. You must have said one, Champak another.'

It gave Champak an opportunity to enter into the family discourse. 'I had a very quiet day all alone. I washed my hair and listened to the hymns relayed from the temple by the radio. Then I said my evening prayers and put the Granth to rest. It was very peaceful.'

Chapter II

The last thing Shunno did every night before retiring was to fill a brass jug with water, put a keekar twig in it, and leave it on a stool outside the kitchen. Every morning while it was still dark she came in, lit the fire, and put the tea kettle on the hearth. She put the keekar twig in her mouth, picked up the jug, and went out into the garden or the vacant plot across the road. She performed her morning functions behind a bush and washed her privates with the water she carried. She scooped up a little mud and used it as soap to rinse her hands. She chewed the twig till one end was reduced to a soggy, fibrous pulp and brushed her teeth with it. She tore off a strip of the bark and scraped her tongue with such vigour that it made her retch and spit. She returned to her quarters and bathed under the tap in the garden and went back to the house to get tea ready. All this she did before the earliest risers, the drongos, had started calling or even a suspicion of grey had appeared on the eastern horizon.

Shunno was a peasant woman and had not changed her way of living in the city. Her regular habits had helped to keep her in rude, rustic health. Although she was fat and nearly fifty, she could work fourteen hours a day without any sign of fatigue. She had never been known to be ill, she had not even known a cold or a headache. Her eyes were clear, with the white and black whiter and blacker than other people's. She had an even row of teeth not one of which had ever given her trouble. She could chew up six feet of sugar-cane at a time. She could crack almonds and walnuts as if her mouth had been fitted with a nut-cracker. Shunno was the despair of men servants employed as additional help. Since she could run the house single-handed, she soon reduced them from being fellow-servants to her own personal slaves. She bossed them till they couldn't stand it any more. They were dismissed for the same reason: making improper advances to her. The compromise had been found in hiring the thirteen-year-old Mundoo whom she could not easily accuse of impropriety and who would submit to her bullying. On New Year's night she had kicked him several times.

Shunno loved to talk, like most women of her age and frustrations. (She had become a widow before she was twenty.) Her sexual instincts had been sublimated in hard work, religion, and gossip. She spared no one, not even members of the family for which she had worked for nearly thirty years. The only reason why she had failed to create misunderstandings between them was because they knew her well.

Despite her tongue, Shunno was a God-fearing woman. She said her prayers, went to the gurudwara and, on religious festivals, helped menfolk in the community kitchen. She was not narrow in her faith. She also went to Hindu temples, bathed in the river every Tuesday morning, respected Brahmins and cows. Even Islam was not beyond her religious pale. She visited tombs of Muslim fakirs, left offerings with their guardians, and consulted them on her imaginary ailments. She never let a beggar, be he a Hindu, Sikh, or a Muslim, return empty-handed from Buta Singh's door.

Shunno's one grievance with life was that no one took her seriously. Although her master and mistress disapproved of her forays into other faiths, they said nothing to her. But the younger members of the family made fun of her. They often insinuated that her visits to the river had motives other than spiritual. And since she was never known to have been ill, it did not take much to twist her accounts of visits to Muslim medicine men.

Shunno did not tell anyone about her new ailment for the first few days. Many times during the previous month she had returned from her early morning performances with a slimy feeling between the thighs; her left hand which she used to wash her bottom felt as if it had been dipped in glue. She had to wash again with fresh water before she felt clean.

On the morning of the first of Jeth (early May), Shunno got up earlier than usual; she had to get the morning tea and the prasad ready. She had also to sweep the gurudwara room and prepare it for the first-of-the-month ceremony. She went to the corner of the garden and after she had finished, washed her person with water she carried in her brass jug. She got the same clammy feeling which she had had before. She decided to get some of the kitchen work out of the way before going to the tap for a second wash. Half an hour later, in the light of the grey dawn, she noticed some red stains on her Punjabi trousers. She examined her left hand; it was also smudged with crimson. She filled a pail with fresh water and hurried to her quarter. She took off her trousers and splashed water between her thighs. It trickled down her legs tinged with red. She felt weak and slumped down on her charpoy. After a few minutes she woke up Mundoo and told him to tell the mistress that she was unwell. That was the first time in the many years of service in Buta Singh's home that Shunno had not turned up at the gurudwara for the first-of-the-month ceremony.

It was Mundoo who brought the steaming tray of prasad. He had changed his shirt and covered his head with a kitchen duster for the occasion. He also felt entitled to stay on in the room instead of being outside with the dog and the urchins of the locality.

As soon as the final prayer had been said and the prasad distributed, Buta Singh asked the question which was in everyone's mind: 'Where is Shunno?'

'She says she is not feeling well,' piped up Mundoo, beaming. 'She looks all right.'

'She came in the morning to light the fire; she put the prasad on the hearth and then went back. I will go and see what is wrong with her. She has never been ill before,' said Sabhrai, very concerned.

'It must be the heat,' added Buta Singh. 'Yesterday the temperature touched 115° in the shade! The courtroom was like an oven.' He made a grimace and went on: 'I was hearing a murder case; the place was packed with Sikh villagers. They obviously do not bathe every day. The smell of sweat and clarified butter was terrible.'

Sabhrai did not like derogatory references to Sikhs and changed the subject abruptly. 'A lot of things are going to happen this month,' she said. 'Beena is going to take her examination; Sher, you've got something on too, haven't you?'

'Yes, the election of the University Union.'

'We ought to have a complete reading of the Granth Sahib. All of you must help.'

'You better get a professional reader. Most of us will be busy and will not be able to do much reading,' pleaded Buta Singh.

'I don't like hiring outsiders to do our prayers; it hasn't the same effect. If none of you can spare the time, I will do it all on my own,' said Sabhrai with determination. They knew they would have to come to her rescue. This was one of the ways she imposed religion on them and although they said nothing, they did not like it. Before they could pursue the matter further, Mundoo came and announced that some people were waiting to see Buta Singh. They had an appointment.

'What are the orders for me?'

This was Buta Singh's way of getting down to business straightaway; it also had the note of humility which, coming from a man of his status, created a favourable impression.

The deputation of Hindu merchants had been sitting cross-legged on the chairs in the verandah talking to the policeman on duty. As Buta Singh came out the policeman sprang to attention, brought his rifle to his shoulder, and slapped the butt in salute. The visitors got up quickly, slipped their feet into their shoes, and greeted him: 'We touch your feet. Sat Sri Akal. . . . Orders? You order and we obey. You are the emperor, we are your subjects.'

It was a proud moment for Buta Singh. His politeness became more exaggerated. He joined his hands to greet them and escorted them to the sitting-room. They took off their shoes and sat down. After a while Buta Singh asked them whether they would like something to drink and, without waiting for a reply, asked again: 'What are the orders for me?'

The visitors again protested that they were the ones to receive orders not give them. After some shuffling of feet, clearing of throats, and nodding to each other, the eldest in the group spoke: 'Sardarji, our request is for a licence to take out a religious procession next week.'

'You know the Deputy Commissioner has promulgated an order banning all meetings and processions,' replied Buta Singh without looking up.

'We know that, Sardar Sahib. We will be honest with you. The Sikhs have had their procession and the Muslims have had theirs; then there was no order to ban them. When it comes to our turn, our kismet is bad.'

'If it is for a Hindu procession, why do you come to me? Go and ask a Hindu official to speak to Mr Taylor. Ask Mr Wazir Chand.'

'Sardar Sahib, for us you are a Hindu. What is the difference between a Hindu and a Sikh? You tell us.'

'Yes, Sardarji,' joined the others in a chorus. 'We are like brothers. No difference at all.'

'I never said there was any difference; I think we are the same community. You started by saying something about Hindus and Muslims and Sikhs.'

'Please forgive us,' said the eldest with his hands joined. 'It was only a manner of speaking. Most of our homes have Sikh forms of worship. We give our sisters and daughters in marriage to Sikhs. We are kinsmen. Why, brothers, isn't that the truth?'

'Truth,' protested one. 'Why, there is no greater truth.' The others nodded approval. The eldest started again. 'Why should we hide anything from you! We did approach Mr Wazir Chand first but he refused to help. He said, "If you want to get anything from Taylor Sahib, ask Sardar Buta Singh." We would not have put you to this trouble if we hadn't been told by everyone in the world that the only man who can do it is Sardar Buta Singh.'

'This is only your kindness. I will do the best I can,' said Buta Singh getting up.

The visitors also got up and slipped their feet back into their shoes. 'When shall we present ourselves?'

'Come and see me some time tomorrow — at the law courts.'

'Sardar Sahib,' spoke another. 'We have pinned all our hopes on you. You do this for us and we will sing your praises the rest of our lives.'

'We will remain ever grateful,' exclaimed the others.

'Acchaji Namaste. . . . Some water or something?' asked Buta Singh mechanically and without waiting for a reply dismissed them: 'Namaste.'

'This is like our own home. We would ask for anything we want. Sat Sri Akal.'

John Taylor was an Englishman and a member of the Indian Civil Service. He was only twenty-eight but these two qualifications had led to his being made the Deputy Commissioner and the virtual ruler of an area larger than two English counties, with a population of nearly a million natives.

Taylor did not belong to the class which had produced the builders of the Empire. He was the son of a schoolmaster. His wife, Joyce, had been a nurse — a very pretty nurse. He had met her at the hospital where he had been sent for a medical check-up before joining the service. From the very start, they found themselves isolated from the English community. They found the snobbery of the senior English officials a little irksome. They did not share their views about the role of Englishmen in India. Although Taylor, as the English Deputy Commissioner, was elected President of the exclusively European Club, he never went to it. His wife avoided the company of other memsahibs and restricted the duties, which her status imposed on her, to purely Indian circles. But their attempts to make friends with Indians were not very successful. The Indians refused to be treated as equals; they refused to be frank and outspoken; and at some stage or other they tried to exploit their association. So the Taylors gave up trying to find friends in India. They spent their after-office hours together — going out riding, taking long walks, or just being at home. They disliked people invading the privacy of their home and Taylor had issued strict instructions that no one was to call at the house except on the day set apart for visitors. He had a repertoire of little tricks by which he put subordinates, who tried to be familiar, in their places. He kept them waiting. He took a long time to answer simple questions; he lit a cigarette or casually knocked tobacco out of his pipe on the heels of his shoe while the other was on pins and needles waiting for a reply. At times he was just abrupt; sometimes even rude.

Buta Singh believed that Taylor had a personal regard for him and would always treat him with special consideration. As minutes accumulated to make half-an-hour and then three-quarters, doubts began to assail his mind. 'Did you give Sahib my card?' he asked the orderly.

'Immediately, sir. Sahib looked at it but said nothing.'

Buta Singh had always tipped the Deputy Commissioner's staff and had no fears about his card having been deliberately withheld. He could not understand why the Sahib had not come out to greet him or ask the chaprasi to show him in. 'Didn't he say whether or not I was to wait; or does he want me to see him in his office at the law courts?' he asked.

'He was having his tiffin with the memsahib. We have orders never to come in when he is at tiffin. But your case is different. I put the card on a plate and took it in. He looked at it but didn't say a word.'

Buta Singh began to feel thoroughly uncomfortable. If it had not been for the fact that Wazir Chand had admitted his inability to get permission for the Hindu procession, Buta Singh would never have taken on the task. He had reasoned that if he failed, it would not do him much damage; if he succeeded, his prestige amongst the Hindus of the city would greatly increase and that of Wazir Chand suffer. He was beginning to doubt the wisdom of his venture. He knew that Taylor did not like people coming to his house unless sent for and he was a stickler for appointments. He had fondly believed that those rules did not apply to him. Now he was not so sure of himself. It could, of course, have an innocent explanation and Taylor might apologize for keeping him waiting; in that case he would forgive him graciously.

'What is it, Buta Singh?'

That is all Taylor said as he came out. He was still in his riding breeches and was smoking his after-breakfast cigarette. His shirt was drenched with perspiration and stuck to his chest.

Buta Singh stood up. 'Good morning, sir . . . I . . . I do not like disturbing Sahib at his residence unless it is something urgent.'

'Well, what is it?'

'Sahib's order banning meetings and processions is being misconstrued by mischief-makers as being directed only against the Hindus because it was promulgated after the Sikh and Muslim celebrations,' said Buta Singh without a pause.

'That is absolute nonsense. I am fed up of hearing about this Hindu, Sikh, Muslim business. Can't you people get these notions out of your heads? The order has nothing to do with favouring one community or the other; and I don't give a damn about what some silly people say. Is that all?' Taylor's cigarette shook in his hand as he took it to his mouth.

'Sir, I felt it my duty to report. A deputation of the city's leading Hindus called on Mr Wazir Chand when they heard that the order was to be passed. They wanted him to request you to postpone its promulgation by a few days. Mr Wazir Chand might have spoken to you about it.' Buta Singh had not intended to take this line; but neither had he expected this kind of reception. Slight inaccuracies did not vitiate a substantial truth.

'Wazir Chand said absolutely nothing. Changing the date of the order would have been a simple matter, but I do not like to take back my orders.'

'Perhaps Mr Wazir Chand got frightened of Sahib's temper,' said Buta Singh a little nervously. Taylor threw the cigarette on the floor and squashed it under his foot. The growl on his face disappeared. 'Why should anyone be frightened of me? It's this heat and the work which make me ratty. I am sorry, Buta Singh, I never asked you to sit down. Do take a chair.'

'No, thank you, sir. You have not had your bath. Your shirt is wet and you might catch a cold if you don't change quickly.' Buta Singh decided to cash in on the changed mood. 'I won't keep you one minute more, sir. And I apologize again for bothering you at home. I know you don't like it, but I felt it was my duty to inform you.'

'Buta Singh, you mustn't misunderstand my temper. I am sorry if I sounded impolite. I did not mean to.'

Buta Singh's face lit up with a broad smile. 'Sir, I have to work with you every day. If I started misunderstanding your anger — which I must say is very rare — our work would stop. I have always said, and will say again, that it is a subordinate's duty to understand his officer's moods as well as his method of work. When you tick me off, I consider it a privilege because then I know I have made a mistake and have been given an opportunity to correct myself.'

This was too much for Taylor. 'Well, well, I don't know if I agree with you, Buta Singh. Now this business of the procession. Don't you think it is wrong to withdraw an order? It can be construed as a sign of weakness.'

'You are absolutely right, sir. I suggest that you let it stay; only give the Hindus special permission to take out a procession along a well-defined route and during hours when there is no chance of a disturbance.'

'That's much the same thing as withdrawing the order.'

'No, sir, not at all. This will be a special dispensation for a few hours. After all you are not banning people going in procession with a wedding or a funeral!'

'That's true. O.K. You make out an order and put it up for my signature in the office.'

'Perhaps Sahib should send for the Hindu delegation and convey the order personally. It will be better than letting someone else do it. That will also avoid wrong interpretations by mischief-makers.'

Taylor thought for a moment. 'I think you are right. Tell them to come and see me at the law courts.'

'Right, sir. I will bring them in personally. Good morning, sir. Change your shirt before you catch a chill.'

Beena had reason to be in a bad temper. Without any reason her mother had started an argument about going to Sita's house. 'Why don't you work at home instead of going to Sita's every day?' she had asked. 'Because Sita is very good at her studies and can help me.' 'Why don't you ask her to come here?' 'Because it is much quieter there. Here there are you and Champak. There, there is no one.' 'What's happened to Madan's wife and child?' 'I don't know; she has gone to her parents.' Then her mother came out with a suggestion which made Beena positively angry. 'Your sister-in-law is left alone in the house when I go away. Today even Shunno is not in. You take her with you.'

'What will she do there?' asked Beena in an exasperated tone. 'We go away to study in Sita's room, what will she do, kill flies?'

'She can knit or read; she is lonely. Anyhow, I do not like you being alone in the houses of strangers. People talk.'

'Talk about what? What do I do there?'

'I do not care; you have to obey your mother. You take Champak with you today and see how it goes. If she does not like it, she can come away.'

Beena walked out of the room in a huff. 'After today, I am never going to Sita's. I don't care if I pass or fail.'

Champak did not protest as much as was expected. Although she was being deprived of a chance of being alone in the house, her curiosity about Wazir Chand's household, which had become the chief topic of conversation over the last month, had been thoroughly roused. Buta Singh often spoke of Wazir Chand, sometimes critically, as people do about their colleagues. Beena was full of the family, particularly Sita. And her husband had begun to see a lot of Madan. She had never met him but had seen him play against the English eleven. 'I am not at all lonely here,' she said in the dutiful tone she adopted in speaking to her mother-in-law. 'But if you want me to go with Beena, I will.'

There wasn't much conversation in the tonga. Sabhrai made some feeble attempts to make up but Beena continued to reply in gruff monosyllables. When they got to Wazir Chand's, the roles between mother and daughter were reversed. Sitting in the verandah was Madan, smoking and reading a newspaper. It wasn't such a quiet place to study after all; Sabhrai felt she had done well to bring her daughter-in-law along. Beena knew her mother would not believe her if she told her that Madan was not usually at home in the mornings. 'Bhraji, you haven't gone to college today?' she asked begging for an explanation.

'I am taking the day off. Sat Sri Akal, auntieji. This is the first time you have entered our home; it will rain today.' He threw down his half-smoked cigarette and crushed it under his foot. 'Do come in.'

'I will another day, son. I am late for the gurudwara. Look after your sisters and see them home when Beena has finished studying.'

'Do you have to say that? Of course, I will see them home. Have absolutely no worry.

The tonga drove away with Sabhrai.

Beena did not bother to introduce Champak. She did not seem to need an introduction or being put at ease. 'You go and work and don't bother about me,' she said making herself comfortable on the drawingroom sofa.

'I will stay here and do my knitting. I have promised to knit your brother a sweater before the winter.'

Beena went off to Sita's room and Champak took her knitting out of her bag. Madan came in from the verandah. 'Would you like something to drink? Shall I send for some cold butter-milk?'

'No, thank you, I am not thirsty. I will ask for anything I want. After all this is like my own home.'

'Absolutely!' he emphasized warmly. 'You must consider this your own home. Don't wait on formalities.'

Madan seemed uncertain of the next step. He went over to the radio set, took off the embroidered velvet covering, and began to fiddle with knobs. He could not find a station on the air and switched it off. Champak went on with her knitting without taking any notice of him. But as he moved towards the door she asked, 'Bhraji, when is sister coming back?'

'She has gone to her parents for the summer. It is very hot here and it wasn't good for her and the little boy's health.'

Madan looked out on to the verandah and slowly opened the door.

'There is nothing wrong with sister's health, I hope?' she asked, putting down the knitting in her lap.

'No, just the heat,' he replied turning back. He realized that his presence was not unwelcome. It was up to him to make the next move. 'Your husband and I have become great friends.'

'Nowadays he talks of nothing but you. He is a great admirer of yours.'

'And I am a great admirer of his. He is a wonderful orator. Today he is only the leader of the students;

tomorrow he will become a leader of the country. I am sure he will be a minister or something really big one day.'

Champak laughed. She took up her knitting again and without looking up said, 'I suppose you have thousands of admirers all over the city since you scored that century against the English eleven. You saved your country's honour that day.'

Madan smiled and sat down in the armchair facing the sofa. 'Have I your permission?' he asked, taking out a cigarette from the case. He lit it without waiting for a reply. He sent a jet of smoke straight at Champak; then tried to fan it away with his hands.

'Where does cricket get you? In five years I will be forgotten. Sher will be the Chief Minister of the Province and you his great lady. When I come to your door you will ask your servant: "Madan? Who is Madan? I don't know any Madan. Send him away."'

'You are making fun of me. How can anyone forget the great cricketer, Madan! You know, Bhraji, one of the sixers you hit, the ball came flying towards me. I thought it would hit me right here in the middle.' She dug her finger in the center of her low cut shirt to indicate the spot. She flung away her thin muslin head-covering, put her arms behind her head and smiled.

Madan looked from the spot between her breasts to her face. Their eyes met and were fixed on each other for a few seconds.

'My husband,' said Champak looking away, 'takes no exercise and has started to get a paunch. You should teach him cricket.'

'I will teach him anything you command; I will be always at your service,' replied Madan putting his hand across his chest and bowing slightly.

'If you make fun of me, I will not talk to you.' Champak took off her shoes and tucked her feet under her on the sofa. She put aside her knitting and said with a deep sigh, 'This will never get done and you know whose fault it will be!'

'I am a great sinner,' answered Madan bowing again. They both laughed. They sat and talked of many things: Sher Singh's election, the growing friendship between the families, the hot weather, films and film stars. Then the clock on the mantelpiece struck twelve and Champak got up; one of her knitting needles fell on the floor. Madan picked it up and came near her to hand it back. 'You are wearing *khas*? On a hot day it reminds one of rain. I think it is the best perfume in the world; better than anything made in France.'

'Is that all you know of perfumes, Mr Madan?' she answered coyly. 'For your information this is French and is called "chasse garde," which means "hunting forbidden." So there!' She tapped him on his chest. One of the buttons of his shirt was open; she buttoned it, then picked a piece of thread off his sleeve and slowly released it in the air.

'Hunting forbidden! What does it mean?'

'Find out for yourself.'

'It's a silly name for a perfume.'

'Isn't it? I am sure the girls have done enough work for the morning. We must get home now. Namaste.'

'Namaste. And don't forget humble folk like us when you are the wife of the Chief Minister,' said Madan joining his hands as if in prayer.

Champak caught his hands in hers and pressed them. 'Don't make fun of me. I don't like it.'

Sher Singh always had a good look at himself in the mirror before taking off his uniform. He examined his profile from both sides and then gave himself a steady stare to study the effect it could have on other people. At these moments he was reminded of newsreels showing busty Russian women soldiers marching fifty abreast through Moscow's Red Square on May Day parades. The crash of bands, the deep-throated chorus, and, above all, the command to salute, gave him a tingling sensation along his spine. If no one was looking, he would stretch his hand sideways and like Hitler clutch his belt with his left hand. Thereafter he looked at himself again in the mirror as each garment came off.

Champak was already in bed waiting for him, so he could not go through the saluting ceremony. However, the Russian troops in the Red Square started a sequence of thought. 'You know what these bastard Communists want to do now?'

'What?'

'They want our peasants to fight the Japanese army. They say we must help Russia to win the war.'

The statement did not register on Champak whose notions of politics and geography were somewhat hazy. She gave a noncommittal answer: 'Funny, isn't it?'

'It's not funny at all; it's serious. For the Communists, one day it is an imperialist war, the next day it becomes the People's War. One day they call the Muslim League a tool of British imperialism, the next day they describe it as the only true representative of the Muslims. One day they decry the demand for Pakistan, the next day they support it. They say what Moscow tells them to say. It is always Russia this and Russia that. They never think of India. I will teach them a lesson one day. My S.V.C. will knock the hell out of them.'

'Incidentally, you have a great admirer.'

Admirers always interested Sher Singh. 'Oh! And who would admire me?'

'Your dear sister's friend, Madan.'

Sher Singh felt a little uneasy. He recalled Beena's going to the pictures with Madan and his sister on New Year's Day and her keeping quiet about it. He was not sure if it meant anything, but it made him uneasy. 'What did he say?'

'He said you were sure to become the Chief Minister one day.'

Sher Singh laughed. The cinema episode could not have meant anything since Sita had also gone with them and Madan was married. But why had she kept it a secret?

'And he said he was going to get his friends to vote for you in the Union elections. He said you were sure to win.'

'Madan is a first-rate chap. We have got to know each other recently but I know he is one of those to whom loyalty to friends comes above everything else. Don't you think so?'

'I have only met him once. You should ask your dear sister. I think she will agree with you. The way she goes on, "Bhraji this and Bhraji that," I think she is a little gone on him.'

'He is a bit of a rascal,' admitted Sher Singh.

'You are telling me! He's a big rascal. The way he looked at me! My God, it made me feel as if I had no clothes on. He had his eyes fixed on my breasts all the time. I couldn't look up.'

Sher Singh knew what the turn of conversation to sexual matters before bedtime meant. 'I don't bother about his morals. I like men who have courage and daring, and he has both.'

'He certainly has daring; I can tell you that after one meeting. I think your mother is quite right in sending someone to keep an eye on Beena — particularly when it is obvious to everyone how she feels about him.'

'Oh, I am hot,' said Sher Singh trying to change the conversation. 'Why can't we sleep out in the courtyard now that the rest of the family sleeps on the roof? It would be much cooler. Even Dyer refuses to stay with me at night.'

'What privacy is there in the courtyard? They can see everything from the roof. There is also that not-so-little Mundoo of yours who sleeps in the courtyard these days. I don't think he likes being on the roof of the servants' quarters next to Shunno.' There seemed no way of stopping Champak from giving a slant to the conversation.

'This heat is terrible,' he grumbled, taking off his vest. 'I feel so sleepy.' He yawned to prove what he had said.

'Just take your clothes off; they make you hot. I am going to strip myself. Have you bolted the door?'

Sher Singh bolted the door. He went into the bathroom to pour tumblers of cool water on his hot, sweaty body and went to bed. Fifteen minutes later he went back to the bathroom to wash himself.

A late moon rose over the line of trees and the day's heat was slowly wafted away by a cool breeze. Buta Singh, Sabhrai, and Beena had their charpoys on the roof. The father and daughter were asleep; Sabhrai sat cross-legged on her bed saying her bed-time prayer. The sound of footsteps coming up distracted her attention. Dyer began to growl but as the steps came closer he recognized them and began to wag his tail. Shunno heaved herself up the stairs invoking the assistance of the Guru at each step. She sat down on her haunches beside Sabhrai's bed and began to press her mistress' legs. Sabhrai finished her prayer, made her obeisance, and spoke to the maidservant in an undertone, 'Where have you been all day? I went to look for you in the servants' quarters in the morning and afternoon.'

'Don't ask me anything,' moaned Shunno. 'It was written in my kismet.' She slapped her forehead and sighed. 'Stretch your legs, I can press them better.'

'What is the matter with you?' asked Sabhrai lying down and stretching her legs.

'Hai, Hai, Hai. Ho, Ho, Ho,' wailed Shunno. 'It would be better if you didn't ask. I could have died of shame.'

'What is the matter?' asked Sabhrai impatiently.

'Bibiji, I am so ashamed, I can't even talk.' Shunno explained her ailment at length.

'How old are you?'

'I don't know; between forty-five and fifty-five.'

'It may be more serious than you think! Bleeding at this age can be dangerous. Did you go to a doctor?'

'It is all right. If it is written that I have to die, I will die.'

'Have you been to a doctor?'

'What do doctors know? Only God knows. I went to the Peer Sahib. He has some miraculous prescriptions which his ancestors have left him. Many women, who had remained barren for years and whose husbands threatened to take other wives, have been cured by Peer Sahib. He is a magician — a divine magician. Sometimes he writes verses from the Koran Sharif and makes people swallow the paper; sometimes he just blows magic formulas in their ears. There is a big crowd there every day — Muslims, Hindus, Sikhs — everyone. I had to wait till I got a chance to speak to him alone. You can't mention such things before others, can you, Bibiji?'

'Did he give you a magic potion?' asked Sabhrai, sarcastically.

'No, Bibiji, he said he couldn't find out the trouble by feeling my pulse. He has asked me to come another day when there is no one and he can examine me carefully.'

'Won't you be ashamed showing yourself to a Muslim rascal?' hissed Sabhrai.

'Na, na,' protested Shunno. 'Don't use such words for him; he is a man of God. He doesn't charge any fee.'

'Go to sleep. I don't want any pressing.'

Shunno took no notice of her mistress' temper and went on pressing. After a while she started again. 'We have heard other things today.'

'Bus, bus, it seems you can't digest your food without slandering people.'

'As you wish. Don't be angry with me later on for not having warned you in time.'

The mistress relented. After waiting some time for Shunno to continue, she lost patience and asked meekly, 'What is it?'

'Don't blame me! We have heard that Wazir Chand's son's wife has gone away to her mother's.'

'She is going to have a baby. What is so important about her going to her mother's to have it?'

'We have heard that she has been turned out; she was old-fashioned.'

Sabhrai made no rejoinder. She had also heard from someone else that Madan had been describing his wife as illiterate.

'Our Beena is growing up fast,' continued the maidservant after a significant pause.

'What's that to you?' snapped Sabhrai; she knew what it was leading up to.

'It is not good to keep a young girl at home. It is time we thought of her marriage. If you find a nice Sikh boy . . . '

'*You* find one and then talk.'

Shunno realized that any talk about Beena would only lead to a snub, so she changed the subject. 'Our queen, our daughter-in-law, is idle all day.'

'What shall I do? Beat her?'

'It is not good to be idle all day. She reads stories and listens to film songs over the radio.' As her mistress did not reply, Shunno went on, 'How long has she been married? Isn't this the second year? There are no signs of a child appearing!'

'You ask her to have one.'

'I? She doesn't even talk to me; as if I was an enemy. She won't let me press her when she is tired. She is always asking Mundoo.'

Again Sabhrai made no comment.

'This Mundoo is getting very cheeky.'

'Is there anyone in the world you do not malign? Whether you are well or ill, you never curb your tongue from gossip and slander.'

'Hai, Hai,' protested Shunno. 'Whatever I say is gossip.'

She pressed her mistress in silence for a few more minutes, then heaved herself up and went down moaning about her age and illness and invoking the Great Guru.

'We Indians have no character.'

When Buta Singh made such statements he excepted himself. But when he added: 'We have still a lot to learn from the English,' the implication was that he had done all the learning there was to be done; it was for other Indians to follow his example. In the past these remarks had been directed to the shortcomings of Wazir Chand's character. Of late Buta Singh had to make his references less pointed because his son and daughter had begun to see a lot of Madan and Sita.

'Some people have boot-licking ingrained in their make-up.' Buta Singh recalled that he had passed that judgement on Wazir Chand more than once and quickly tried to generalize it, 'All these magistrates are great lions in their own homes. When it comes to facing the Sahib, you should see them: each anxious to push the other in front. When Taylor is there, they can't utter a squeak.'

'This has come because of centuries of slavery. Our country has never been free and we have developed a servile mentality. We are frightened of power. Rarely do we get someone who can stand up to it: someone like Shivaji, or Rana Pratap, or our own Guru, Govind Singh.' Sher Singh's heroes were the tough men of Indian history who had fought the Muslims.

Buta Singh acknowledged his son's compliment. 'Those were great men called upon by destiny to save their country. I am talking of common people like us. Take this business of getting permission for the procession. Not one of these Hindus, who give battle with their tongues, would face Taylor and get him to revise his decision. They had to come to me.'

'Did he grant them permission?' asked Sabhrai.

'Of course! Didn't take a minute. It would have been a little awkward if he had asked me why a Sikh had to speak on behalf of the Hindus.'

'Sikhs have always had to help the Hindus,' answered his wife proudly. 'That is nothing new.'

Buta Singh felt the mantle of 'Defender of the Hindus' descend on him. His tone became generous and patronizing. 'There are other things about these English which one must admire. When Taylor realized his order was a mistake — I pointed that out to him —

he did not hesitate one moment to alter it. No personal pride or anything.'

'It isn't by accident that they are sitting on half the world as rulers,' joined Sher Singh. 'Look at the way their delegates come to negotiate with Indians who have been put in jail by his own King's Viceroy. No personal pride or anything,' he concluded with his father's words.

'We Indians have a lot to learn from them.'

Sher Singh sensed that the remark was directed to him. 'They too have something to learn from us,' he said, taking up the challenge.

'What?'

He did not answer or look up.

'What?' repeated Buta Singh, 'can Indians teach Englishmen?'

'Oh, many things. Like . . . like . . . '

'Like what?'

'Like hospitality . . . tolerance . . . '

'Rubbish! Ask the eighty million untouchables what they think of the tolerance of the caste Hindus. Ask the Hindus and Sikhs about the tolerance of the Muslims.'

'You can find examples like that everywhere. Most white people are anti-semitic. It's not only Hitler who has been putting Jews in gas chambers, the Russians have killed many. Everywhere in Europe and America there is prejudice against them and only because they have better brains and talent than the others. We do not have any racial discrimination.'

'No? What is untouchability if not racial?'

'We do not kill our untouchables.'

'Because they have never had the courage to revolt. What religion of the world other than the Hindu — and I include the Sikhs in the Hindus — has degraded humanity in the same way?'

The friendly family discussion turned into an acrimonious debate. Sabhrai did not like it. 'Why must you start arguing at home? Don't you get enough from the lawyers in the courts?' she asked angrily.

'One must not get things wrong,' answered Buta Singh lamely and got up. 'One should be able to see one's faults and learn from other people. Being contented with one's lot is not good enough.'

Sher Singh did not reply. He knew anything he said would irritate his father more and occasion another long sermon. But as soon as Buta Singh left, Sabhrai provoked him into another argument. 'Why do you have to contradict your father in everything he says?' she asked him aggressively. 'It is not nice to argue with one's elders; you should listen to what they have to say.'

'I wasn't arguing. I was . . . '

'Sherji never argues,' interrupted Beena. 'Other people argue with him.'

They started laughing.

'And why are you so much against the English? What have they done to you?' asked Sabhrai coming back to the subject.

'I am not against them; I am for my own country. If they stayed in England, I would have nothing against them.'

'Is that what you say at your meetings? Do you tell the British Government to go back to England?'

'That, and other things.'

'Well, don't say them in this house. We eat their salt, and as long as we eat it, we will remain loyal.'

Sher Singh's temper shot up. 'Who eats whose salt? They suck our blood.'

'This is no way to talk, son,' remonstrated Sabhrai gently. 'You are welcome to your views, but do not say things which you know may embarrass your father. At least we eat *his* salt.'

Sher Singh got up. Sabhrai felt she had upset her son. 'Tell me, son,' she asked, putting her hand on his shoulder, 'what will you get if the English leave this country?'

'I? Nothing. But we will be free.'

'Then what will happen? What sweetmeats will we get?'

Sher Singh could not answer simple questions like these; at least not in words his illiterate mother could understand. He became lyrical —- 'Spring will come to our barren land once more . . . once more the nightingales will sing.'

Chapter III

In June the sun scorches
The skies are hot
And the earth burns like an oven.
The waters give up their vapours,
Yet it burns and scorches relentlessly.

When the sun's chariot passes the mountain tops,
Long shadows stretch across the land.
The cicadas call from the glades,
And the beloved seeks the cool of the evening.

If the comfort she seeks be in falsehood,
There will be sorrow in store for her.
If it be in truth,
Hers will be a life of joy.
Spake the Guru: My life and life's ending are at the
    will of the Lord

To Him have I surrendered my soul.

The Guru had left out reference to the dust in his
description of the month of Asadh (May/June). First
there were the devils spiralling their way across the
parched land. They were followed by storms which came
with blinding fury, flinging dark brown earth in fistfuls
in people's faces. Some summers, as in the summer of
1942, there were no dust-devils or dust storms but only
dust. The sky turned from a colourless grey to copper red

and a fine hot powder started to fall. It fell gently day after day and covered everything under a thick layer of khaki. It got into the eyes till they hurt; it got into the mouth and one felt the grit between the teeth; if one turned the end of a handkerchief on one's fingertip inside the ears or nostrils, it came out muddy. Trees stood in petrified stillness with the weight of dust heavy on their leaves. There was neither sunshine nor shadow. The sun had become a large orange disc suspended in an amber sky; its light was dissipated in the atmosphere. It was intensely hot without even a suspicion of breeze anywhere.

Sabhrai wiped her forehead with a towel and pressed it on the Holy Book. She spread the cover on it and looked up at her family. They were all there including the dog and they were all well and happy. That was enough for her.

Her husband ran his hand gingerly behind his neck and remarked: 'I've never had prickly heat like this before. It feels like a thousand thorns stuck into the back.'

Sabhrai took no notice of the complaint. They had spent several disturbed nights and everyone's nerves were a little frayed. 'Will you say the supplicatory prayer?' she asked, heaving herself up. 'Don't forget to thank Him for Sher's success at the elections. Also mention Beena's examination: if the Guru wills she will pass even if her papers have not been good.'

The family stood up. Buta Singh stepped in front. He shut his eyes and raised his face to the ceiling. With his hands joined across his navel he recited the names of the ten Gurus, the important shrines, and the martyrs. He thanked the Guru for his son being elected President of the Students' Union and invoked special assistance for his daughter and blessings for the rest of the family. They all went down on their knees, rubbed their foreheads in front of the Holy Book once more, and sat down in their places. Shunno stirred the prasad with a dagger.

'Last night it was like an oven,' commented Sher Singh. 'I could not sleep at all. I must have drunk at least twelve tumblers of water but the thirst would not go.'

'It can't last very long. The monsoon has broken in Bombay and it should be reaching the Punjab in another fortnight. As a matter of fact, Mr Taylor, who is a keen bird-watcher, told me that he had heard the monsoon bird calling. He said this bird comes all the way from Africa with the monsoon winds and wherever it goes the rain is sure to follow. Now the college is closed, why don't you go to the hills for a few days? Sher, you should take Champak and Beena to Simla. You can rent a house for a couple of months; your mother and I will come over later.' Buta Singh cupped his hands to receive prasad from Shunno.

'I have just taken over the Union and even though the colleges are closed, there is a lot of work to do. Madan said his father has rented a large house in Simla and only he and his sister are going for the present. He suggested our sharing it with them. It may not be a bad idea if Beena and Champak went with them now; I will take off a few days in September before the colleges re-open.' Sher Singh took his share of the prasad in his cupped hands.

Before Sabhrai could say anything, Buta Singh agreed that it was a good idea. 'Of course, I will have to stay in a hotel — Cecil or Clarke's. In Simla one meets many senior officials of the Punjab Government and the Government of India, and a good address is most important. You come to some arrangement with Wazir Chand's family: take half the house and pay half the rent. I will see Taylor and discuss summer plans with him.'

The attitude of Buta Singh and his family to the Wazir Chands had undergone a change. Buta Singh had so completely triumphed over his colleague both in the eyes of the bureaucracy and in the estimation of the local populace that he could afford to adopt a patronizing attitude towards him. Sher Singh and Madan were constantly seeing each other during the elections and there was no doubt in anyone's mind that Sher Singh's easy success was in large measure due to Wazir Chand's son. The opposition that had come from Sabhrai was silenced by Beena's persistent refusal to go to Sita for help in her studies, and a not too subtle insinuation that her poor performance at the exams was a result of her mother's attitude.

The Buta Singhs decided to call on the Wazir Chands to settle the business of going to Simla.

The arrival of Buta Singh and his family created quite a commotion in Wazir Chand's house. They had turned up without warning. To emphasize the degree of familiarity that had developed between them, they trooped in without waiting to be announced.

'Anyone there?' shouted Buta Singh leading the way; Sabhrai, Sher Singh, and Beena followed behind him. They went through the sitting-room into the courtyard. Wazir Chand was lying on his belly on a fiber mattress with only a loin-cloth on his person. A servant was vigorously massaging his buttocks and legs with oil. Beside him seated on a chair was his son Madan shaving himself in front of a mirror placed on a stool; one side of his face was still covered with lather. His mother had just emerged from the lavatory at the far end of the courtyard and was scrubbing her water-jug with ashes. Sita, the only one who was dressed and ready, fled to her room utterly embarrassed.

'Oho,' said Buta Singh jovially. 'You are having yourself massaged.'

Wazir Chand shook off the servant and got up hurriedly. He unwound the dirty dhoti on which he had been resting his chin and wrapped it round his legs; he spread a newspaper across his greasy, hairy chest. Madan wiped off the lather with a towel and stood up; his face looked like a lawn, only half of which had been mown.

'Don't disturb yourselves,' protested Buta Singh. 'This is like our own home. We are always this way.'

Sher Singh and Beena looked at each other and smiled.

'Sardarji, come into the sitting-room. Oi, ask Sita to come out,' ordered Wazir Chand.

'I will get her,' volunteered Beena and rushed away to Sita's room. Wazir Chand put on a soiled shirt and conducted his guests to the sitting-room. Servants brought in trays of dried fruit and seltzer. Despite Buta

Singh's protests that they had just had breakfast, that this was like their own home, that they would ask for anything they wanted, they were talked into sampling the nuts and drinks placed before them.

The conversation started with the terrible heat and plans to escape to the hills. Then the women made a group of their own and got into a huddle on one side. Buta Singh and Wazir Chand dropped their voices to a conspiratorial whisper to discuss office gossip and politics. 'They are getting a hell of a beating these English, aren't they? Four of their aircraft-carriers have been sunk, the Germans have swallowed most of Europe and Russia, the Japanese have them on the run in the East. How long do you think they can hold out?'

'One can never tell,' answered Wazir Chand cautiously. 'So far they seem to be getting the worst of it. But their broadcasts always talk of victories.'

'Don't believe a word! You think they would be willing to talk of a settlement with us if all were going well?'

'You maintain that the English always win in the end,' said Wazir Chand with a mischievous smile. 'Have you begun to change your views?'

Buta Singh felt cornered. 'You will agree that so far they have always won the decisive battles. One never knows how things will turn out, they may still turn defeat into victory.' Buta Singh realized that Wazir Chand had made him contradict himself. He tried to retrieve the situation. 'What is more important than the fate of the English or the Germans or the Japanese is the future of this country. How can our leaders persuade the English to give us freedom if the Muslims do not side with us?'

Buta Singh's zeal in collecting war funds was a popular subject of discussion in magisterial circles. Words like 'freedom,' 'our leaders,' were new in his vocabulary. Wazir Chand decided to keep Buta Singh on the defensive. 'What does Taylor have to say about it? You see more of him than anyone else.'

'Sends for me morning and evening,' complained Buta Singh. 'You can see he is worried. He is always asking me about British proposals and my views on the Muslim demand for Pakistan. I tell him quite frankly what I think.'

'Your position is different,' conceded Wazir Chand. 'You are the only one he really confides in.'

'You are making fun of me,' said Buta Singh, thoroughly flattered. 'Believe me, he listens to what I say because he gets things straight from me; I don't butter my chapatis for him. He has sent for me again this morning.' Buta Singh glanced at his watch: 'Actually we came to discuss this matter of sharing the house in Simla; I believe you have rented a large one.'

'Sardar Sahib, it is your house; you are most welcome. What could give us greater pleasure?'

'That is very kind of you, but we must share the rent.'

'No, no,' protested Wazir Chand, taking Buta Singh's hands in his. The two magistrates squeezed each other's hands with great affection. Buta Singh looked at his watch again. The conversation died down.

Wazir Chand's wife spoke in a timid, low voice: 'Sherji, you don't ever come to see us.'

'What a thing to say!' said Madan before Sher Singh could answer. 'He is busy being a leader; he has no time for social calls.' He turned to Buta Singh's wife and added: 'Auntie, we are going to ask you for sweets the day Sherji becomes a Minister; he is bound to become one one day. I've got sister Champak to promise us that already.'

'If brothers like you wish him well, then he will achieve everything,' answered Sabhrai. She turned the conversation to what was uppermost in her mind: Madan's relationship with his wife. 'How is our daughter-in-law keeping? You get good news of her?'

'She is with her mother and you know how daughters are in their mothers' homes!' answered Wazir Chand's wife.

Sabhrai was not satisfied. 'I hope she will be going to Simla. It should be good for her health.'

Wazir Chand came to his wife's rescue: 'Of course! The plans are that Madan will first take up his sisters. After he has made all the arrangements for their comfort, he will go and fetch his wife. By then, I hope I will be there or Sherji or Sardar Sahib. There ought to be some man there all the time. Don't you think so?'

'Of course, of course,' agreed Buta Singh. 'I wish Sher could go now, but he insists on staying here for some time. My own arrangements are a little uncertain. If I go at all, it will only be for a day or two to leave my wife and then to bring her back.'

They got down to discussing the plans again. Buta Singh and Wazir Chand went out together and after much protesting on either side agreed to share the rent of the house.

The chaprasi returned the visiting-card and held up the heavy chick for him to pass under. 'Go in, Sardarji, the Sahib is waiting for you.'

Buta Singh put the card back in his wallet, adjusted his tie and coat, and went in. It was dark; all the doors and fanlights were blocked with thick *khas* fibre thatching. A cool spray came through each time the coolies outside splashed water on them. A pleasant damp smell of fresh earth pervaded the courtroom.

A table lamp cast a circle of light on a sheaf of yellow files which Taylor was reading. He wore a white open-collar shirt, khaki shorts, and sandals on his feet. A silver tankard of iced beer lay in front of him; froth trickled down its sides and mixed with the beads of frost on the metal. Several feet away on a lower level there was another circle of yellow light under which Taylor's reader sat quietly turning over case files.

'Come in, come in, Buta Singh. Come right in,' said Taylor pushing a chair beside him.

'Good morning, sir. How cool you have made it here! You have brought Simla down to this hot place. No need to go to the hills.'

Taylor felt slightly uneasy. He knew the conditions in which his Indian colleagues worked. Small cubicles packed with litigants and lawyers squabbling and shouting each other down; smell of sweat and stale clarified butter churned about vigorously by the ceiling fan. No curtains to keep out the glare; no *khas* to lessen the heat and bring in the aroma of the damp earth. Just bare white walls with red betel spit splattered on the corners and a calendar bearing a photograph of the

Governor of the Punjab looking down upon the scene through his monocled eye.

'I would break down under the heat if I didn't have all this,' explained Taylor. 'It is a matter of getting used to it. You Indians can take it because you eat the right food, wear the right clothes . . . not you Buta Singh,' he added laughing as he noticed the other's stiff-collared shirt, necktie, silk suit, and thick crepe-soled shoes. 'I mean the man in the street.'

'Even so, Sahib, it doesn't stop us getting prickly heat, sore eyes, and bleeding through the nose. Last two nights I had a servant rub the soles of my feet with the skin of an unripe melon; and still they burn as if on fire. I am sending my family to the hills to escape this heat.'

That gave Taylor the chance to introduce the subject he had wanted to discuss with Buta Singh for some days. 'Very good idea! The youngsters must have finished with their colleges. A long three-month break every year is a very good idea.' After a pause he added, 'I was glad to see your son was elected President of the University Union. He can go off to the hills feeling pleased with himself.'

Buta Singh was flattered at Taylor's knowledge and interest in his family. 'Yes sir, God has been good to us. We have much to be grateful for.'

Taylor became more explicit. 'What are his immediate plans?'

'Sir, we were planning to go to Simla. I really wanted to know what your programme was for the summer before deciding.'

'I don't think I will take any vacation this summer. Neither should you just yet. Send the family with Sher Singh and join them later.'

'Sher is not free yet. You see, sir, as President of the Union he has a lot of work to do. He is a very serious-minded young man.'

'You tell him from me that it is not wise to work during the summer months. Ask him to see me. I'll talk to him.'

'Yes, sir, thank you, sir. I will tell him. All work and no play makes Jack a dull boy.'

Buta Singh purred with gratitude at Taylor's concern for Sher Singh. He was quietly tapping his knees with his hand when Taylor got up and extended his hand. 'Well, goodbye, Buta Singh. And don't forget to give my message to your son. Tell him to drop in whenever he has the time.'

Buta Singh went out into the glare of the noonday sun; it was some time before he could see properly. It took him yet longer to get over the fact that Taylor had sent for him only to ask about his family. Then an uneasy suspicion crossed his mind; perhaps there was more in Taylor's tender inquiries about Sher Singh than he knew.

For the first time in two months, Champak had the house almost to herself. Although Mundoo was there he scarcely mattered.

As soon as the family had dispersed, Champak bolted the doors of the house from the inside and retired to her room. She changed back from her Punjabi dress to her kimono. She switched on her radio and stretched herself on her bed under the ceiling fan.

Mundoo finished the little work Shunno had left for him and dozed against the wall. He heard the music coming from the young mistress' room and sat up. Champak watched his reaction through the chick curtain and turned down the volume. After straining his ears for a few minutes, Mundoo got up, came to Champak's door, and sat down on the floor beside the threshold. Champak got up and went into the bathroom and shut the door behind her. Mundoo heard his mistress leave the bedroom. He lifted the chick curtain over his head to shade him from the sun. He put his head against the door and shut his eyes in musical rapture.

Champak bathed and washed her hair. She was in a carefree mood and kept company with her radio music, singing at the top of her voice. Mundoo heard her singing and splashing water; he felt assured that his listening would not be interrupted for some time. As soon as Champak stopped, he sat up. One of his favourite songs was coming over. The mistress would surely take a couple of minutes with the towel. Mundoo thought he could risk it a little longer.

Champak decided that it would be cooler under the breeze of the ceiling fan. She stepped into her bedroom with her long hair and naked body dripping with water. Mundoo edged back thoroughly frightened.

'Why don't you ask before you come into the room?'

Mundoo murmured something incoherently.

'Fool! Hand me the towel.'

The towel lay on a chair facing her dressing-table. Mundoo went across the room and gave it to her.

'You can sit inside and listen,' said Champak and went back to the bathroom. Mundoo came in and sat down beside the table on which the radio was placed.

Champak came back wearing her thin cotton kimono. She had a towel about her shoulders to take the drip from her wet hair. She went to her dressing-table with its three full-length mirrors and sat down on a chair facing them. From the corner of her eye she noticed Mundoo looking at her reflection. She casually undid the belt of her kimono and put her feet on the dressing-table drawer. The kimono fell on either side of her legs, baring her to the waist. She dabbed talcum powder from the neck downwards to her breasts, belly, and thighs. Then threw her head back and let her wet hair fall behind the chair. She shut her eyes to enjoy the cool breeze and the music.

Mundoo sat and stared at the reflection in the mirrors. He felt hot and the palms of his hands became wet with perspiration. His little virginal mind was swamped with lustful longing. All he could do was to stare, squeeze his hands between his thighs, and drool at the mouth. The torment ceased after a few minutes; he felt tired and ill. He got up to go back to the kitchen.

'Press my legs. I am very tired.'

Champak got up from her chair, flapped the sides of her kimono, and tied the belt. She lay down on her belly clutching a pillow between her arms.

Mundoo began pressing his mistress' feet and ankles with his damp hands.

'Here,' ordered Champak, slapping her calf muscles. 'It hurts here.' She drew up her kimono to her thighs and spread out her legs. The boy pressed without daring to look up. After a few minutes he looked up to press the other leg. His mistress was bare up to her buttocks. She seemed fast asleep. The boy was overcome with a maddening desire. He clutched his mistress by the waist, then sank back exhausted.

'What is the matter with you?' asked Champak waking up.

'Nothing, Bibiji,' answered the boy trembling.

'Go back to the kitchen. You don't know how to press.'

Champak let out the boy and bolted her bedroom door. She switched off the radio and fell asleep.

When she woke, the shadow of the wall had spread across the courtyard. Sparrows were gathered by the hundreds for their evening twitters before going to roost. All the family were in except her husband.

Champak's mood changed when her husband came back. She had slept all day, and was wide awake and full of herself. After a perfunctory inquiry about what he had been doing, she came back to her favourite subject — herself. 'I had a very quiet day. All your family was away so I washed my hair and read and read and read. Did you know John Barrymore was dead? He died yesterday. I was very sad. He was my favourite film star. I wish we had someone like him in the Indian films. Our films are just singing and dancing. Nothing else. That reminds me, you must do something about this Mundoo, you really must.'

'What has he been up to?'

'Without knocking or warning he came into the room. I had nothing on, not a stitch. My God!'

Sher Singh knew that this sort of conversation always ended in the same thing and he wasn't in the mood.

The fellow said nothing. Just gaped at me stupidly with his mouth wide open as if I were something to eat. I ran into the bathroom and put on my dressing-gown.'

'Why didn't you tick him off?'

'I did. I told him if he came into my room again without knocking I would have him whipped. He simply said he had come in to listen to the radio. He has got film music in his blood. It's these films that give him ideas. How old do you think he is?'

'I don't know; thirteen, fourteen, or fifteen.'

'I used to be so innocent at that age. We were brought up so strictly and Mummy did not tell us one single thing about life. This fellow, I am sure, knows all about sex already. Don't you think so?'

Sher Singh did not like after-dinner conversation turning to sex, so he changed the subject abruptly. 'It must be the heat or something. I have never felt as tired out as I do today,' he said, speaking through a yawn.

'I'll press your legs and you will sleep much better. Take off your clothes; it is so hot.'

Sher Singh was late for breakfast. Shunno knocked at the door twice to say that the others were waiting. He quickly wound his turban (his father objected to people coming to the sitting-room or dining-room bareheaded), brushed his little beard and tied a muslin band round his chin to press it. He hurried to join the family at the breakfast table. He interrupted his father's monologue with a loud 'Sat Sri Akal' meant for everyone.

'Sat Sri Akal,' replied his mother. 'Now that he has no college to go to, Sherji finds it hard to open his eyes before midday.'

'I came back rather late last night. Our meeting did not end till then.'

Buta Singh resumed his discourse. 'As I was saying, these Englishmen take a lot of interest in other people, and it is not just curiosity, it is a genuine concern with their problems. Now Taylor knows all of you by name, what you are doing, how you have fared in your examinations — everything. He has an excellent memory.'

'They have learnt from the Americans,' answered Sher Singh. 'They have reduced human relationships to a set of rules. They say you must know the name of the person you are talking to and use it as often as possible. You must know his or her interest and talk about them and never of your own. They write down whatever they have discussed with anyone in their diaries and refresh their memories before the next meeting. It does not mean much because their real desire is to create a good impression about themselves. They are not one bit concerned with the affairs of the person they happen to be talking to.'

Buta Singh did not like the way his son twisted everything he said in favour of Taylor. 'I don't know what you mean. Mr Taylor asked me about your election and where you planned to go for the summer. He also asked you to come and see him. He does not take that sort of interest in everyone nor invites people to see him. Many rub their noses on his threshold and are not allowed to enter.'

'He must have politely mentioned my name.'

Buta Singh flared up. 'I don't understand this attitude. Even if he mentioned your name out of politeness, you can at least pay him a courtesy call.'

'What will I say to him?'

Buta Singh was too angry to be coherent. 'I don't know what is happening to young men today. I wonder when you will learn about the world.'

Once more an academic discussion had turned to an unpleasant personal argument between father and son. Sabhrai stepped in. 'Why don't you go to see the Deputy Commissioner if he wants to meet you?'

'I did not say I will not see Mr Taylor,' protested Sher Singh. 'I simply asked what use it will be and you all start getting angry.'

'Don't worry, I will send him,' said Champak smiling. 'I will make him ring up for an appointment today.'

'Good,' pronounced Buta Singh. 'When a man is friendly and also happens to be an important officer, one should take advantage of it. Ring up his PA, tell him who you are — mention my name — and say the Sahib wanted to see you. He will give you an appointment.'

When Sher Singh rang up the Deputy Commissioner's office, Taylor himself answered the telephone. Sher Singh's English crumbled to a breathless stutter punctuated with many 'sirs.' Taylor brusquely ordered him to come on Tuesday which was the visitors' day.

Visitors' day came a week later. Sher Singh had expected to be received alone. When he got there, the Deputy Commissioner's regular hangers-on were already waiting their turn to be called. There were village officials in their starched turbans and baggy trousers, with their pistols strapped on their sides and cartridge belts running across their chests. There were fat businessmen from the city in their thin shirts and dhotis. There were officials in silk suits and ties. They sat in a row of chairs in the verandah. Sher Singh had great contempt for such people; but here he was sitting alongside them waiting his turn to be summoned. His father had terrified him into submission. He had visiting-cards specially printed so that one could be sent in to the Deputy Commissioner. He had his own silk suit altered and made Sher Singh wear it instead of the militant-looking open-collared bush shirt made of coarse hand-spun cloth. The process of humiliation was carried a step further by the reception Sher Singh got at Taylor's bungalow. One of the regular callers, a colleague of Buta Singh, recognized him and proceeded to introduce him to all the others. 'Wah bhai, wah,' he went on after the introductions were over. 'We used to ask how long will it be before this disciple of Gandhi will become his father's real son! Today in your European outfit you look like the heir of Sardar Buta Singh.'

'Yes, Sardarji,' drawled another who looked like a common informer: stiffly starched turban with its plumes waving in the air and a shifty, cunning look in his lecherous, antimonied eyes. 'What is there in Gandhi's followers? When an Englishman says, "Git awt you biladee," they will run like jackals. Sardar Sher Singh, your father is a wise man. You should follow in his footsteps.'

Sher Singh did not say a word. He was angry with his father for having sent him and angry with himself for having come. He felt angrier with his wife — he always felt angry with her when he could not find reasons for his temper — for not having stopped him from coming. And of course he felt angry with Taylor for having suggested his calling on a Tuesday and belittling him by keeping him waiting with the crowd of sycophants. 'Never again,' he kept saying to himself. This time he would go through the ordeal even if it meant sitting out till the last snivelling, fawning caller had had his say, but 'never again.'

Sher Singh was still immersed in his angry thoughts when the orderly came to say that the Sahib would receive him. Him, Sher Singh, before any of the crowd of corrupt businessmen wanting to be made honorary magistrates; before the boot-licking peasant informers begging for the privilege of being seated beside the Deputy Commissioner at formal functions! It could be because he was Buta Singh's son; it could also be because he was the leader of the students. In either case it was something which raised him above the sort of people who called on Taylor. Sher Singh's temper cooled a little.

The orderly conducted him through the verandah, lifted the chick, and peered in. Taylor was dictating to his stenographer. The orderly asked him to wait till the Sahib had finished.

Taylor finished dictating. The stenographer read out what he had taken down and left. Taylor picked up the first visiting-card on his table, turned it about, and put it down. He lit his pipe, and after looking vacantly into space for some time, tapped the bell on his table. The orderly raised the chick and hustled Sher Singh into the room.

'Good morning, sir!' said Sher Singh a little nervously. Taylor picked up the visiting-card again and scrutinized it carefully. He did not hear the greeting.

'Good morning, sir,' repeated Sher Singh a little louder.

'Hm?'

'Good morning, sir,' said Sher Singh a third time.

Taylor looked up and smiled. 'Oh, good morning, Sher Singh, good morning. Didn't notice you come in. Do sit down,' he said, pointing to a chair.

'Good morning, sir,' stammered Sher Singh for the fourth time, 'thank you, sir.'

'Well, how are you? And how is your good father? I haven't seen him for some days.'

'Very good, sir. Very good, sir. Thank you.'

'I am glad. And how are your politics? You are a leader of the students, aren't you? Your father told me you had become President of the Students' Union. He is very proud of you.'

A kind word from anyone one fears or hates has quicker and greater impact than it has from another — and Sher Singh had worked up both fear and hatred for Taylor. The Deputy Commissioner's friendly tone and praise won him over completely. He did not know what to say. 'It is nothing, sir, nothing,' he replied with gratitude. He could hardly believe his own ears when he heard himself say, 'It is all the kindness of people like you. The students were being led astray by these Communists and other political groups. At a time like this, when the enemy is at our gates, we should be united and strong. The way the English are standing up to their adversities should be a lesson to us.'

'Things are not going too well for us, are they?' queried Taylor. He picked up a shiny metal tube from his table and tossed it in the air several times. Sher Singh was not sure what it was but he was fascinated by the object. Taylor went on: 'It could put ideas in the minds of people who do not like us. Of course, we can rely on our friends. The Sikhs have a long tradition of loyalty to the British. We trust them more than any other community in India. And you know, your father is my closest colleague. He is a very good man.'

'Yes, sir. Thank you, sir.'

Taylor smiled looking straight at Sher Singh. He put one of the tubes to his lower lip, blew into it and made it whistle. It was an empty cartridge. Sher Singh went pale.

Taylor continued in his friendly manner: 'Well, I mustn't keep you from your work,' he said. 'It's nice of you to have come. Drop in any time you want to see me about anything — not on a visitors' morning like today — any other day. And if I can do anything for you, don't hesitate to ask me.'

Sher Singh stood up and saw two other cartridges lying on the table beneath the table lamp.

'Nice of you to have called.'

'Goodbye, sir. Thank you very much, sir.'

'Goodbye. Remember me to your father. What do you Sikhs say — Sat Sri Akal. That's right, isn't it? I am told it means "God is truth." '

'Yes, sir.'

'Sat Sri Akal.'

Sher Singh walked out of the room and left the bungalow without saying goodbye to the other visitors. He brushed off the orderlies who ran after him to collect their tip. As soon as he was out of the gate, he pulled off his tie and thrust it into his coat pocket; then took off the silk coat and hung it on his shoulder. He walked aimlessly down the road till he found a quiet spot. He sat down on the grassy curb with his head between his knees. He was angry, humiliated, and frightened. He wanted to cry but no tears would come into his eyes. He sat like that for a long time till the anger and humiliation receded to the background and only fear remained. Fear of what Taylor might do to him, fear of what the whole family would have to say for the way he had disgraced his father.

For the first time in many years, Sher Singh went to the big temple in the city to pray.

Chapter IV

To know India and her peoples, one has to know the monsoon. It is not enough to read about it in books, or see it on the cinema screen, or hear someone talk about it. It has to be a personal experience because nothing short of living through it can fully convey all it means to a people for whom it is not only the source of life, but also their most exciting impact with nature. What the four seasons of the year mean to the European, the one season of the monsoon means to the Indian. It is preceded by desolation; it brings with it the hopes of spring; it has the fullness of summer and the fulfilment of autumn all in one.

Those who mean to experience it should come to India some time in March or April. The flowers are on their way out and the trees begin to lose their foliage. The afternoon breeze has occasional whiffs of hot air to warn one of the days to come. For the next three months the sky becomes a flat and colourless grey without a wisp of a cloud anywhere. People suffer great agony. Sweat comes out of every pore and clothes stick to the body. Prickly heat erupts behind the neck and spreads over the body till it bristles like a porcupine and one is afraid to touch oneself. The thirst is unquenchable, no matter how much one drinks. The nights are spent shadow-boxing in the dark trying to catch mosquitoes and slapping oneself in an attempt to squash those hummings near one's ears. One scratches and curses when bitten, knowing that the mosquitoes are stroking their bloated bellies safely perched in the farthest corners of the nets, that they have gorged themselves on one's blood. When the cool breeze of the morning starts blowing, one dozes off and dreams of a paradise with ice cool streams running through lush green valleys. Just then the sun comes up strong and hot and smacks one in the face. Another day begins with its heat and its glare and its dust.

After living through all this for ninety days or more, one's mind becomes barren and bereft of hope. It is then that the monsoon makes its spectacular entry. Dense masses of dark clouds sweep across the heavens like a celestial army with black banners. The deep roll of thunder sounds like the beating of a billion drums. Crooked shafts of silver zigzag in lightning flashes against the black sky. Then comes the rain itself. First it falls in fat drops; the earth rises to meet them. She laps them up thirstily and is filled with fragrance. Then it comes in torrents which she receives with the supine gratitude of a woman being ravished by her lover. It impregnates her with life which bursts forth in abundance within a few hours. Where there was nothing, there is everything: green grass, snakes, centipedes, worms, and millions of insects.

It is not surprising that much of India's art, music, and literature is concerned with the monsoon. Innumerable paintings depict people on rooftops looking eagerly at the dark clouds billowing out from over the horizon with flocks of herons flying in front. Of the many melodies of Indian music, Raga Malhar is the most popular because it brings to the mind distant echoes of the sound of thunder and the pitter-patter of raindrops. It brings the odour of the earth and of green vegetation to the nostrils; the cry of the peacock and the call of the koel to the ear. There is also Raga Desha which invokes scenes of merrymaking, of swings in mango groves, and the singing and laughter of girls. Most Indian palaces had specially designed balconies from where noblemen could view the monsoon downpour. Here they sat listening to court musicians improvising their own versions of monsoon melodies, sipping wine and making love to the ladies of their harem. The commonest theme in Indian songs is the longing of lovers for each other when the rains are in full swing. There is no joy fuller than union during monsoon time; there is no sorrow deeper than separation during the season of the rains.

An Indian's attitude to clouds and rain remains fundamentally different from that of the European. To the one, clouds are symbols of hope; to the other, those of despair. The Indian scans the heavens and if cumulus clouds blot out the sun his heart fills with joy. The European looks up and if there is no silver lining edging the clouds his depression deepens. The Indian talks of someone he respects and looks up to as a great shadow; like the one cast by the clouds when they cover the sun. The European, on the other hand, looks on a shadow as something evil and refers to people of dubious character as people under a shadow. For him, his beloved is like the sunshine and her smile a sunny smile. He escapes clouds and rain whenever he can and seeks sunnier climes. An Indian, when the rains come, runs out into the streets shouting with joy and lets himself be soaked to the skin.

The fact that the monsoons come at about the same time every year gives expectation a sort of permanent place in the Indian's mental calendar. This does not happen with other people, e.g., the Arabs, who also thirst for water and bless its descent. (If the Arabs had the monsoon turning up with the same regularity, their calendar would have taken note of changes of seasons instead of being linked with the vagaries of the moon.) All the different calendars current in India are a dexterous combination of the lunar and the solar systems. As a result, the correspondence between the month and the season is much closer. On the official day heralding spring, the chill winds of winter mysteriously vanish and a warm breeze begins to blow. Similarly, while the coming of the monsoon may be any day in June or July by the Roman calendar, more often than not the first of Sawan will see it in full force all along the Western Ghats and well inland up to the plains of the Punjab.

Sawan is the month for lovers. Just as spring turns a young man's fancy to thoughts of love, in Sawan an Indian girl longs to be in her lover's arms. If her lover is not there, she languishes away singing songs of sadness. That spirit is expressed by the Guru in his composition on the monsoon, in which, following the literary tradition of the time, he describes God as the Great Lover and the devotee as His mistress yearning for union with Him.

> The season of rains is here
> My heart is full of joy

My body and soul yearn for my Master.
The Master is away and if He return not,
I shall die pining for Him.

The lightning strikes terror in my heart.
I stand alone in my courtyard
In solitude and in sorrow.
O Mother of Mine, I stand on the brink of death.
Without the Lord I have no hunger
Nor any sleep;
I cannot bear the clothes on my body.

Spake the Guru: She alone is a wife true
Who loseth herself in the Lord.

The monsoon had burst some time after midnight.
The thunder and lightning was enough to wake the
dead but people had just lain in bed pretending that
they were asleep. It came as usual: first a few heavy
drops and everyone announced to everyone else, 'It is
going to rain,' then suddenly it began to pour. There
was shouting on all the rooftops and much bustle and
activity as servants ran from their quarters to help bring
the charpoys and bedding down into the verandahs. It
took some time to get back to sleep again — but not too
long. Nerves which had been frayed by the heat were
soothed. And the sound of water spouting down from
the roof, the gurgle of the gutters and of the rain falling
in torrents was like a lullaby.

'Today we have Simla here,' said Buta Singh. He
made the remark in the hope that his son would start

some conversation. When Sher Singh said nothing, Buta Singh made another attempt. 'What wonderful weather we are having,' he repeated looking out of the door of the temple room. The chicks had been rolled up. The rain pock-marked the puddles as it fell.

'Yes,' answered Sher Singh without looking up; he held his father chiefly responsible for what he had suffered at Taylor's hands, and had avoided meeting him for some days. Buta Singh had sensed that the meeting had not been a success and wanted to know what had happened. 'How did your interview go?'

'It was on the morning meant for visitors; there were many others there.' The tone of resentment was unmistakable.

'Did you have to wait long?'

'No! He sent for me before any of the others.' Now father and son were on the same ground. Sher Singh mellowed at the thought that Taylor had sent for him first.

'He is specially kind to me,' added Buta Singh glowing with pride. 'One should take full advantage of his friendship. You should not bother about what people say. After all you are the President of the Students' Union and may be seeing him in connection with the students' demands.'

Sher Singh recalled Taylor playing with the empty cartridge and the two lying on his table.

Sabhrai interrupted their conversation. 'You have plenty of time to talk about these things later on; why start on them in the gurudwara?' she said crossly. She opened the Granth and, without scanning it silently before reading as she was wont to do, began to recite:

O, Black Buck, why lovest thou
The pasture of fenced-in fields?
Forbidden fruit is sweet but for a few days
It entices and ensnares
Then leaves one sorrowing. . . .

Sabhrai had brought a pen and paper to take down the passage to send to her daughter and daughter-in-law who were away in Simla. The verse made her a little uneasy, but it was the Guru's word and she copied it down as it had come. Shunno distributed the prasad to her husband and son and the children outside.

It was obvious that Sher Singh was not in a mood to talk; Buta Singh made no further attempt to make him do so. Sabhrai broke the silence at the breakfast table. 'I wonder what the girls are doing today?' she asked.

'The monsoon couldn't have got to the hills yet,' answered her husband. 'They must be having a good time strolling about on the Mall looking at the shop windows or meeting friends.'

'I wasn't thinking of that. I was wondering if they'd know it was the first of the month and go to a temple or at least say their prayers.'

There were no rickshaws available to take them out to the picnic. Madan had looked for them at the stands and on the roads and drawn a blank: all had been reserved by the English folk the day before. 'They give bigger tips than we do,' he explained.

'We can't walk all the way to Mashobra and back,' complained his sister. 'It is more than seven miles from here. And now we have the lunch things ready.'

'The best I could do was to reserve bicycles in the Carpenters' Bazaar,' said Madan. 'He had only three left. One of us could take the other on the back.'

After all the preparations, the girls were in no mood to spend the day at home. They set out with their lunch packed in a basket and their raincoats slung across their shoulders. In Simla, most people carried raincoats as a matter of style; news of the advancing monsoon had provided the habit an additional excuse. They came to the shop owned by the Sikh who combined making furniture, toys, and walking-sticks, with hiring out cycles. Of the three bicycles, two were ladies': these were taken over by Sita and Beena. Madan took the man's.

For the first mile the road climbed steeply, so there was no question of anyone cycling. When they came to the flat stretch they noticed that there were no carriers on any of the cycles. The only possible way Champak, who could not cycle, could get a lift was by riding on the handlebar of Madan's cycle. Nothing was said on the subject. But, instead of mounting their cycles, they went on walking. Madan was in great form. He made funny remarks about the people they passed — in Punjabi about the English and in English about the Punjabis.

Mashobra bazaar and hotel were crowded with holiday makers so they went a little farther to an old rest house in the midst of pine trees. Madan found an isolated spot above the roads. They hauled their cycles up the hillside and flung themselves on the bed of pine needles.

They ate their lunch and again spread themselves on the ground for an afternoon siesta. It was pleasant lying in the sun, breathing the warm, resiny odour of the pines and listening to the breeze soughing through the trees. There were a few white clouds. Lammergeiers circled lazily, high above in the deep blue of the sky. In the valley below a barbet started calling in its agitated, breathless way. Then a woman started to sing in a plaintive voice which seemed to fill the valley to the brim. Beena sat up to listen. She looked at her companions; they seemed to be fast asleep. She got up and quietly walked away in the direction from where the song was coming.

The hillwoman stopped singing as soon as she saw Beena and began to call to her goats, 'Hurrieyeh . . . urrieyeh. Aoh, aoh, aoh.' The goats paused in their grazing and looked up.

'Why have you stopped singing? I came to hear you.'

'What singing, Bibi? This is only to while away the time. We poor people can't go to the cinemas and learn new songs . . . aoh, aoh.' The goats looked up again, saw their mistress busy, and resumed their nibbling. The woman sat down on her haunches. She was old and full of wrinkles but her smile had the gay abandon of youth. She had a flat gold coin of the size of a rupee on one side of her nose and her arms were full of cheap glass bangles. 'What can we sing, Bibi!' she repeated. 'Aoh, urrieyeh.'

'Your song was better than the songs in the films. Why don't you go on?' asked Beena sitting down a little distance from her. The old woman just looked down at her feet.

'Have you a family?' asked Beena to encourage the other to talk.

'Family? Don't ask me anything. Five daughters!' she replied, slapping her forehead. 'It was written on my forehead; I cannot grumble.' She smiled baring a set of pearl white teeth.

'What's wrong with having five daughters?'

The peasant woman spat on the ground between her legs. 'One has got to get them married; that costs money. We can't pay our debts and now we have to borrow more because the eldest is thirteen. We are marrying her off next month. You can't keep a young girl in the house, can you? *You* must be married.'

'No, I am single.'

'You rich people have no worries. It's us poor folk who can't get enough to fill our bellies. Five daughters and nothing to give to any one of them.' She smacked her forehead again. 'It is all written there' — and smiled again. Her worries did not last long.

Beena took off one of her gold bangles. 'Give this to your eldest for her dowry. And now sing me a song.' Beena flung the bangle on the ground.

The hillwoman picked it up and placed it on her open palm. 'Bibi! You are unmarried and will need it yourself. Take this back.'

'No! I don't take back anything I have given. Now sing.'

The woman came up to Beena, touched her feet, and began a loud sing-song of blessing. 'Bibi, may all your wishes be fulfilled! May you get a handsome bridegroom; may you be the mother of seven sons; may you. . . .'

'Stop! stop!' laughed Beena. 'You have seven sons yourself; one will be enough for me. Now sing.'

'I will sing you a song of a young girl waiting for her lover.'

She began to hum. When she had the notes correct she put the palm of her hand across her left ear and started to sing. Once more her soft, plaintive voice rose above the roar of the stream and the crying of barbets and flooded the valley like the sunshine. Beena shut her eyes and listened to the invocation to the gods to grant a young girl's wishes: to bring her lover back home in time to hear the koel calling in the mango groves and see the rain falling in torrents; to make him take her till every part of her body was full of pleasure and full of pain.

The singing stopped suddenly. Beena opened her eyes. The old woman had drawn her veil. Beena looked up. Madan was standing beside her. 'What sin have I committed that I should not be allowed to hear the singing?' he asked with a smile.

'Hai Bhraji, I didn't hear you. I thought you were asleep.'

'How can sleep come to me when you are away!'

Beena's face coloured up. The hillwoman got up, wrapped her grass in a bundle, and called to her goats. 'Aoh, aoh. Urrieyeh. Bibi, a thousand blessings on you. We will always pray for you.' She hurried down the hillside driving the flock of goats in front of her.

'Are you angry with me? You haven't spoken to me all day.'

Beena stood up. Madan took her hands in his and pressed them against his heart. 'You don't love me,' said Madan with a leer.

'How can you say a thing like that? I like you more than anyone else. . . . I also like your wife and your sister. I am very fond of you all,' she replied. She could not bring herself to utter the word 'love.'

Madan let go her hands and assumed a very hurt expression. 'Let's go back.'

'Please don't be angry with me,' pleaded Beena. She came up to his side and took his hand. He did not reply; he withdrew his hand from hers and started to walk back. 'Please don't be angry with me, Bhraji, please!' she pleaded tearfully. 'I'll do anything you want me to do, but don't be cross with me. I will do anything. . . . '

Madan stopped and turned to her. He held her firmly by her arms. 'You swear you will do anything I ask?'

'I swear.'

'Come to my room tonight when everyone is asleep.'

Later in the afternoon more clouds appeared in the sky and a black wall came up on the southern horizon. There were flashes of lightning which could be seen across the bright sunlight.

'I think the monsoon is here at last. We should get back home before it starts,' said Sita.

They sat up and saw the black clouds towards the south looking like a range of mountains. The cicadas had begun to call. Then the bells of St. Crispin's Church in Mashobra began to toll for evensong.

'We must have tea at Gables Hotel,' said Madan.

'They have excellent sandwiches and cakes. They charge you just the same whether or not you eat them.'

'In which case we better eat all they give us,' said Champak laughing. 'We have no dinner ready and it will be too late to cook anything.'

They got their things together and began to walk homewards. The road was too rough to cycle and was crowded with people going to Gables Hotel for tea. By the time Madan found a table and got a bearer to serve them, the wall of black clouds from the southern horizon had spread over the sky and a strong breeze sprung up. People started to leave. Rickshaw coolies and syces of horses were agitating to get their clients to move on before the downpour started. They were amongst the last to be served. Madan was in a bad temper. He did not mince his words with the bearer. 'You serve Indians after the English people have finished! Is their money better than ours?'

The bearer grinned sheepishly. 'No, sir, for us all are the same. They were in a hurry; it might start raining any moment.'

'Don't Indians get wet?'

The bearer shuffled his feet uncomfortably.

'Jao — go' roared Madan, 'get me the bill.'

Madan's outburst gave him a sort of right to command. He proceeded to order everyone. 'I think you girls should be on your way,' he told his sister and Beena. 'I shall be slower as I have to bring Champak. We may catch you up at the Carpenters' Bazaar. But don't wait for us. Go home and get something hot ready; tea or something.'

The two girls got up. 'Don't go too fast,' warned Madan. 'The road will be crowded with horses, rickshaws, and mule caravans.'

'We can look after ourselves,' replied Sita. 'Don't be too long.' They waved a farewell and left on their cycles.

Madan scrutinized the bill carefully before paying. When the bearer brought him his change, he left a large tip on the plate and asked for a packet of cigarettes. The bearer brought him the cigarettes. Madan lit one, stretched his legs on another chair, and relaxed. After everyone had left, he stubbed his cigarette, looked up at the sky. 'We'd better be moving,' he said at last and got up.

They walked up the road to the Mashobra bazaar and stopped to survey the scene. Twilight was rapidly sinking into the night. Across a range of hills, the lights of Simla sparkled in stellar profusion all over Jacko Hill. Shopkeepers were putting up the shutters of their shops; smoke oozed through the crevices of the wooden planks smelling of wood and spices and tobacco. There were muffled sounds of the hubble-bubble of the hookah, of coughing and spitting and subdued conversation. The chirping of millions of cicadas was like the deafening roar of a waterfall.

Madan folded his raincoat over the bar of his cycle and smoothed it with his hand. Champak came on the other side. He put his arm around her waist and gently raised her on to the raincoat. He put his right leg across to the other side and got on the saddle. Once more he put his arm round Champak's waist and brought her closer to him till her head touched his chin and her thighs were between his knees. He let the cycle roll down the hill.

They had hardly gone a hundred yards when it began to rain. 'We will get wet,' said Champak turning her face backwards.

'We'll stop under the cliff which is sheltered from rain.'

When they came to the cliff, they saw many people with bicycles taking shelter. Madan slowed down but did not stop. 'I know a house farther down the road which has an arched entrance thickly covered with wild roses; that will be better.'

The house was another half-mile. By the time they got to it their clothes were completely wet. Madan put the bicycle against the wall and opened the gate. They went in and stopped under the arch made by the creeper. There were no roses, but honeysuckle, which grew with it, was in full bloom. Its acid-sweet smell was heavy in the dark, leafy tunnel.

'I am absolutely drenched,' said Champak holding out her shirt in the middle. 'How foolish of us to sit on the raincoat instead of wearing it. You put it on before you catch a chill.'

'We can share it,' answered Madan. He spread the raincoat over his shoulders and put his arms around her waist. She leant back and let her head rest on his chest.

'Your shirt is soaked,' she said turning back. She opened the slit below the first button and drew her finger across his chest. 'You will catch a cold,' she murmured turning away from him and pressing her head back on to his chest.

'You are also wet,' replied Madan in a whisper. He undid the top button of her shirt and let his hands slip on to her warm, rounded breasts. She turned her face up to him; their mouths met with hungry passion. Madan gently pushed her against the wall on the side and kissed her on her eyes and glued his lips on hers. The breath in his nostrils became heavy.

Champak wriggled out of his grasp: 'What will the girls say if we are late?'

'What will they say? They must have been held up by the rain! What else?' He waited for her reaction. She flung her arms about his neck and bit him fiercely on the nose. Madan kissed her on her nose, chin, and neck; then buried his face between her breasts. She pushed him back. 'Not here,' she whispered. 'Somebody will see us.'

Madan became impatient. As he moved towards her his shoulder brushed against a pole supporting the arch on which the roses and honeysuckle grew. A heavy shower of raindrops came down from the leaves. 'You see,' said Champak laughing, 'the gods also say not here. Come along.'

Madan caught her by the arm. Before he could pull her towards him, a tinkle of bells came round the corner and a line of mules carrying wooden crates filed past. The muleteers coming behind paused by the gate and then moved on. They had hardly gone out of view when half-a-dozen rickshaws came round the bend. There was more tinkling of bells. 'Hosh . . . bacho,' shouted the coolies as they ran past on their bare feet.

'Even the coolies say, "Careful . . . keep off,"' said Champak teasing. 'If you behave like a good boy, I will come to your room after the others have gone to bed.'

Sita and Beena did not wait at the Carpenters' Bazaar and went on home to get out of their wet clothes. They changed into their nightdresses and made themselves some tea. Madan and Champak came in an hour later.

'We stopped under the cliff hoping the rain would stop. It was jammed with people. So we came on,' said Champak holding up the hem of her shirt to show how wet it was.

They went to their rooms to change. Madan came back wearing his full-sleeve sports sweater and white flannel trousers. Champak joined them a few minutes later. She wore a bright red kimono. She had put on a fresh paint of lipstick and loosened her long black hair about her shoulders. 'Absolutely wet,' she explained, running her fingers through it and tossed it back. She settled down on the sofa and crossed her legs lotus fashion like a female Buddha.

They had their tea and discussed the monsoon. Beena didn't say a word. Madan lit a cigarette. He did not know how to put her off. Should he take her aside and apologize to her for having made the unbrotherly proposal in a rash moment? Before he could make up his mind Champak yawned and got up. 'I don't know about you people, but I am very sleepy. It is this fresh air and the rain. Sat Sri Akal.' Sita and Beena who shared a room also left. Madan got up with a sigh. Beena, he decided, was not the sort who came into men's bedrooms. He switched off the lights in the house and retired to his room.

Beena turned on the table lamp and saw a letter from her mother lying beside it; the servant had left it there.

She got into bed and tore open the envelope. As usual, most of it invoked the Guru's blessings for someone or other. In the end she mentioned how the monsoon had burst the night before the first of Sawan and how cool it had become. Then followed the passage from the Granth:

O, Black Buck, why lovest thou
The pasture of fenced-in fields?
Forbidden fruit is sweet but for a few days
It entices and ensnares
Then leaves one sorrowing . . .

There was a postscript asking her to read it to Champak and also to write back soon and give a detailed account of how they were getting on in Simla and whether or not Madan's wife had joined them.

Beena put the letter under her pillow and switched off the table lamp. The confusion that already existed in her mind became worse confounded. The desire to go into Madan's room brought a feverish longing in her body. It was followed by visions of Madan's wife and child; and the hot perspiration turned cold and froze on her. Then came the figure of Madan in his cream-coloured, hand-knitted sports sweater and flannel trousers — tall, handsome, and overpowering — stripping her and taking her as a man should take a woman; and the fever wracked her system. Once more the implications of what would follow — her mother's cold censorious eyes, the words in the letter burning through the thickness of the pillow . . . 'Forbidden fruit is sweet but for a few days. It entices and ensnares, then leaves one sorrowing.' The images followed each other in quick succession, alternately rousing hot passion and immersing her in cold water. After an hour of sleepless tossing in bed, her mind became possessed by one figure, a mammoth one, of Madan smoking, smiling, and beckoning her. Others receded to a dim background and the fever took complete possession of her.

She heard Sita's steady breathing. She whispered her name several times to make sure. She got out of her bed, picked up the letter from under the pillow, and tiptoed out of the room. She decided to see if Champak was also asleep. She could say she had just seen her mother's letter and brought it to give to her.

The rain fell on the corrugated tin roof with a deafening roar and drowned all sounds of creaking wood and opening and shutting of doors. Beena called softly to Champak and then tiptoed to her bed. It was empty; even the bedcover had not been removed. She went to the adjoining bathroom and slowly pushed open the door; it too, was empty. She tiptoed through the sitting-room to Madan's room. The door was shut. She put her palms gently on it and pressed. It was bolted from the inside. She put her ear against it and heard sounds of human voices. She stood rooted to the ground like a statue. All longing turned to cold, sickening hate. She went back to Champak's bedroom and left her mother's letter on the pillow. She opened her bedroom door and went out on to the balcony. She stood in the pouring rain staring steadily at Madan's window. An hour later a light came on in his room and was extinguished a few minutes later. Another light came on in Champak's room which also went off after a couple of minutes. And all was dark and silent save the thunder of rain on the roof.

The meeting with Taylor did not help to settle the issue for Sher Singh; it only introduced an element of fear to the confusion that already existed. At the two extremes were the Deputy Commissioner and the terrorists: one stood for the status quo with the power to maintain it; the others, for change and the insecurity that is the price of change. In the case of terrorism, the price could be one's life. Presiding over the two extremes was his father with his conveniently dual morality: 'Keep up with both sides.' For him loyalties were not as important as the ability to get away with the impression of having them. To be found out was stupid, even criminal. There was also his temper, of which Sher Singh was as scared as he was of the police. He had his tacit approval of his association with the Nationalists, but he knew that if Buta Singh learnt that he had got mixed up with the terrorists, his father would disown him and throw him out of the house. In addition to these factors, there was his own temperament. Despite his love for his country, he knew he was not the sort who ever burnt his bridges himself.

On the point of principle, Sher Singh felt that his mind was quite clear: he was a Nationalist and although he had worn a silk suit and tie when he called on the Deputy Commissioner, that was to save Taylor's feelings. Or was it the fear of his father? He could have told Taylor that he did not believe in the hocus-pocus of traditional Sikh loyalty to the British. In proportion to their numbers,

more Sikhs had gone to jail and to the gallows in the
freedom movements than those of any other community
in India — Hindu, Muslim, or Christian. In any case, talk
of loyalty might have made some sense in the nineteenth
century, it was beside the point in 1942. Britain had to
get out of India herself, or be kicked out, and Sher Singh
would say that to Taylor's face. Could he? What about
his father's views, his career in the service, and his hope
of finding his name in the next Honours list? And the
unique honour he was getting in the way of an armed
police guard outside his house — the sentry who sprang
to attention and smacked the butt of his rifle even when
Sher Singh passed by with his college friends? Couldn't
it somehow happen that these opposing factors could be
combined into one harmonious whole? He visualized
scenes where his Nationalist and terrorist colleagues
honoured him as their beloved leader, where Taylor read
an address of welcome, and his father proudly looked
on. Such were the dreams with which Sher Singh tried to
dope himself. They were based on the non-discovery of
one party by the other.

Sher Singh tried to dismiss the cartridges on the
Deputy Commissioner's table from his mind. Taylor
was known to shoot; they could be from his own rifle.
And many people liked playing with empty shells.
He tried to reassure himself that a village headman
wouldn't dare to report against the son of as powerful
an officer as Buta Singh. Deep inside him he also
knew that there were flaws in his reasoning. There was
evidence to prove that he was being watched. A new
sentry had replaced the old one.

The new sentry was politer than the last one and even saluted visitors who came to the house. He asked their names and business before letting them enter. He also became friendly with Shunno and Mundoo, and both the servants got into the habit of gossiping with him when they were free from work. Then one of the terrorists let him down. He used to come to see Sher Singh off and on and was known to Mundoo. One day he turned up with a false beard and moustache and wearing dark glasses. He announced himself to the sentry by a Muslim name. Even the thirteen-year-old Mundoo recognized him. Before Sher Singh could make up his mind whether or not to tell Mundoo not to talk about it to the sentry, the boy had done so. This was the last straw.

Sher Singh decided to get rid of the arms till suspicion had been allayed. But his troubles had only begun. He tried to arrange a meeting. None of the boys would agree to have it in his own home. One had a sister getting married; another had just lost his aunt and there were mourners in the house. One's father was already suspicious; another was sure his house was watched by the police. Sher Singh asked them to meet on the canal bank outside the town and come on their own cycles. They grumbled about the heat and the distance and only agreed when Sher Singh lost his temper and gave them a sermon on the greater battles to come. But neither the sermon nor the bad temper would persuade them to take over the illicit arms and keep them in their homes. 'They are safer in your house than ours. No one will dream that Sardar

Buta Singh's son can be a terrorist, no one will dare to search a magistrate's home.' Sher Singh repeated with exasperation that he was wanting to remove the arms precisely because he was already under suspicion. They offered him much advice but refused to budge from their position: 'They have to be with either you or Madan; and Madan is away.'

Sher Singh left them, raging and cursing wildly. He realized later that by his behaviour he had turned fellow conspirators into potential informers. If there were trouble, he would be the only one involved. The headman, and perhaps Taylor, knew only of him; the arms were also in his possession. He simply had to get rid of them.

He decided to throw everything into the well in the garden, then changed his mind because it was too obvious a place and the first thing anyone looking for the arms would do would be to send a man down into the well. He planned to put them in the jeep and dump them into the canal. Before he could do anything about it, the jeep was taken away. The driver said that it was wanted for emergency service elsewhere. He could not risk taking the stuff in a taxi or a tonga and once more he reverted to the plan of throwing them into the well. One evening he went out to reconnoitre. He discovered that the sentry who stood by the gate all day, slept by the parapet of the well at night. So the rifles, pistols, and hand-grenades remained where they were. Sher Singh just tried to forget their existence.

Then the village headman came to call on him.

Buta Singh had strong views about people coming to see him in his house — particularly if they were unimportant. His principle was that the only place for business was the office: the home was for rest and the family. 'Otherwise,' he used to say, 'fellows not worth the price of a broken shell could destroy the peace of the home.' He had issued instructions to his servants to tell callers to see him at the law courts. Naturally he was angry when Mundoo casually announced at breakfast, 'Sardarji, there is a peasant waiting to see you. He has been waiting since the morning. He says he has come all the way from his village.'

'Haven't I told you a hundred times not to allow peasants in the house! Tell him to see me at the courts.'

'Not you, Sardarji. He wants to see the small Sardarji,' answered Mundoo turning to Sher Singh.

'Me? What peasant wants to see me?' Sher Singh got up from the table and went out to the verandah. He saw the village headman sitting by the gate talking to the sentry. After a few moments of reflection he went back to join his parents at the breakfast table. Before they could ask him any questions, he ordered Mundoo to take a tumbler of buttermilk and some chapatis for the visitor.

'Who is the man?' asked Buta Singh.

'Just a villager we met when we were out on the canal bank one day. He was very good to us and gave us tea and food.'

'We? Who's we?'

'Madan and I.'

'Of course! One should always return hospitality,' said Sabhrai, backing her son.

'That is all right,' said Buta Singh, 'but one should not encourage these people too much. They always try to take advantage.'

Buta Singh went off to the law courts and Sabhrai to the kitchen. Sher Singh stayed on to plan his line of approach. He felt cross with Madan for having got him into this mess and having gone away to Simla. But there it was and he had to face the situation alone. At least he could find out whether or not this fellow had told the police or Taylor about the shooting of the crane and given the Deputy Commissioner the fired bullets. He would have to be tactful. Perhaps the best approach would be to give him hope of getting something or other from Buta Singh and keep him hoping till things were easier.

Sher Singh opened the offensive with an enthusiastic greeting. 'Wall, wah,' he exploded warmly, 'you are sitting outside and this your own home! Come inside.'

The headman had just finished the tumbler of buttermilk that Mundoo had brought him. He belched loudly and brushed his moustache with the back of his hand. He got up and made a quick move to touch Sher Singh's feet. Sher Singh stopped him half-way, put his arm round the other's shoulders, and conducted him to the sitting-room. The headman left his shoes by the threshold and went in. He smoothed the sofa with his hands and slowly sank into it. Sher Singh sat down beside him. The headman took his host's hand in his. 'What wonderful palaces you live in!' he exclaimed, looking from the carpet, to the pictures on the walls, the radio set covered in embroidered velvet, up to the whirring ceiling fan.

'What palace? This is our poor home that you have blessed by putting your feet in it. Tell me what service I can do for you. More buttermilk or tea? Our buttermilk is not as good as yours. You get the best milk, butter, and yogurt.'

'Sardarji, there is no *ours* and *yours*; it is all given by the Great Guru, the True Emperor. You order me and I will bring you an excellent milch buffalo — twenty seers of milk a day and thick with cream. Next time I come I'll get you a tin of pure clarified butter. Your heart will rejoice.' He squeezed Sher Singh's hands with great affection.

They talked of the joys of village life, of crops and cattle. Sher Singh got no closer to the real subject. His patience began to run out; he glanced at his watch.

'You working people!' exclaimed the headman giving Sher Singh another sympathetic squeeze. 'You have to go somewhere. I only came to have a sight of you. Now I have been blessed with that, I can return happily.'

Sher Singh sniggered; then came to the point — first with the bait. 'If you want my father to do anything for you, tell me. I can speak to him. If you want to be on the panel of assessors in Sessions trials, or entitled to a seat at the Commissioner's durbars, or anything like a gun licence . . . just anything.'

'Sardarji, all I want is your kindness. The Great Guru, the True Emperor, has given me all I want. I am a headman and an assessor; I am entitled to sit on a chair at formal occasions; I also have a gun and a pistol. I have cows and buffaloes; plenty to eat and drink and no debts to pay. If I want anything who else can I go to except you! All I want is your kindness.' He smacked Sher Singh on the thigh and added, 'All right, you go to your important business.'

'It isn't all that important,' answered Sher Singh. He knew he was losing the game; he had grossly underestimated the peasant's cunning. He made a headlong plunge. 'Friend,' he whispered, 'you didn't by any chance tell Taylor Sahib about our shooting party of the other day?'

'I tell Taylor Sahib about you? Sardarji, how can you say such a thing?' The headman looked utterly scandalized.

'I know you couldn't have told against your brother. Taylor had empty bullets lying on his table and I thought they might have been mine.'

'Here, Sardarji, are the bullet cases,' said the headman untying the knot of a dirty handkerchief. There were three: on Taylor's table there were also three. Sher Singh had emptied his magazine which took six bullets. He stretched out his hand to take the cases. The headman withdrew the handkerchief and retied the knot. 'No, Sardarji, they are my property. They remind me of the lucky day when I met you.'

Sher Singh felt cornered and helpless. And that in an encounter with a slovenly Sikh peasant with a shaggy, unkempt beard; a rustic whose clothes were full of grease, whose skin had layers of dirt on it and whose head was undoubtedly full of lice.

'Sardarji, who were those Hindu boys with you that day?' asked the peasant again taking Sher Singh's hands in his.

'Friends,' answered Sher Singh. He wasn't going to give the fellow any more information even if they had let him down. 'They were not all Hindus,' he added quickly. He recalled introducing them with Muslim names.

The headman didn't seem perturbed. 'One of them was a gentleman; the tall chap in trousers . . . You know the boy who introduced us!'

'Yes, he is an important officer — a lieutenant in the army.'

'Wonderful!' exclaimed the headman. 'Big people like you should only have big friends.' After a short pause he remarked, 'He looked like a college boy.'

'Yes, he looks younger than he is.'

They sat in silence for some time. Sher Singh felt like ordering the fellow out of the house or having the servants beat him up. He decided to keep calm and make one more attempt to get round his adversary. He got up abruptly and went to his room. He came back with five ten-rupee notes stuffed in his trouser pockets. 'All right, Lambardarji, Sat Sri Akal . . . and here is a little present for your children from me.' He thrust the money in the headman's hands.

'Sardarji, what is this? I am your slave. I have no children and if I had any they would also be your slaves. You don't have to give me anything.'

'You have come to my house for the first time; you must have something, otherwise it will be an ill omen. Buy some sweets for your wife and relations.'

Fifty rupees proved too much for the Lambardar. He accepted them with lavish expressions of praise. 'You are an emperor . . . I shall always sing your praise.'

Sher Singh paid the money but the headman didn't give him a chance to ask for the return of the spent bullets. He kept up a flow of flattery till he left the house.

Sher Singh's illusions about Taylor not knowing of his activities were shattered. He also realized that he had paid the first installment of blackmail money and many more would undoubtedly follow.

Chapter V

S abhrai was possessed of that sixth sense which
often goes with people of deep religious
convictions. It had been proved so often that her
family believed that she had some sort of intuition
which told her of events to come. Once she had returned
from her village many days before she was expected,
just as her husband was being taken to the hospital for
an emergency operation to have his appendix taken out;
she had left long before the telegram summoning her
had been delivered. Once again she had come to her
son's bedside, who, in her absence, had been suddenly
taken ill with typhoid fever. On her arrival she had
not shown any surprise but behaved like a doctor who
had been sent for and was expected to get down to his
job straightaway. She had got down to hers at once:
with softly murmured prayers and gentle ministrations
of her hands which had the healing touch. There
were many other instances. Perhaps they were mere
coincidences to which men of science would attach
little importance. Her family had learnt to know better.
Therefore, when she suddenly declared her intention to
go to her daughter in Simla, neither her husband nor her
son asked her for the reason.

The monsoon had settled down to a routine of rain.
People no longer risked sleeping in the open or on their
rooftops; too often had a clear starlit sky suddenly
become overcast and without warning it had begun
to pour. Buta Singh, Sabhrai, and Sher had taken to

sleeping in the verandah under a ceiling fan. Dyer slept on the floor beside his young master on a trough of sand on which water was sprinkled from time to time. The servants slept in the humid heat of their quarters.

Sabhrai always felt uneasy when all the members of her family were not with her. She talked about those who were away, wrote them long letters full of quotations from the scriptures and sermons to be good. She thought of them in her prayers — particularly with the last one she said before going to sleep. She was doing this the night before she announced her intention to go to Simla. She sat cross-legged in her bed telling the beads of her rosary. After the prayer she shut her eyes and thought of her family by turn. For many days her main concern had been her daughter, Beena. That evening she could think of nothing else and even at prayer her mind had strayed from her God and her Gurus to her daughter. When she went to bed the argument went on in her mind. Although Beena was not alone, she was unprotected. She could be the victim of Madan's wiles. Madan's wife had probably not turned up in Simla. Even if she had, she was not likely to be able to keep her husband straight. For some reason men were inclined to be more promiscuous when their wives were pregnant. Sabhrai tried to drown these ugly thoughts with more fervent praying. But they persisted and when she finally went to sleep somewhat exhausted, they turned into a nightmare. She dreamt that her daughter was being pursued by a band of hooligans wanting to ravish her and was frantically calling for help. As the pursuers gained ground, Sabhrai's agitation changed from dream to reality. When they bore upon her child, she yelled at them and opened her arms to protect her daughter. One of them tried to kiss Sabhrai by force. She began to moan. Dyer got up and came to her bedside and sniffed enquiringly in her ear, then licked her on the nose. Sabhrai woke up with a start and smacked the dog on the face. Her husband and son also woke up.

'What is the matter?' asked Sher Singh turning to his mother.

'This Dyer of yours. He put his cold nose against my face. Don't know what's come over him.'

Dyer was told off by all three and slunk back to his place. Father and son resumed their snoring. Sabhrai returned to her prayers.

At the breakfast table next morning she was quieter than usual. When her husband and son had finished discussing the morning's news, she said, 'We haven't heard from Beena for some days.'

'She must be having a good time. After examinations no one wants to be worried with reading or writing — not even letters,' answered her son.

The concern on Sabhrai's face indicated that she had other things on her mind.

'You must be imagining she is ill. No one falls ill in the hills,' assured Buta Singh.

'Has Madan's wife joined them in Simla?' she asked.

'I don't know, but I can find out,' answered Sher Singh.

'I would like to know.'

Neither father nor son followed the trend of her thoughts. That evening when Sher Singh told her

144 / KHUSHWANT SINGH

that he had found out from Wazir Chand's house that
Madan's wife was still with her parents, Sabhrai stated
firmly, 'I should go to Simla.'

'I asked Wazir Chand myself,' replied Sher Singh
somewhat nonplussed. 'He said Madan's wife would
rejoin her husband after having her baby which is
expected in a month or two.'

After a pause, Sabhrai repeated: 'I ought to go to
Simla. Beena wants me.'

'Why do you get so bothered and impatient?'
protested her son. 'Champak is there; so are Sita and
Madan. And if there were anything wrong, they would
send us a telegram.'

'No, I will go tonight.'

To such determination there was no answer. It only
aroused apprehension: anything that could bother
Sabhrai so much was not to be trifled with. Buta Singh
waited for his son to volunteer to accompany his
mother. Sher Singh did not look up from his plate. 'All
right,' said Buta Singh at last, 'I will send one of my
orderlies with you.'

Sabhrai reached the house in Simla as the siren boomed
across the hills and valleys to announce the middle of
the day. She found the doors and windows wide open
with no one about. She left the orderly to haggle with
the rickshaw coolies and went in. The sitting-room had
not been swept; the dinner table was littered with the
remains of the morning's breakfast; one teacup had
cigarette stubs floating in a mixture of tea and ash. The

next room was obviously her daughter-in-law's: on the table beside the bed was a photograph of her son. The door of the room beyond that was shut. Sabhrai opened it gently. One bed was empty; her daughter was fast asleep in the other. She had a woollen scarf round her neck and was breathing heavily through her mouth. Her nose was raw and there were marks of dried tears on her cheeks. She had a heavy cold.

Beena opened her eyes as Sabhrai's soft hand touched her forehead. Sabhrai sat down beside the pillow and took her daughter's head in her lap. Beena clutched her mother by the waist and burst into tears. Sabhrai began to chant:

'The True, The True
The Great Guru.'

The mother pressed her daughter's head as she chanted. The girl cried, sobbed, sighed, and then fell silent.

'You have no fever?'

Beena shook her head.

'When did you catch the cold?'

'Night before last. We were all drenched.'

'The True, The True
The Great Guru.'

Sabhrai was still with her daughter when Madan and the two girls returned. She heard the servant tell them of her arrival and Madan's loud guffaw, 'Wah ji wah! It is our good kismet that has brought auntie to our home. Where is she?'

'I will get news of my Sardarji,' added Champak jovially. 'He is such a bad correspondent.'

The three came into the bedroom, led by Madan. They bowed to her to receive her blessings.

'Auntie, you did not write about your coming; I would have come to receive you at the taxi stand.'

'No, son, it was only yesterday that I decided to leave; there was no time to write a letter. And I do not like sending telegrams.'

They sat down on Beena's bed. 'First tell me the news of my Sardarji. Why didn't you bring him with you? I don't like it here without him. Now you have come, I can go back,' said Champak.

'Everyone is well. Sherji is very busy with whatever he is doing. He leaves early morning and seldom turns up for dinner.'

'He's got into the rut of leadership,' explained Madan. 'It is very demanding, but it will take him far, very far.'

Sabhrai changed the subject abruptly. 'Madanji, have you good news of your wife?'

'It is quite some time since she wrote,' he replied without any hesitation, 'but you know what girls are when they are with their mothers! All must be well otherwise I would have certainly heard.' He did not let Sabhrai pursue the subject further. 'Auntie, we must celebrate your arrival. I will take you all to Davicos for tea. They have a European band and all the world turns up. It will do Beena good; fresh air is good for a cold.'

Beena waved her hand to say no.

'I think I will stay with Beena,' said Sabhrai.

'Bibiji, you go, I will stay with her,' insisted Champak.

'No, no, no,' protested Beena angrily, 'I don't want anyone to stay with me. I have no fever. I will sit out in the garden in the sun. I don't want to meet people; I can hardly talk. My nose is clogged.'

'That's settled then,' said Madan triumphantly. 'I will book a table. We will steal some of the sandwiches and small cakes and bring them home for Beena.' He laughed at his own joke.

After lunch they left Beena at home and went out for tea. The sun had come out after two days and people came out of their homes as ants emerge out of their holes after rain. The Mall, on which the big stores and restaurants were, was crowded. The Viceroy sped past in his Rolls Royce. The Muslim Chief Minister of the Punjab strode down the slope like an elephant at a ceremonial parade; he wore a white turban whose stiffly starched plumes waved in the air. He was surrounded by a horde of bowing and scraping ministers and civil servants. Behind him followed a train of liveried coolies, bearing his crest on their blue turbans, pulling brightly polished rickshaws. Fashionable women, both English and Indian, strolled about showing off their clothes and exuding expensive French perfumes. Batches of college students went up and down the three hundred-yard stretch of road displaying their college badges and eyeing girls. It was like a fashion parade where everyone was both the mannequin and the audience. Madan had his admirers all along the route. He stopped every few yards to greet them and exchange the three stock questions which people ask each other at holiday resorts: 'When did you come up? Where are you staying? How long will you stay?' And then rejoined Sabhrai and the girls.

Davicos Restaurant was jammed. The air was thick with cigar smoke, perfume, and the smell of whisky. Sabhrai drew one end of her shawl across her face.

The steward conducted them to their table at the farther end of the hall close to the orchestra. Madan surveyed the room, waved to the people he knew, and sat down. 'Auntie, you would hardly believe there is a war on and these English chaps are getting the beating of their lives,' he said to Sabhrai.

Champak answered, 'When they work, they work hard. When they have a good time, they have a really good time. So my Sardarji says.'

'You don't know what the Germans and the Japanese are doing to them! And so far they have had the Indians to go to the front to receive the enemies' bullets. That won't last for long. When it starts here, they will forget about having a good time; then they will think of their maternal grandmothers.'

Sabhrai looked up sharply. Before she could speak, the bearer came with the tray of teacups and started laying them out on the table. As soon as he left, Madan started again, 'Auntie, you think we Indians can do nothing! Wait and see what happens; you just wait and see. We will give them a shoe-beating such as they have never had before.'

Sabhrai did not want to be rude to Madan; nor let him get away with saying things she did not like. She remonstrated gently, 'Son, your father and uncle would not like to hear you talk like this.'

'Auntie, you have old-fashioned ideas.'

'I am an old woman.'

They had their tea without further conversation. Madan turned his chair away to look at the crowd and resumed waving and smiling to his friends.

The setting sun broke through the clouds and came streaming through the large bay windows of the restaurant. It was a magnificent view. Immediately below them was the unshapely mass of grey and red of the tin roofs of Simla's bazaar. Kites dive-bombed into the narrow streets and reappeared with food in their talons. They fought in the air and went whirling down in pairs. Beyond the bazaar yawned an enormous valley with its terraced fields and tiny farm houses; in the centre of the valley was a silver stream with its banks flecked with white where the washermen had spread their clothes to dry. Beyond all these were the vast plains of Hindustan with the river Sutlej winding its way through the golden haze like a gilded serpent. The sun went down behind a range of low hills. Twilight spread over the city and the mountains like the hand of benediction. Some English people came across with their whisky glasses to admire the scene; many Indians followed their example.

Sabhrai got up. She did not like to be surrounded by people smoking and drinking. The evening star was up in the deep blue sky and it was time for prayer once more.

The bill had to be paid so Madan suggested their going ahead. Champak volunteered to stay and come with him; it was her only chance to agree to explanations if any were called for. Sita went home with Sabhrai.

Madan and Champak came out in the brightly lit and crowded street. They went across to the ridge which was less crowded. There were many benches on the sides but they were all occupied.

'Can't we find any place where we can be alone for a few minutes?' asked Champak, taking Madan's hand.

'Let us go to the tennis club,' he replied. 'After dark there is no one there.' He marvelled at the woman's daring.

They went down a steep road and came to the club. The courts were absolutely dark and deserted. They found a bench and sat down. Madan pulled Champak onto his lap. He pressed his lips on hers and his hands sought the cord of her trousers. Champak pushed him back rudely and stood up. 'I did not come for this,' she hissed angrily. 'I am not a bazaar woman who sleeps with men in the open.'

'I am sorry,' replied Madan tamely. 'I thought you wanted to say something to me alone.'

'Say, not do,' she replied. She sat down beside him and took his hand in hers. She put her head against his shoulder. 'I am so worried and you don't care at all.'

'What are you worried about?'

'Why do you think the old woman has turned up suddenly?'

'I don't know. But why should that worry you?'

'You don't know her. She gets to know things that no one else knows. Besides, I think Beena suspects and she may tell. I am going mad, I will kill myself.' Tears rolled down her cheeks. 'Why did I do it? Why, why, why!' she sobbed.

'Why does Beena suspect?'

She told him of the letter left on her pillow the night she had come to him.

Madan put his arm round her shoulders and kissed her on the ear. 'Beena will never tell. You take it from me, never.'

'How are you so certain?' she asked, looking up with her tear-stained eyes.

Madan kissed her tears away. 'Because she wanted to come to me herself. I did not agree. She can never say a word against you.'

Champak's concern changed to anger. 'The slut! How can she raise her eyebrows at me? Or her old, pious mother point an accusing finger at me?'

'I told you no one can say anything.' Madan raised her on his lap and once more his hands went exploring. They did not meet any resistance — nor any response.

'Nevertheless I have been bad. It was absolute madness.' She kissed him on his lips and got up. 'No more of this. Never again.'

Chapter VI

In the absence of Sabhrai, Shunno automatically became the mistress of the household. She played her role well. She pandered to Buta Singh's whims and mothered Sher Singh. She also resumed bullying Mundoo. She nagged him all the time and occasionally smacked him. With no one left to complain to, Mundoo decided to repeat the trick which had earlier on put Shunno out of action for twenty-four hours. At the end of a day when he had enough of Shunno's tongue — she had even pulled his ears till he had screamed — he took all the gum and red ink from Beena's table and emptied it into Shunno's jug of water.

Shunno took her responsibilities seriously. Despite the recurrence of the mysterious disease, she attended to her master's breakfast, prepared the dinner, and told Mundoo to warm it before serving it. She asked for permission to be absent for the day. Buta Singh was too well-bred to ask a woman questions about her illness. He offered to get a doctor from the municipal hospital. But Shunno did not believe in Western-trained doctors and their bitter medicines. She had faith in vaids and hakims brought up on ancient Indian and Arabic systems. She had more faith in the prescriptions of holy men who combined spiritual ministrations with medicine. Peer Sahib was such a man.

•

Peer Sahib was a young man under thirty years of age. He had inherited the guardianship of the tomb of an illustrious ancestor — respectfully referred to as Hazrat Sahib — who had made many converts to Islam in days gone by. Hazrat Sahib had lived in the open under a jujube tree. When he died he was buried under the shade of the same tree and his tomb became an object of worship. People came from distant towns and villages and it started drawing a handsome income in offerings. The mud and brick of the tomb was replaced by marble slabs and a red headstone with a niche for an oil lamp. Then a large brick courtyard was built to enclose it. And, finally, rooms were put up for the guardian of the shrine who was always chosen from amongst the descendants of the Hazrat Sahib's brothers. The incumbent had to devote himself to the study of the Koran, the Traditions, Islamic law, and medicine. He also had to remain celibate, and succession went from uncle to nephew.

Like his predecessors, Peer Sahib spent most of the day praying and giving spiritual guidance to the men and women who flocked to the tomb. He did not know much about medicine, but since most of the people who came to consult him were more sick in mind than in body, he was able to minister to their needs. His following, though largely Muslim, had also a sprinkling of Hindus and Sikhs.

Shunno had chosen a good day to call on the Peer Sahib. The three-day celebrations of the anniversary of the illustrious ancestor's death had ended and the crowds had departed. There were only a few people sitting under the shade of the jujube tree which was alive

with the twittering of sparrows. The tomb was draped
in a green cloth on which were strewn rose petals and
copper coins. The courtyard was littered with paper and
crumpled plates made of leaves sewn together. Seventy-
two hours of non-stop singing, dervish dancing, prayer,
and sermon, had left everyone and everything exhausted.
Shunno joined the group by the grave.

'Peer Sahib is asleep. He won't be up for a long
time,' said one of the women. 'The anniversary of the
Hazrat Sahib's ascent to heaven ended yesterday, and
Peer Sahib is very tired.'

'I will wait. I have come a long distance from the
city.'

An hour later, Peer Sahib emerged from his room
in the corner of the courtyard. He was a tall, wiry man
with closely cropped hair. Unlike most Muslim divines,
he did not grow a beard; only a scissor-trimmed stubble
spread from one ear to the other. He had a thin moustache
which fell below his chin on either side in the fashion
of the Mongol, Genghis Khan. He wore large earrings
and a necklace of amber beads of the size of pigeon
eggs over his black silk shirt. He was handsome in an
austere sort of way — high cheek-bones and sunken
eyes. He had no loose flesh over his big, bony frame.
Women found him compelling since he carried an air of
spiritual disdain towards their sex.

He filled his brass jug from a pitcher which stood on
a stool beside his door and washed his face. He gargled
noisily and spat the water on the wall; then splashed
more water on his head, face, and hands and held up
his hands in the air to dry (the Prophet had never used

a towel). He came to his congregation praising Allah in his rich, bass voice.

'Salaam, Peer Sahib; may Allah bring plenty to you!' exclaimed the Muslims and put offerings of a few pice each on the tomb. Shunno touched the holy man's feet and placed something wrapped in a towel in front of him. Peer Sahib looked away. Shunno removed the towel and uncovered a silver plate with slices of coconut and five shining rupees. Five rupees was many times more than the measly copper pice the faithful had offered. Peer Sahib saw them from a corner of his eye; but he was not one to express interest in money — particularly when it came from an infidel woman. He looked up to the sky and said: 'May Allah be merciful to you, my daughter, and fulfil your wishes. The offerings are not for us; we have nothing to do with money. If you want to give something in the name of the Almighty, place it on the tomb of our revered ancestor, now sitting in the lap of Allah.'

Shunno did as she was told. It gave her a peculiar pleasure to have a man, young enough to be her son, call her daughter.

'It is time for our evening prayer. Ask what you have to ask; then we must devote ourselves to the praise of our Maker.'

The women asked what they wanted, got the Peer Sahib's blessings, and departed with their children and menfolk. Shunno waited until the last one had left; her troubles could not be mentioned in public.

'Daughter, what is it you desire?'

'You are a Man of God who can remove all affliction.'

'Allah is the remover of ills; we are only his slaves. What ails you, my child?'

Shunno only shifted her weight from one leg to another.

'We haven't much time. The sun is setting and we must pray. If it is a child you want, we will give you an amulet to wear when you are being intimate with your man. If Allah is pleased, your womb will fill again and again.'

Shunno blushed. She nearly fifty and children! How far this young man of God was from worldly things! Perhaps he did not know the first thing about sex. Such were the pure in heart!

'Peer Sahib, my man was summoned by the Great Guru thirty years ago,' she explained. 'I do not want a child. My troubles are of a different sort.' She drew her veil across her face and hurriedly whispered her ailment to the holy man. 'You are the only one who can cure me. I have no faith in English-trained doctors, nor in hakims or vaids. If you make me well, I will give you all you want. I will give marble for the headstone of the tomb of your great one.'

Peer Sahib pondered in silence.

'Daughter, this will need careful examination. Would you not rather see a lady doctor?'

'You are the knower of all secrets; what is it that I can hide from you? I have no fear.'

'Then wait till we have finished our evening prayer.'

The Peer Sahib bolted the door of the courtyard. He washed himself once more and faced west towards Mecca. He put his hands to his ears, turned his face to

the heavens, and in his rich mellifluent voice beckoned
the faithful to prayer. His voice floated across space
with no one to hear it, for habitation was a long way off.
Peer Sahib himself hearkened to his call and proceeded
to whisper his prayer and go through the series of
genuflections. He sat on his shins with his palms open
as if he were reading them like an open book. He
turned his face to the right and blessed those on his
right side. He turned his face to the left and blessed the
rest. He rubbed his face with his palms and stood up
still praising Allah. The short twilight gave way to the
night. The sparrows on the jujube tree were silent. Only
dogs barked in the distance.

Peer Sahib brought an earthenware lamp from his
room, lit it, and placed it in the niche in the headstone
of the tomb. He whispered yet another prayer for the
peace of the departed soul, again holding his hands
in front of him like an open book. He went back and
brought another oil lamp. 'Daughter, let us see your
trouble,' he said holding the lamp up to his shoulder.

'Here? In the open?'

'The door of the courtyard is shut. No one comes
here after sunset.'

'If you look away, I can take my clothes off.'

The Peer Sahib turned his face to the wall. Shunno
undid the cord of her trousers and underwear and slipped
them below her knees. She laid herself on the floor beside
the tomb and covered her face with her hands.

'See.'

The holy man turned and saw a fat middle-aged
woman lying bare from the navel to her ankles. He held

the oil lamp in his left hand and sat down beside her. The aroma of jasmine and sweat filled his holy nostrils; the infidel woman had perfumed her privates. '*Aaoozo Billahé Minash Shaitanur.* . . . I seek the protection of Allah from Satan,' said he getting down to his job, 'there is no power except that of God . . . *Allah Billah.*' With his large calloused peasant's hands he stroked the soft flesh of the woman's underbelly and the sides of her thighs. There was no visible evidence of any disease.

'Turn over.'

Shunno turned over baring her enormous wrinkled behind. The Peer Sahib's healing hands went gently over the sagging buttocks down to the back of her thighs and up again. He explored the depths with his fingers and saw what there was to be seen by the help of the oil lamp. He could not find a clue to Shunno's mysterious ailment.

'Turn over.'

Shunno complied once more. Peer Sahib came over and examined more carefully. His scrutiny was no longer confined to clinical ends. With the vows of celibacy to which he was committed, sex got little chance of natural expression. He had had to be satisfied with his own devices or occasionally take liberties with little boys sent by their mothers to learn the Scripture. These were not the normally accepted expressions of sex and therefore did not violate the rules of celibacy as he interpreted them. Neither did intercourse with an infidel woman who might in this way be brought on the right path. And it was obvious she had come with something of the sort in mind. So the Peer Sahib put the other lamp also on his ancestor's grave and obliged.

Shunno made a nominal protest at the start: 'Na, na, someone will see,' and then accepted the inevitable. She had almost forgotten what sex was. Her instincts had been buried under a thick pack of conventional morality prescribed for a Hindu widow — religion, charity, gossip about sex, but no sex. Here was a man twenty years younger, strong and virile with an untamed lust savagely tearing off the padding of respectability with which she had covered herself. He stirred up the fires of a volcano which had all but become extinct. It was all wrong, but it was deliciously irresistible. It was like an itch which begs to be scratched till it draws blood.

The two lay on the hard brick floor of the starlit courtyard till the early hours of the morning with only the slumbering sparrows and the winking oil lamps on the Hazrat Sahib's tomb to witness the goings on. Not a word of affection or explanation passed between them.

Shunno repeated the visit several times with several shining silver rupees. Her temper improved: she stopped nagging or beating Mundoo. Instead she brought him sweets from the bazaar. There was no reason for Mundoo to take recourse to bottles of gum and red ink.

The cure was a complete success.

Neither her intuition nor her shrewd insight into human character gave Sabhrai a clue as to what had passed between Beena and Madan — or between Madan and Champak. For one, Beena's cold led her off the scent; she believed that it was her daughter's illness which had been mysteriously conveyed to her. And she was pleased to have yet another confirmation of the prowess of knowing whenever any member of her family needed her. For another, Madan completely won her heart with his attentions. At the breakfast table he read out the news and translated it for her in Punjabi. Her own family had hardly ever taken any notice of her in their political discussions which were carried on exclusively in English. When they went out, he preferred walking with her rather than with the girls. He introduced her, an old-fashioned Punjabi woman, to his college friends always adding: 'You know the mother of our future Chief Minister, Sardar Sher Singh.' It did not sound as if he were pulling her leg. Her suspicions were completely allayed. She settled down to enjoying the blue skies and the pine-scented air of Simla. She hoped that her husband and son would join her. But neither said anything about his plans. When the exam results were announced, there was an exchange of telegrams. Both her children had passed: Sita, as expected, in the first division and Beena in the third. From then on there was little communication between the family. But the days went by pleasantly.

A month later, events took place which not only shook the country but almost destroyed Sabhrai's family. Neither her sixth sense nor the Guru speaking through the Holy Book gave her any warning. She learnt of them from the headlines of the daily newspaper read out by Madan.

The fresh cold air of Simla had been getting the better of Sabhrai and she had been getting up later and later every day. One morning she had only finished her bath when the servant came in to say that breakfast was on the table. She did not want to keep her hosts waiting and decided to postpone her prayers.

Madan never smoked in front of Sabhrai. That morning he did not throw away the cigarette he was smoking nor get up from his chair. 'Listen to the rumblings before the earthquake, auntie,' said he, and proceeded to tell her of the breakdown in the negotiations between the British and Indian leaders. He told her that the Nationalists had called a meeting at Mahatma Gandhi's hermitage to decide on the next step. Meanwhile the police had begun arresting demonstrators; in Dacca alone over seven hundred had been arrested in one day. There had been riots in many towns.

He stubbed out his cigarette and lit another. 'These bloody English won't learn till they get a real shoe-beating,' he said angrily.

'Is there any trouble in the Punjab?' asked Sabhrai.

'There have been a few arrests including some in Simla yesterday. But no rioting or violence — not so far.'

'Not by the people perhaps, but by the police,' added Sita. 'Last evening I saw a boy volunteer — he couldn't have been more than fourteen or fifteen — come up the steps of the lower bazaar to picket an English store on the Mall. A European sergeant hit him full in the face. He fell and must have rolled down at least a dozen of those horribly steep steps when one of the crowd came to his help. The sergeant went down and arrested the picket as well as the man who had helped him. I saw them taken to the police station. The boy must have had some of his teeth knocked out; he was bleeding profusely. There was an uproar on the Mall and many shops closed in protest.' Sita seldom spoke this way. Her cheeks were flushed.

'Bastards,' muttered Madan in great anger.

After a pause Champak said: 'I suppose this will go on and on.'

'This sort of thing never stops,' replied Madan.

'Then I must get back to my husband. He mixes with such queer types and gets excited very quickly. Bibiji, don't you think I should go back? I will do exactly as you tell me.'

Sabhrai did not say anything. Champak sensed that her mother-in-law would not object. 'If you give me permission, I will leave tomorrow.'

'You have never travelled alone,' interrupted Sita. 'These are dangerous times; Madan Bhraji can go with you. We can look after ourselves for a few days.'

'No, no!' protested Champak. 'He can put me in a taxi. I am bound to meet somebody at the Kalka railway station who can see me home.'

'That is out of the question,' stated Madan in a tone of authority. 'Of course, I will go with you. You are not the only one who wants to see Sherji; I also want to see my brother. He is doing all the work amongst the students and I am having a good time in Simla. I will send him up for a few days' rest.'

It was agreed that the two would leave the next day.

Madan went to the bazaar to book places in the taxi which was to take them down to the plains. Most of the Indian bazaar was shut. All European and some Muslim-owned shops on the Mall were open. Nationalist volunteers in Gandhi caps came up the long flights of stairs to picket them. Knots of people collected at a safe distance to watch.

Madan saw the scene narrated by his sister enacted before his eyes. Encouraged by the audience, one of the volunteers shouted defiantly, 'Victory to Mahatma Gandhi,' and waved his tricolour flag. A white sergeant walked up to him. The volunteer cowered down and covered his face with his arms. The sergeant hit him from below on the chin and sent him flying backwards down the steps. Two constables ran after him and brought him back handcuffed. His nose was bleeding and he cried like a child. Madan's blood boiled within his veins; his hands itched to get round the sergeant's throat.

All that afternoon and evening and the next day, till it was time to take the taxi, they talked nothing but politics. A national crisis had overtaken them and completely swamped their personal problems. Beena did not dare to sulk or even hint that Champak and Madan travelling together might cause people to talk. It seemed treasonable to mention such trifles — particularly when Madan seemed so concerned with the fate of his country and Champak so worried about her husband.

Rumours of road blocks and attacks on trains had caused a lot of cancellations; Champak and Madan had the taxi all to themselves. The momentous events taking place in the country and their own secret desires seemed to create a conflict in their minds which made talking of either one or the other somewhat difficult. They sat in silence at the two ends of the rear seat looking at the mountainous scenery — the lush green hillsides and endless stretches of valley lost in the haze of tropical sunshine. Champak, who normally took this journey badly, was able to do the sixty miles of tortuously winding road without feeling sick. They came down from the cool breezes of fir and pine of the high Himalayas to the hot, dusty plains of the Punjab.

The railway station at Kalka was crowded with English soldiers and coolies. From the hill cantonments of Taradevi, Kasauli, Dagshai, and Sanawar, British soldiers and officers had come down in lorry loads to go to distant towns to quell the disturbances which had broken out. The European refreshment room was packed with officers drinking iced beer under the mad whirl of ceiling fans. Madan, who had always preferred going there rather than to any of the Indian varieties (Hindu vegetarian, Hindu non-vegetarian, or the Muslim), went straight to the Hindu non-vegetarian. He asked Champak to order the dinner and went out to buy the railway tickets.

At the ticket-booth he was informed that all the first and second class accommodation had been reserved for the officers and soldiers. In the inter and the third class there were no reservations — nor any privacy. Madan bought two seconds despite the clerk's warning that he would find no berths on the train. He went to the platform on which his train was standing. A group of Indian ticket-collectors were busy checking reservations. Madan took the youngest by the hand, put his arm round his shoulders, and drew him away to a quiet spot.

'Brother, I have to have a second class coupé at any cost and you have to find it for me.' He slipped a ten-rupee note into the collector's hand.

The collector gave the note a quick glance and thrust it into his pocket. A ten-rupee tip for a man whose monthly salary was Rs 50 was nothing to scoff at. Madan also looked familiar and important; he spoke with the tone of confidence which goes with authority. 'It is going to be extremely difficult,' replied the collector. 'The whole train is packed with British tommies; their reservations were made two days ago. But I'll try.' After a pause he asked: 'Are you by any chance Mr Madan, the famous cricketer?'

'The same, your humble servant,' replied Madan with a bow.

They shook hands.

The collector took out the ten-rupee note and put it back in Madan's hand. 'Keep this. Put your luggage in this second class coupé and I will put a reservation slip in your name.'

Madan forced the note back into the collector's pocket. 'What I give once I never take back. After all, getting British soldiers out of a train in these times is not easy. It needs a man of courage to do that.'

The flattery worked. 'Mr Madan, if you can hit them for sixers, I can write them down on my penis. You will say one day that you met Mussadi Lal, the ticket-collector of Kalka. My name is Mussadi Lal.' He slapped his chest in a gesture of defiance. They shook hands once more.

Mussadi Lal took out a key from his pocket and unlocked the glass frame alongside the door of the compartment. He took out the card marked 'Reserved for B.O.R.'s No. 171/172,' tore it up and flung the bits in the air with contempt. He wrote out another one in the name of Mr and Mrs Madan and put it in its place.

'Here!' he said slapping his chest again. 'What will you say!'

They shook hands a third time.

'Mr Mussadi Lalji, I'll sing your praises. If there were a few more brave people like you, India would have been free many years ago.'

The collector accepted the compliment; they shook hands for the fourth time and said goodbye.

Madan joined Champak for dinner. He ordered two bottles of beer and drank them in the Hindu refreshment room which had no licence to sell liquor nor a permit to allow consumption of alcoholic beverages. Madan was above these petty rules and regulations; and now he was celebrating his victory over the British Army.

He ate his dinner with relish and relaxed with a cigarette. When it was finished, he got up, took Champak by the elbow: 'Let's go.' On the way to the compartment he bought some betel leaves charged with lime paste, cardamoms, and scented betel nuts. He ordered a couple of iced bottles of lemonade to be left in the coupé and told the coolie to spread the bedding rolls on the berths. He left Champak to change while he took a stroll on the platform.

The train was due to leave at midnight but most of the upper class passengers had retired and put up the shutters of their compartments. The inter and third classes were also quiet with people dozing on each other's shoulders. The hawkers had packed up and left. The platform was deserted except for the railway staff.

Many soldiers were still in the refreshment rooms drinking beer when the guard's whistle summoned them to the train. They trudged out in the sweltering heat with their heavy packs on their backs and their sten guns slung on their shoulders. Most of them found their berths indicated on the counterfoils they carried. Only two remained. They went up and down the platform peering at reservation slips to find one that matched their own. The engine-driver blew the warning whistle. The soldiers began to shout for the guard. Instead of the guard, they found Mussadi Lal walking quickly away towards the end of the platform.

'Hey you, Babu. Where's our berths?'

'Sir?'

'Them places to sleep on you know! *Charpoy bashin!*' One of them shut his eyes and put his cheek against his hand. 'Unnerstan?' The other showed him the counterfoil. Mussadi Lal examined it carefully and consulted the reservations in his book.

'Sir, I have no record of this reservation. There is no place on the train. You can go by the morning express.'

'Mawhnin? Wot you talkin Babu? Court martial if we don't get there tomorrer. Court martial you know?' The soldier unslung his sten gun, stuck the nozzle in Mussadi Lal's belly and explained 'Tatatatatatattat — bang.' He fell back a step to indicate the effect of the firing. 'Unnerstan? Give us them berths or we'll stick the gun up your tail. Hurry-*juldi.*'

The guard blew his whistle and waved his green lantern. The engine gave another blast and jerked the train into movement.

'Sir,' stuttered Mussadi Lal, 'there is no time now. I will ask the guard to let you sit in his compartment. He may find you a place at the next station.'

The tommies began to shout. 'We are fighting for the King and country. Our f . . . King and your f . . . country and you can't find a charpoy on this 'ere trayn?'

Many shutters were let down and genteel ears heard the inebriated tommies blaspheme and curse on the deserted platform. The shutters were quickly put up. The train began to gather speed.

'Where's the f . . . guard's van?'

Mussadi Lal and the two soldiers ran to the tail end of the train. The guard stood in the open door of his van. Mussadi Lal breathlessly explained to him in Hindustani, 'Let these whites who sleep with their sisters get in till they can find a place. They are drunk and may let off their guns. One never knows with these people!'

The soldiers leapt into the guard's van hurling insults to the King and country. Mussadi Lal waved them a goodbye and then shook his arm from the elbows to make an obscene gesture. 'Ride on my pony if there is no room on the train,' he roared.

The occupants of the soldiers' berths did not hear the abuse. The musical hum of the fan and the tipity, tipity, tap of the wheels beating time drowned all unpleasant noise. A cool breeze came through the shutters smelling of the green rain-washed forest. Champak went into the bathroom and took a shower. She came back wearing her transparent kimono. She went to the window and let down the shutter. A gust of wind blew the kimono on either side, baring her from her feet to her waist. Her hair flew wildly like the snakes on Medusa's head. Madan got up, switched off the lights, and came towards her.

'Can't you bear to see me as I am? Why do you want it dark?'

Madan pressed the switch. Champak took off her kimono, tossed it on the rack and lay down on the berth.

'Now you can switch off the lights if you want to.'

Madan stared at the girl stretched out on the white bedsheet. He had never seen a woman like that — not even his own wife.

'Don't look at me like that; it makes me ashamed of my nakedness,' said Champak turning her back and hiding her face. 'You look as if you had never seen a woman.'

Madan switched off the light and came to her. 'No, I have never seen one with absolutely nothing on — never,' he said hoarsely.

'I still have my wrist-watch.'

Chapter VII

Sher Singh saw the morning paper before his father. He read the news of the arrests of the Indian leaders and of the strikes and demonstrations taking place all over the country — except in the Punjab. At the breakfast table he read out the headlines to his father. They were discussing the consequences of the action taken by the Government when an orderly came with a message asking Buta Singh to come to Taylor's bungalow at once.

Sher Singh took the paper to the sitting-room and scanned the details. As he went from page to page he realized that everywhere in India the people were protesting; only the Punjab was peaceful. He thought of his own inactivity. He too was doing nothing except lie on the sofa and get worked up. Just then Mundoo brought the post and handed him a letter. It was a cyclostyled circular in English with the caption, 'A Manifesto of the Hindustan Socialist Republican Army.' It drew attention to the arrests of the leaders and asked the youth of India to rise and rid themselves of foreign rule. It did not mince its words. 'Shoot English officials and the Indian toadies who serve them. Destroy roads and bridges; cut telegraph and telephone wires; create chaos and paralyse the administration. This is your sacred duty. Long live the revolution.' Sher Singh examined the postmark. The letter had been posted the evening before from the city. He had heard of the terrorist organization which went under the name of the Hindustan Socialist Republican Army but had never met anyone who belonged to it. Could someone have told them that Sher Singh was a secret sympathizer?

Sher Singh stayed at home and brooded. He listened in to the news over the radio each time it came on. Each time it was the same story — demonstrations, violence, arrests everywhere — everywhere except in the Punjab. Wasn't it time for him to throw caution to the winds and strike a blow? He was like the rest of his countrymen, frittering away his energies in quarrelling with his colleagues. How could he get them to collaborate in any plan of action which required courage and daring for its execution? He spent that day and night in these thoughts and decided that the hour of trial had come. At some time or the other in their lives, men had to gamble with fortune. Those that won, became great; those that lost, lost; those that refused to take the chance, made up the mass of mediocrity.

Next morning one of the boys of his group turned up at the house. He walked straight into his room. 'Sher Singhji,' he said without a word of greeting or explanation, 'the time for quarrels is over, we have to do something.'

'Do what?' asked Sher Singh sitting up.

'Something or other. You are our leader, we will follow you.'

Sher Singh ran his fingers through his thin beard, pulled out some hairs and examined them thoughtfully. After a minute he answered, 'O.K. I will be in your house in half-an-hour. Ask the others to come too. Tell them to come at different times with books on their carriers; there are bound to be a lot of policemen about.'

A few minutes later, Sher Singh cycled out of the house with his hockey kit on the carrier behind him. In the bag were also six hand-grenades which had been lying with him for many months.

All the boys who had taken part in the shooting practice were there; only Madan was missing. Since he was in Simla, and there was no time to waste, they got down to business. The first thing they did was to take an oath of secrecy. They spread out the Indian tricolour flag on the table and put their hands on it. Someone produced a picture of Mahatma Gandhi and set it in the centre.

'No, not Gandhi,' said Sher Singh. 'What has he to do with bombs and pistols? We are not launching a campaign of passive resistance. We will take the oath in the name of our martyrs. Have you a picture of Bhagat Singh?'

The host fetched a card with the photograph of the handsome, clean-shaven Sikh terrorist who had been hanged twelve years earlier and laid it on the flag. They took the oath to liberate their country from foreign rule. Then Sher Singh got down to explaining the line of action. 'The call is to destroy means of communication,' he said. 'A few bridges blown up, a few roads barricaded, and the British Army will be stuck where it is.'

'How is a bridge blown up?'

'They are heavily guarded. We'll have to kill many soldiers before we can tamper with a bridge.'

'I have never blown up a bridge,' replied Sher Singh, 'but we can learn. We will try our hand on something small and unguarded. I have six hand-grenades. I am sure they will knock down one of the canal bridges. Later on we can have a go at a bigger one — perhaps a railway bridge.' Sher Singh opened his bag and showed them the grenades.

'What do you do with them?'

Sher Singh unfolded a piece of paper on which he had written down the instructions and read them out.

'Let us blow up the little bridge near where you shot the crane.'

'That's what I had in mind too,' agreed Sher Singh. 'It is in a deserted spot. We can test the power of these grenades without anyone bothering us.'

They agreed to go back to their homes and meet in the afternoon outside the city. Sher Singh decided to stay where he was rather than go back home and be seen again by the sentry at the gate of the house.

The group reassembled a few hours later and made for the canal. They wore coloured sports shirts and carried their hockey sticks. They passed many policemen on the way but no one took any notice of them. When they reached the bridge, there was still daylight. Some of the boys took off their clothes and jumped into the canal; others went with Sher Singh to examine the bridge. It was barely ten feet wide, made of red bricks. The thick layer of dried dung showed that it was mainly used by cattle. They came back and joined the bathers.

The sun set and the short twilight quickly darkened into night. There was no moon. It was silent except for the croaking of frogs. Sher Singh took out his flashlight and produced one of the grenades. 'I suppose the first honour goes to me,' he said gravely.

'Sure, leader. But tell us how it is done,' they said closing round him.

They went down the canal embankment to take cover. Sher Singh stood up. He pulled out the pin of the grenade with his teeth, counted five, hurled it on the bridge, and sat down. The grenade bounced off the parapet and fell into the water with a loud splash and exploded. It sent a jet of water flying into the air. The next one, thrown by one of the other boys, exploded on the bridge and sent up the debris all round. So did the remaining four. The boys ran up through the dust and the smoke to see the damage they had caused. Sher Singh flashed his torch. There were big dents in the centre of the bridge and the parapet had been knocked off at several places; but it was still serviceable. They mounted their bicycles and sped back as fast as they could.

Sher Singh went to the bazaar near the railway station where there was a row of eating places. He sat down on a steel chair on the pavement and ordered himself a plate of meat and raw onions; he ate onions to his heart's content when his wife was away. The cook slapped a few chapatis and baked them in the oven. Sher Singh had his dinner on the pavement along with a motley crowd of peasants and labourers, and listened to the music coming over the radio. He heard the nine o'clock news. He heard about the Allied victories in the face of Fascist advances and the calm in the country despite thousands of arrests. It did not irritate him any more. He knew they were lying.

Sher Singh got home after 10 p.m., his mouth still on fire from the chillies and raw onions he had eaten. Finding his wife at home was not a pleasant surprise. She made it unpleasanter. 'Hullo, hullo, when did you turn up? You did not send any word!'

Champak was too angry to talk. She just looked out of the window. Sher Singh came to her and put his arms round her shoulders. 'Don't be cross. How could I have known you were coming?'

'This is what you do when I am away.'

Champak covered her nose with her handkerchief; the reek of raw onions was overpowering. Sher Singh kissed her on the back of her neck and then on the cheeks. She shook herself free. 'Now I suppose it is my turn. I am just the wife you can have whenever you want . . . after you've had your own good time,' she said bitterly. The suspicion of infidelity amused Sher Singh. He became more amorous. 'I am not like one of those chaps . . . like your Madan,' he said laughing. 'That type go about sleeping with anyone they can. For me it is only you. I was at a meeting, that is why I am late. If I had known you were coming I would have left it and come straight home.'

The reference to Madan changed Champak's attitude. 'I've been waiting for you all day. I nearly died of worry,' she complained. 'You must not be out late these days. These are dangerous times.'

Sher Singh promised not to be late again. They forgave each other in their usual way. Only Champak kept thinking how different this was from the evening before. That man's breath was perfumed with cardamoms and scented betel nuts; and this man's! She could not avoid smelling the onions even when she breathed through her mouth.

The orderly took Buta Singh's cycle from him and stood it against the wall. Buta Singh unfastened the metal bands he wore round his shins to save his trousers being soiled and put them in his pocket. 'Have the others come?' he asked.

'Yes sir, but not all; the Sahib is waiting for them. He has ordered me to inform him as soon as everyone is here. Please sit down.' He held up the heavy khas fiber chick. Buta Singh ducked under it and joined his fellow magistrates. They stood up to shake hands with him.

'Buta Singh give us some news. You are in the know. What itches the Sahib today?'

It was a Muslim colleague and with Muslims it was not wise to be honest about politics. They pretended to be against the idea of Pakistan when they were with non-Muslims but gave it their support in every way they could.

'It must be the arrests of the Nationalist leaders. I suppose he expects trouble in the city,' answered Buta Singh.

'The police brought papers of some of these Gandhi disciples to my house yesterday,' continued the Muslim a little maliciously. 'I sentenced them to six months' detention under the Defence of India Rules.'

Buta Singh knew that if the papers had concerned a Muslim supporter of Pakistan, the same magistrate would have argued with the police. In that case the police would undoubtedly have arranged to bring the papers to somebody like Wazir Chand or himself and they would have taken pleasure in locking up the Muslim for six months. That was the accepted method of dispensing justice from the lowest tribunal to the highest.

Four magistrates, including Wazir Chand, arrived together. The newcomers greeted the others very cordially and took their seats — the Muslims with the Muslims, Hindus and Sikhs with the Hindus and Sikhs. That sort of division took place automatically.

Wazir Chand embraced Buta Singh and the two sat down next to each other. Their families had brought them closer than they believed possible.

'Did daughter Champak reach home safe and sound?' asked Wazir Chand.

'Champak! Is she back? I left home very early.'

'Yes, Madan escorted her from Simla; that is why I am late. She wanted to come back to Sher. Youth, you know! How long can a young wife keep away from her husband?' Wazir Chand smiled mischievously.

'It is good she is back. Sher has been very lonely and working too hard with his student organizations. Everything else O.K.?'

Wazir Chand wagged his head contentedly and then asked in a whisper, 'What is all this about?'

'I suppose he wants us to do special duty. He's expecting trouble after the arrests of the leaders.'

The chaprasi came out and asked the magistrates to come into the sitting-room. He held the chick up for them and they filed in. Taylor got up and shook hands with them. He was smoking his pipe and looked completely unruffled: he was keeping up the tradition of the British Civil Service of appearing calm in times of crisis. He pretended that it was the sort of meeting he called on the eve of religious festivals. He did not ask them to sit down but dismissed them with a short speech: 'Gentlemen, I am sorry to have sent for you at short notice. You have no doubt read the news of the arrest of some political leaders. We are not concerned with the rights or wrongs of the decision; we have to carry out the orders of the Government. Our hands are strengthened by the fact that the Government of the Punjab thoroughly disapproves of the position taken by the leaders of the Nationalist Party and fortunately the Nationalists have very little following here. We are not expecting any trouble from our own people but mischief-makers may come in from other provinces. We have to be vigilant. We have powers to detain people on suspicion. These powers are not to be abused; but we must not hesitate to make use of them whenever necessary. We have to co-operate with the police in maintaining law and order. If you have any information of importance or need my advice, come to me without hesitation. That is all for the moment. Thank you.'

Taylor turned away without shaking hands again. He paused at the door. 'Buta Singh, do you mind waiting. I want to have a word with you.'

A minute later Taylor came back to the sitting-room and asked Buta Singh to sit down beside him on the sofa. He knocked his pipe against his heel and blew in it. He filled it with tobacco, lit it, pressed the tobacco with the matchbox, and took a few puffs with noisy 'Urn ums.' Buta Singh was quite used to the trick; it no longer played on his nerves. He waited patiently for the Englishman to begin.

'Buta Singh, I am a little worried and want your advice.'

'Whatever little service I can perform! I am at your disposal.' Buta Singh rubbed his hands with obsequious eagerness.

Taylor produced a copy of a cyclostyled leaflet. Buta Singh read the exhortation by the Hindustan Socialist Republican Army to rise against the British. 'The Police Commissioner has given me this thing,' continued Taylor. 'The envelope bears a city postmark. He says we can presume it was also printed here. That is the most he can say. It may be the doing of some one individual who may do nothing more. It is also possible that there is some sort of organization in the city which has violent aims and is planning to put them into effect. If that is so it must be tracked down and its plans nipped in the bud.'

'Before it can do any mischief,' added Buta Singh.

'Precisely.'

They both became silent. Buta Singh expected Taylor to tell him what he wanted him to do. Taylor believed the hint was good enough. Then, seeing that Buta Singh had not taken the cue, added, 'Can you help in tracking down these people?'

'If Sahib assigns me this duty, I will carry it out. I should have thought this sort of job is more for a policeman than for a magistrate.'

Taylor relit his pipe; it did not need relighting. Could he make the suggestion directly or would Buta Singh take offence? 'Buta Singh, I wasn't thinking of official action. These chaps are obviously some young hotheads who have got a little worked up. If we knew who they were, we could keep an eye on them and save them from their own acts. Even talk to them in a friendly way.'

Buta Singh realized what Taylor was driving at; he kept his eyes fixed on his feet.

'Don't misunderstand me, Buta Singh,' said Taylor quickly. 'I am not suggesting anything dishonourable. Your son could do a good service to his friends and his country. You know we are anxious to get out of India and hand over the reins of power to you people as soon as the war is won. But we will not leave the country to the Japanese or the Germans. And these acts are calculated to do just that — hand over India on a silver platter to the Fascist powers.'

Buta Singh did not look up.

'I seem to have upset you, Buta Singh; I am sorry. Let's forget about it. I'll let the Police Commissioner handle it in his own way.'

'I will speak to my son, sir,' answered Buta Singh at last.

'No, no, don't. Just forget about the whole affair.' Taylor got up abruptly and shook hands. Just as Buta Singh was going out of the room, he called him back. 'Oh, I almost forgot. Last time your son came to see me, he asked for a licence for a rifle. I have made one out for him. Give this to him with my compliments. Goodbye. And don't bother about what I said.'

Chapter VIII

Taylor did not have to do any more than ignore Buta Singh and the strain became too much for the old man. He came unbidden a week later and assured the Deputy Commissioner that he would get the required information. Another week passed. Buta Singh's resolve to speak to his son remained unfulfilled for the simple reason he never saw him. When he left for the law courts the boy was still in bed; when he came back, he was away. He had dinner with his daughter-in-law. Every time he asked her, 'Where is Sher?' she replied 'I do not know' — and nothing more. Night after night he whiled away the hours doing his files waiting for his son to return. Night after night, he nodded, dozed off to sleep, woke up again, switched off the light, and went to bed resolved to broach the subject the next day. There were many questions he wanted to ask. When had Sher Singh decided to buy a rifle? Why hadn't he mentioned it to him? Why hadn't he told him that he had asked Taylor for a licence? It did cross Buta Singh's mind that the boy might be up to no good in wanting the weapon; it did not occur to him that he might already be owning one illegally. Buta Singh planned to utilize the situation to get round his son to try to get the required information. No, that was a horrid expression. To cooperate in keeping peace and order and save India from a Fascist invasion. Sher Singh might not see it that way unless it was put tactfully. It was worth waiting for. If Sher Singh did what he was asked, the New Year's Honours list would certainly have something for his father.

Then came the first of the month. Buta Singh resolved that was to be the day. Three days before the date he told the servants and Champak that everyone was to be present at the gurudwara in time. On the morning itself, he was up before anyone else and went to the servants' quarters to get Shunno and Mundoo to sweep the room and put things ready. He knocked on his son's bedroom door and told him not to be late. He had decided to bring up the subject casually at breakfast as a sort of follow up of the discussion on the morning's news.

Things seemed to go as planned. Everyone turned up at the gurudwara as told. Sher Singh looked fresh and cheerful. So did Champak. She wore a close fitting Punjabi dress which accentuated the largeness of her bosom and narrowness of her waist. It was odd, thought Buta Singh, how the girl he saw every day without taking much notice of her looked more fetching one morning than on another! There were several children outside, with Mundoo as usual bossing them and the dog. Shunno brought in the tray of prasad and placed it in front of the Granth. Buta Singh picked up the fly-whisk and began to wave it over his head with one hand; with the other, he looked for the right page to read. He was not used to conducting the prayer and it made him slightly nervous. He found the chapter and put the fly-whisk down. He removed his beard-band and brushed his moustache off his lips. He placed his forehead reverently against the Book and shut his eyes to say a private prayer for the fulfilment of his own wishes. His eyes were still shut when he became conscious of someone entering the gurudwara. The man had prostrated himself before the Granth. He stood up and announced his arrival by greeting everyone at the top of his voice, *'Wahe guru ji ka Khalsa, Wahe guru ji ki Fateh.'* ('The Sikhs are the Chosen of God, Victory be to our God.') It was the village headman.

Buta Singh's face flushed with anger but he kept it under control. This was a temple where anyone could come and worship and there was nothing he could do about it. He read the passage for the month quietly to himself, made his obeisance, and left. Champak followed him.

At the breakfast table Buta Singh kept the newspaper in front of him to cover the scowl on his face. He did not want to be irritable with Champak, but he could not help saying with suppressed wrath: 'I don't understand the sort of people your husband mixes with! Low, third class types! He should use his intelligence a little more.'

Champak did not look up from her plate.

Buta Singh could not bring up the subject that morning. He swore to himself to do it in the evening even if it meant sitting up later than before.

That night Buta Singh waited a long time for his son to return home. Once again the vigil was in vain.

Sher Singh took the headman to the sitting-room and ordered breakfast for him.

'Sardarji, why do you put yourself to all this trouble?' asked the headman, munching a thickly buttered toast. He wiped the butter off his moustache with the hem of his shirt and gave it a twirl. 'You should not have bothered. This is like my own home.'

'You've come from such a long distance,' answered Sher Singh in the same tone, 'this is nothing.'

'Why nothing, Sardarji? This is everything! All I want is your kindness.' He picked up the tumbler of buttermilk, cleared his lips of his billowing moustache, and drank it up in one long gulp. He emitted a loud belch which tapered off into praise of the Great Guru, the True Emperor. He combed his beard with his fingers and placed a heavy hand on Sher Singh's knee. 'Tell me some news.'

'What news? Life just goes on.'

The headman belched again and stroked his beard patiently. 'Oh, congratulations!' he said as if he had just recalled something.

'Congratulations for what?'

'Congratulations for what! This is no way to talk to friends. You know very well; the gun licence. Taylor Sahib's clerk told me he had issued one for you and given it to your revered father.'

'Oh, when?'

'Again you hide things from friends! When we first met you said you had a licence and now I discover you have been given one only fifteen days ago. You ask the big Sardar, your father.'

Sher Singh wondered why Buta Singh had not questioned him about the rifle. Nor had he handed him the licence given by Taylor. Did he know that the rifle was already in the house? In any case Sher Singh was relieved that the headman would not be able to blackmail him any more.

'Here, friend, what do you say! You were worried about these things.' The headman thrust the three empty rifle bullets in his hand. Sher Singh wanted to fling them in the peasant's face, call him a dirty pig, spit at him, and kick him out of the house. But he quietly took the shells and put them on the table. This was the last time he was going to see this fellow, why not let the meeting end peacefully?

The headman gave no indication of wanting to leave. He combed his beard, twirled his moustache, and slapped Sher Singh's knee. 'Tell me some news.'

'What news? Life just goes on.'

'Wah ji wah! Great men do great deeds.' The peasant smiled mischievously and pinched Sher Singh's thigh. What was he up to now? 'Great deeds, great men,' he said with a sigh. He continued after a significant pause: 'Tell me, you know how to make bombs?'

'Bombs?'

'Bombs.'

'How should I know anything about making bombs. Why, do you need some?' asked Sher Singh, laughing nervously.

'Is this friendship or a chaff of chick-peas? Our little canal bridge is full of holes. Had the poor thing done any harm to anyone? My best bullock broke its leg in one of the holes. It had cost me Rs 300. I said, it doesn't matter if my 300 are drowned; this is my friend's hobby! But these canal chaps have been trying to find out. They came to ask me. You see, the bridge is within the area of my village. I said nothing to them.'

Sher Singh felt cornered once more. It was humiliating for a well-to-do, educated, rising politician like him to be put on the spot by an illiterate, uncouth, peasant informer. 'Sardar Sahib, I will say nothing about you. Once one makes friends, come what may, one must prove true to that friendship. Don't you agree?'

Sher Singh agreed.

'I could never say anything about you,' the headman repeated. 'But who are these Babus with you? Something should be done about them.'

Sher Singh wanted to yell like a madman. Instead he maintained a sullen silence. The headman continued: 'I ask nothing of you, but these Babus must pay for my bullock. I will say nothing to the canal people; they can go and have their mothers raped, but these Babus. . . . '

'I will get you the money.'

The headman clasped him by both the knees. 'No, brother, not you. If I take anything from you, may I be cursed as if I had eaten the flesh of the sacred cow. But these Babus, are they relations of ours? If you tell me who they are, I could get the money from them myself.'

'No, I will get it for you. This evening at seven o'clock at the bridge.'

There wasn't another place within cycling distance of the city which was as desolate as the spot near the little bridge over the canal. For several miles on all sides the land was flat as a pancake. It also looked like a pancake: a stretch of yellow with a layer of fine powdery saltpetre. Nothing grew on it except bushes of calotropis and thorny saguaro cactus. There was also the marsh. Most of it was a muddy swamp with reeds growing in some places. The only evidence of human life was a footpath along the canal bank which no one ever seemed to use, and the little bridge, which if used at all, was probably used by stray cattle. The flat waste of saltpetre, scrub, and swamp had an eerie loneliness about it.

The boys came in their sports kit carrying their hockey sticks as they had done a few days earlier. Near the bridge, they divided themselves in three groups. Two groups, of four each, took their positions fifty yards on either side of the bridge behind calotropis bushes. The remaining four, including Sher Singh and Madan, sat in the open on the bridge. The bridge had no holes in it as alleged by the village headman. Nor did Sher Singh have the Rs 300 to pay him for the bullock which had broken its leg.

Sher Singh looked at his watch. It was 7:15 p.m. The sun had set. In another ten minutes the twilight would darken into night.

'Perhaps you should have come alone. He might have taken fright seeing four of us here,' said one of his companions a little wearily.

'Of course I could have come alone. I've told you several times he was most keen to meet you. He certainly isn't the sort who would be frightened of people like us. You know what Sikh peasants think of city dwellers! And this chap, you might remember, is a few inches taller than Madan and fat and full of hair; he looks like a gorilla. I wouldn't like to meet him alone in the dark.' Sher Singh laughed a little nervously. 'If he doesn't turn up in another ten minutes, we will go back. He can have his mother raped.'

They all hoped the ten minutes would pass quickly and they could go to their homes.

Suddenly, the Lambardar appeared from behind them. The boys jumped when he greeted them with a loud *'Wahe guru ji ka Khalsa, Wahe guru ji ki Fateh.'* A leather belt charged with cartridges ran down from his shoulder to the waist. At the lower end was a holster with the black butt of a revolver sticking out. 'The entire congregation is here,' he said cheerfully and sat down beside them.

'You said you wanted to meet them; that is why they are here. I said to myself, "If my brother asks a favour, I should do it for him."' Sher Singh introduced the boys — this time with their correct names.

The headman shook hands with the three boys. 'What have I to do with names? All I want to know is that they are my brother's friends and that is enough for me,' he said with a broad smile.

The twilight was fading rapidly and, as usual, it was the peasant who was more at ease. 'Tell me some news,' he said quite unconcerned and slapped Sher Singh on the thigh.

'What news? Life just goes on.'

Madan changed the tone of polite humbug.

'Lambardara, you said your bullock had broken its leg in a hole in the bridge. There are no holes in the bridge.'

The headman was quick to react to the rude tone: 'What do you know about bullocks, Babuji? You stick to your shopkeeping and account books.'

'You want us to pay you Rs 300 for a damaged bullock. We have brought the money but we must have proof before we pay. Show us the hole in the bridge and your lame bull.'

For a moment the headman believed the money was in his grasp. Then his shrewd rustic sense told him they were bluffing. 'I don't give any proofs. This is not a court of law.'

The tone cleared the atmosphere. They all stood up.

'In one breath you call Sher Singh "brother," ' said Madan sharply, 'in the other you want to make money off him. What sort of bastardy is this?'

'Keep your tongue in check. You know who you are speaking to?'

'Yes. A police informer. The son of a pig. . . . A raper of his mother.'

The Lambardar's hand went to his holster. Before he could draw his weapon two of the boys fell on him. He shook them off like a wounded wild boar shakes off pie dogs at the end of a chase. Madan and Sher Singh covered him with their pistols.

'Put your hands up or I'll shoot you like the filthy dog you are.'

The headman extended his arms towards Sher Singh as if to embrace him. 'Brother, you also have become angry!' he said appealingly.

Sher Singh stepped back and fired. The headman bent over with a loud 'Hai.' His hand moved to his gun.

The boys behind him saw and gave warning. Madan
fired a second shot. The headman let out another loud
'Hai,' sagged down on his knees and slowly stretched
himself on the path. Blood poured out of his wounds.
His last words were not addressed to God or the Great
Guru but to his killers. 'I'll sleep with your mothers. .
. . I'll sleep with your sisters. . . . I'll. . . . ' It made it
easier for them to finish him off. Each one of the boys
fired a shot in the headman's body so that the crime was
shared. They unstrapped the holster and the cartridge
belt and dragged the corpse down the slope towards
the swamp. It was warm and twitching. An occasional
gurgle came out of the dead man's throat. They dumped
it into a ditch and covered it with earth and stones. They
dug up and relevelled the path where he had fallen and
bled. They washed their hands in the canal and made
for the city as fast as they could.

There was a brief farewell at parting. The boys were
to leave the city immediately for different destinations.
Madan was to return to Simla.

Sher Singh was left alone to face his amorous wife,
his ill-tempered father — and himself.

Chapter IX

In a country of 400 million people living in congested rusticity, events like births and deaths are reduced to their proper insignificance. That does not mean that the birth of a son does not occasion joy or the death of a kinsman no grief. They do. Only the rejoicing at the arrival of another infant in a family which has to live on the produce of ten acres of impoverished land becomes progressively more a matter of form than of reality. After the first child or two, births are simply looked upon as something which follows nocturnal pastimes as day follows night. Since there are no other diversions in the village and it is not easy to restrict sexual intercourse to a few messy days in the month, one child comes after another as the new year comes after the old. Its arrival is accepted with resignation as a blessing of the Almighty, Omniscient God who knows what is best. But little importance is attached to it. In the case of death, the reactions are somewhat confused. There is sorrow at the loss of a loved one; there is also relief that there is one mouth less to feed. In any case God seems to manifest His power more at death than at birth. (Human beings have a not too unimportant role in creating new life: it is only rarely that they become instruments of destruction. Killing is largely God's monopoly. When the Lord giveth, He lets mankind have some share in the giving. But when the Lord taketh away, He does it at His own sweet will.) So deaths are accepted with even more resignation than births — and with as little fuss.

Jhimma Singh was one of many brothers. Being the eldest, he inherited the official function of headman of the village from his father. Thereafter he acquired possession of most of his father's property. He loved his brothers and arranged marriages and employment for them as farm labourers in newly colonized lands a few hundred miles away to the north-west. Malicious tongues spread poison and turned the brothers against him. They took him to court to get possession of their share of the land. But providence, assisted by clever lawyers, triumphed over their evil designs. Then they tried violence. That too went against them. They were imprisoned on charges of attempted murder and Jhimma Singh was given a revolver to defend himself. He gained the confidence of the local police officials by his hospitality; they let him look after the affairs of the village and Jhimma Singh became virtually its ruler. Anyone who has had to live the hard way, literally fighting for survival at every step, doesn't set much store by values like truth, honesty, loyalty, or patriotism. Neither did Jhimma Singh. Each little success meant more envy and more danger from the envious. He had to seek the help of the police to protect him. In turn they expected him to keep an eye on miscreants. He became a paid informer.

Jhimma Singh's only failure in life was the inability of any one of his three wives to produce a child. After the first had remained barren for five years, he married her niece. Following a few years of fruitless matrimony with the niece, he cast his protective mantle on a young widow whose provocative figure and dark eyes had given Jhimma Singh visions of many sons. She also let him down. Now the land he farmed, the land he leased out to tenants, his own brick-built house, his wives' jewelry, and his account in the savings bank, which was said to have grown from some hundreds to fabulous thousands, was his to give away or squander. This prosperity hurt his fellow villagers, particularly his relations. Although everyone feared him and some even sided with him in his lawsuits, not one of them loved him.

It wasn't very surprising then that for a week no one should have bothered about his disappearance. He was known to go away to the city for two or three days without telling his wives. As in the past, they assumed he had been called away on urgent business. After a week they became anxious and started going round to other homes asking the women to find out from their menfolk if they had seen Jhimma Singh. When no one came forth with any news of him for another week, the anxiety changed to alarm and a report was lodged at the police station by one of the tenants at the urging of Jhimma Singh's first wife. It mentioned the enmity of his brothers and their previous attempts to murder him. Once again the brothers were arrested, interrogated, and beaten up. Nothing came of it. No corpse, no case. They were set at liberty. The Police Commissioner was notified that the most trusted informer in the district had disappeared — probably murdered by one of his many relations and no trace could be found of either the victim or the murderer. The Commissioner sent the file to the Deputy Commissioner to have the case closed as 'untraced. ' He was a little surprised to find that instead of the usual words 'Seen. File,' with the illegible initials, there was an order asking him to come over to discuss the case. What followed startled the Police Commissioner,

The Deputy Commissioner handed the Police Commissioner a warrant to search the house of Sardar Buta Singh, the seniormost Indian magistrate of the district. He gave him another one, to arrest Sher Singh. Taylor refused to disclose his source of information. All he said was: 'Be gentle with the old man. I suggest you send him over to see me and then search the house. You may find something. In any case, take his son to the police station and give him the works. Get some of your tough Anglo-Indian sergeants to handle him. It will not be hard to make him talk.'

Buta Singh had firmly decided to speak to his son after the headman had left. That evening Sher Singh came home early but straightaway retired to bed complaining of a severe headache. Next morning, he did not turn up for breakfast and Buta Singh went to see him in his room. The boy looked pale and jaundiced and would not speak at all. A doctor was sent for but he could not diagnose anything. Nevertheless it was plain to anyone that he was very sick; one could scarcely bring up a delicate subject with him in that state of health. After many days in bed, his health improved and he started moving about the house. He still wore a sallow, furtive look and avoided meeting people. Buta Singh waited patiently. At last came the first of the month. The father came to the conclusion that matters had been allowed to drift for too long and the time had come to settle the business once and for all. He would talk to his son after the morning ceremony.

Autumn had set in and there was a nip in the morning air. Inside the gurudwara it was cozy because of the thick carpet and the incense. Sher Singh, Champak, and Shunno were inside. Mundoo, as usual, was lording it over the children and the dog outside. Buta Singh uncovered the Holy Book to start reading. He saw the figure of a policeman through the chick. He kept his temper under control and proceeded to look for the appropriate passage. He pressed his forehead reverently on the Book and looked up once more. There was yet another policeman outside talking excitedly to Mundoo. He took off his shoes and came into the gurudwara. This was too much for Buta Singh. He hollered angrily at the top of his voice: 'What is your business?' The constable saluted and said: 'Huzoor, the Police Commissioner is waiting for you outside in his car. The Deputy Commissioner has sent him to fetch you. It is most urgent. I crave forgiveness for disturbing you in the gurudwara; I was ordered to do so.'

The reference to the Police Commissioner and Mr Taylor changed Buta Singh's tone. He did not proceed with the reading. He left at once and asked Champak to carry on. Shunno followed her master; she wasn't going to be left out of things.

'You do the reading instead of your father,' said Champak with a smile.

Sher Singh did not smile back. 'I can't. I am not feeling too well.'

'What is the matter?' asked Champak.

'I don't know. I don't feel well.'

Champak put her hand on his forehead. 'You have no fever but you have cold-sweat. I'll get Mundoo to make your bed. You come and lie down. Mundoo Oi Mundoo,' she cried. 'The policemen seem to have frightened away the servants.'

She went out and shouted for the boy again. Mundoo came wailing. 'A policeman beat me. They have come inside the house. When I asked them what they were doing, one fellow slapped me.'

Sher Singh went deathly pale. Had they found out? Had one of the boys told on him? His wife looked at him for some explanation. 'I will see what is happening,' he said weakly. 'You go to your room.'

There were policemen all over the place: in the courtyard and the sitting-room; in the garden and at the gate. Sher Singh came out in the verandah followed by Dyer. Two white sergeants were sitting in the armchairs with their legs on the table, smoking. A head constable stood by them with handcuffs dangling from his belt. A policewoman in a khaki sari was leaning on a Black Maria in the porch. 'You want to see my father?' asked Sher Singh timidly.

'You Buta Singh's son?' asked one of them knocking the ash off his cigarette.

'Yes . . . sir.'

'Head constable, search this fellow. And send someone inside to search his woman.'

The two resumed their smoking. The policewoman went inside. The head constable took Sher Singh by the hand. Sher Singh felt he ought to protest. He mustered up all the courage he had and spoke: 'What is this about? How dare you put your hands on me! What authority. . . .'

One of the sergeants got up slowly from his chair and came up to him. 'You want to know what authority we have to search you?'

'Yes,' answered Sher Singh through the spittle that clogged his throat.

'Man, this bugger wants to know why we want to search him,' said the sergeant turning to his companion. 'We better tell him.'

Without warning the sergeant struck his knee sharply into Sher Singh's privates. As he doubled over with pain, the sergeant hit him on the face with the back of his hand. Sher Singh's turban came off and fell on the ground; his long hair scattered about his face and shoulders.

'Cheeky nigger. That'll teach. . . .'

The sergeant could not complete the sentence. Dyer leapt at him with savage fury and knocked him down. He tore the collar off the white man's coat and went for his throat. The constable lashed out with his iron handcuffs; the other sergeant laid out with his swagger stick and kicked the dog with his hobnailed boots. Policemen came running with their iron shod bamboo poles to beat him. At last the Alsatian gave up. Blood flowed from his face and back, the bone of one of his legs had been fractured.

'I'll shoot the bloody pariah,' raged the sergeant getting up and drawing his pistol. His coat was torn, his face scratched and bitten.

The other sergeant put his hand on the pistol. 'No, mun. Old Deecee will kick up a hell of a row if you shoot the bloody cur. You know how mad these f . . . Englishmen are about dogs!'

The sergeant put back his pistol in the holster and wiped the blood off his face: 'Suppose I'll have to have anti-rabies shots. A Sikh's dog is bound to be mad.'

It took two constables with their long bamboo poles to keep the battered Alsatian at bay.

Sher Singh slumped on the floor of the verandah with his arms covering his face and began to cry. He hated himself for crying but he could not stop. The two people he feared and loathed most, Anglo-Indians and Muslim policemen from northern Punjab, had insulted and beaten him in his own home and all he could do was to cry like a child. Even his dog had shown more fight.

'Take this bloody patriot to the station and put some red hot chillies up his arse,' ordered the sergeant to the head constable. 'If he has any illusions of being a magistrate's son, knock them out of him.'

The head constable put the handcuffs on Sher Singh's hands and said gently: 'Come along, Sardar Sahib.' Sher Singh rolled up his hair into a chignon and picked up his turban. His eyes were inflamed with hate and humiliation. When he tried to stand there was a stab of pain in his testicles. He held them with his manacled hands and slumped down again. The head constable took the turban from him and put his arm round his waist and helped him up on to his feet. He whispered in his ears: 'Be a man. Don't degrade yourself before these white bastards.' Sher Singh limped into the van.

The search lasted an hour. They ransacked every room in the house. A man was sent down the well. They found nothing — not even the rifle for which Taylor had made out a licence in Sher Singh's name. The illicit arms remained unnoticed in the pit in the centre of the empty garage.

The policewoman came out to report that she had searched Champak and her belongings but had recovered nothing. The sergeants rode off on their motor cycles. The two policemen who had been keeping the Alsatian at a safe distance took their seats in the van. Sher Singh heard the defiant barking and snapping of the dog following the Black Maria till it gathered speed on its way to the police station.

The Police Commissioner dropped Buta Singh at Taylor's house. There were no other magistrates present nor were there any chairs laid out for them. Taylor's bearer came out and held open the wire-gauze door. 'The Sahib is at *chota hazri* and wants you to join him.'

Buta Singh had been inside Taylor's drawing-room but no farther. Mrs Taylor came in to greet him. 'Come in, Sardar Sahib, and join us for breakfast.' She led him to the dining-room.

'Very kind of you, madam. I had my tea before coming,' answered Buta Singh lying. 'Very kind of you. Good morning, sir.'

'Good morning, Buta Singh,' answered Taylor putting down the morning paper. 'Come and join us. You have met my wife before, haven't you? Joyce, you know Mr Buta Singh.'

'Of course! One more cup of tea won't do you any harm.'

'No harm,' sniggered Buta Singh. 'No harm. Thank you. Very kind of you, madam.' Buta Singh sat down and allowed himself to be talked into having eggs and bacon, toast and marmalade, and three cups of tea. He could now bring up Taylor's breakfast menu casually with his colleagues and his family. It would be fun talking about bacon in front of the Muslim magistrates. Had Taylor some special favour to ask for this reception? Probably to pursue the subject of getting information from Sher Singh.

When breakfast was over, Taylor conducted Buta Singh to his study. He didn't light a cigarette to time the interview but took out his pipe and tin of tobacco.

'Sahib seems to have something special on his mind this morning. What service can I render?'

Taylor lit his pipe. 'I wanted to have a general talk with you about things; one seldom gets the time to do that. I also have to ask you about a particular subject which we will come to later on. I hope you don't mind my being personal. How long. . . . '

'Nothing personal, sir,' interrupted Buta Singh. 'I have no secrets to keep from you. Ask me anything you like.'

'I was going to ask how long had your family been connected with the British Government?'

'Sir,' warmed Buta Singh, 'sir, we can almost go back to the days of Sikh rule. On the annexation of the Punjab and the disbanding of the Sikh forces my great grandfather, who was a subedar and had fought against the British in the Anglo-Sikh wars, joined the British Army. He served under John Lawrence. He also fought under Nicholson in the Mutiny of 1857 and was awarded a medal for the capture of Delhi; we still have it in the family. My grandfather was also in the British Army. He rose from the ranks and retired as a Jemadar — in those days to be a Jemadar was a big thing for an Indian. My father did not join the army, but he recruited many soldiers in the 1914–48 war and our family was given lands in the Canal Colonies. I have kept up the tradition of loyalty to the British Crown and will do so till the day I die.' He became breathless with the excitement he had generated in himself. It did not seem to affect Taylor who coolly lit his pipe once more.

'What about your son?'

'What about my son? He may hobnob with the Nationalists but he will have to be loyal to the British as long as Buta Singh lives,' he replied, smacking his chest. 'Otherwise I will disown him. After I am dead, he can do what he likes.'

Taylor still seemed unimpressed. 'I appreciate your sentiments of loyalty, Buta Singh, but I do not agree with you about the future of India; and I am British. I feel we should pull out of this country as soon after the war as we can and let you Indians manage your own affairs. I, for one, have no intention of continuing in the Indian Civil Service a day after the cease-fire. In fact I am not on the side of Mr Churchill but on that of Mr Gandhi and Mr Nehru — except, and this is important, I do think the war has to be won first. Otherwise the Nazis and the Fascists will put the clock back for you and for us. I may be wrong, but that is my belief.'

Englishmen like Taylor confused Buta Singh. It wasn't entirely his fault. He had only known Englishmen who believed in the British Empire as they did in the Church of England; who stood to attention even if a bar of their national anthem came over the air while somebody was fiddling with the knob of a radio set; who believed that 'natives' were only of two kinds — the Gunga Dins, whom they loved like their pet dogs because of their dogged devotion to the Sahibs, and the Bolshies, whom they hated.

'Mr Taylor, you may be right. I am an old man and I cannot change. I am for the British Raj. If it goes, there will be chaos in this country as there was chaos before the British came.' Buta Singh felt mean. There were limits beyond which flattery should not go; his frequently did. Only if the Englishman accepted it, he would feel better.

'What does your son have to say on the subject?'

That gave Buta Singh the opportunity to redeem himself. 'Of course he disagrees with me and is more of your point of view. He is young and you know what youth is!'

'Yes,' answered Taylor absent-mindedly. 'But what do you do when there is a conflict of loyalties? What would you do if you discovered that he had been mixed up not only with the Nationalists but also with terrorists?'

Insinuations about duplicity made Buta Singh angry. 'I would disown him. I would throw him out of the house,' he replied emphatically.

'You are a harsh judge, Buta Singh. Children are meant to be understood, not thrown out when there is a difference of opinion.'

'We teach our children to respect and obey their parents,' said Buta Singh. 'I am sure European parents do the same, sir.'

'It may be a hard thing to say, but, despite the close living in joint families and the formal respect paid to the elders, there is less contact, understanding, or friendship between parents and their children in India than in Europe.'

Buta Singh didn't understand the trend of the conversation. Taylor seemed to be beating about the bush. Then out of the blue he came out with a wholly irrelevant question. 'Did you know Jhimma Singh, headman?'

'Jhimma Singh? No, who is he?'

'I hope he is; he certainly was. A big, burly, black chap. Apparently he knew your son and was on visiting terms with him.'

'Oh yes, sir, I know,' answered Buta Singh. 'I think he came to my house some time ago when I was at prayer in the gurudwara. I remember him. I didn't know his name was Jhimma Singh. What about him, sir?'

Taylor went through the process of emptying, refilling, and relighting his pipe. Sometimes these tactics worked.

'What about Jhimma Singh, sir?'

'I have reason to believe that the day he came to your house was the last day he was seen alive. Further, I have reason to believe that your son, Sher Singh, was perhaps the last man to see him alive.'

Buta Singh's face fell. 'What is this you say, Sahib?'

'Jhimma Singh was a headman and a police informer. He had been informing me about your son's activities with a group of boys who practiced rifle shooting near his village. You recall I gave you a licence for one! I hoped that it would bring the whole business out in the open and you would have put a stop to it. Well, it didn't work out that way. These lads then tried to blow up a bridge on the canal. Jhimma Singh told me about that too. The only one of the gang he knew was your son. Then suddenly he disappeared. I am pretty certain he has been murdered. I may, of course, be wrong.'

Buta Singh sank back in his chair and covered his face with his hands. Large tears rolled down his cheeks and disappeared in his beard. 'My nose has been cut. I can no longer show my face to the world,' he sobbed.

Taylor took the Sikh magistrate's hairy hand in his own. 'Buta Singh, this is extremely unpleasant for me but I have to do my duty. Let me tell you all. Your house is being searched in your absence now. I have also ordered Sher Singh to be taken into custody. We have nothing to go on except what Jhimma Singh has told me and that, you as a magistrate know, is not enough. If Sher Singh had anything to do with the headman's disappearance it is for him to tell. It is on him we have to rely for information about his accomplices as well. If he gives it, I may consider granting him a King's pardon. Of course, if he had nothing to do with the affair, or refuses to talk, the case will not be reopened.'

'How shall I face the world?' moaned Buta Singh and again covered his face with his hands. Taylor got up and asked the bearer to get a cold drink. Mrs Taylor came in carrying a tray with three glasses of orange juice. She put it on the table and sat down on a chair beside the magistrate. She put her hand gently on his knee. 'Mister Buta Singh, pull yourself together and have a drink. I was told the Sikhs were brave people! This is not being very brave, is it?'

Buta Singh blew his nose and wiped his tears with his handkerchief. Mrs Taylor held the glass of orange juice for him. 'Come along, drink it. And don't fret. What's happened has happened.'

The magistrate's hand shook as he gulped down his glass of orange juice. He brought up a deep sigh. 'How can I thank. . . . ' He broke down again and started to sob in his handkerchief. The Taylors sat quietly and let him cry his heart out. Then Taylor spoke in a firm voice: 'Buta Singh, I have given you fifteen days' leave. Your house will continue to be guarded as before. If you want to be spared the embarrassment of visitors you can tell the policeman to keep them out. You can see your son as often as you want to. You can give him whatever advice you deem fit; it is for you to decide. I repeat, if he is willing to give us the names of his accomplices, he will be made a Crown witness and be granted the King's pardon. If not, he must face the consequences of his act.'

•

In the Himalayas it is not the advent but the end of the monsoon which is spectacular. There are not months of intense heat which turn the plainsman's longing for rain into a prayer for deliverance from a hot purgatory. People of the hills look upon the monsoon as they do on other seasons. One brings snow, one the blossoms, one the fruit; also one brings the rain. For another, in the mountains the monsoon is heavier and for days the hills and valleys are blotted out by sheets of rain. It is misty, damp and cold, and people pray for the sunshine. Their prayers are answered some time in September or October. The monsoon is given a grand farewell with fireworks. Thunder explodes like firecrackers and lightning illumines the landscape as if flares were being dropped from the heavens. The sky is no longer a mass of shapeless grey; it is an expanse of aquamarine full of bulbous white clouds which change their shapes and colours as they tumble away. The mists lift as if waved away by a magic wand, unfolding rain-washed scenery of snow-capped mountains on one side and an infinity of brown plains intersecting a thousand golden streams on the other. The air is cleaner. It has the crispy cold of the regions of perpetual snows; it also has the insinuating warmth of the regions of perpetual sunshine.

Some days of autumn have more of 'God's in His Heaven' than others. This was one of them. When they came out into the garden, the sun had just come up over the hills and touched the snow range across the valley with a glow of pink. The forests of deodar stood on the mountainside patiently waiting for a long day of mellow sunshine. There wasn't a cloud in the deep blue sky: only lammergeiers drifting lazily with the noiseless ease and grace of gliders. It was too good to be true; and like all times that are too good to be true, there was mixed with the sense of elation, an apprehension that it would not last long, and perhaps, not end as well as it had begun.

They had their breakfast in the garden where the dew lay like whitewash on the lawn. The borders were thick with chrysanthemums, sunflowers, and hollyhocks. After breakfast they went for a stroll on the Mall. The crowds had considerably thinned as most of the government offices had shifted back to the plains and some of the larger stores had closed down for the month. They walked up and down the road a couple of times and then went into Davicos for coffee. After the coffee, Madan took the girls with him to watch the finals of a football tournament played on the race-course in the valley at Annandale. Sabhrai went down to the temple in the lower bazaar to spend the rest of the day.

When Sabhrai returned home late in the afternoon, the servant handed her a telegram; it had been delivered some hours earlier. She tore it open and looked at the hieroglyphics. 'What does it say?' she asked anxiously.

'I can't read English,' replied the boy, a little surprised that she should ask him.

'Go and ask somebody to read it and come back quickly.'

The boy went to the neighbours' homes and came back half-an-hour later to say that the masters were out and none of the servants could read. Sabhrai took the telegram from him. She paced up and down the verandah; she walked up to the gate and came back; she went down the road a little distance, came back home, and paced up and down the verandah again. She looked at the telegram over and over again. The only letters she could piece together were those that spelled her husband's name; the rest made no sense to her. At long last Madan and the girls came home. Sabhrai met them at the gate with the telegram. Madan read it out aloud first in English and then translated it for her in Punjabi. She was right, it was from her husband.

'Return immediately. Buta Singh.'

S abhrai's sixth sense told her nothing about the drama that had taken place. She realized that nothing could be wrong with her husband because he had sent the telegram. Whatever had happened had happened to her son. If he were sick or had met with an accident, his wife was there to look after him. Why should Buta Singh send for her in this manner unless Sher Singh was dying or was already dead? The more she thought of it, the more certain she became that the telegram had something to do with her son; and that he was either in mortal danger or had succumbed to it. She sat up in her bed and prayed all through the night. Next day on her way down to the plains and again all night in the train, her thoughts and prayers were for her Shera.

It was still dark when she woke up Beena and asked her to wash, change, and roll up the beddings. She asked her to come and sit beside her. 'Pray for your brother,' she said to indicate that she had an inkling of what had happened. They sat cross-legged on the berth wrapped in their shawls and recited the morning prayer. The black nothingness outside the window-pane became a dimly-lit landscape beyond continuous waves of telegraph wires which rose and fell from pole to pole. The sun came up over the flat land and lit up the yellow squares of mustard, the solid greens of sugar-cane, and blocks of mud villages. They came to the suburbs of the city. Mud huts gave way to brick buildings, and open fields to evil smelling ditches where men sat on their haunches, shamelessly baring their bottoms and relieving themselves.

The train drew in on a noisy crowded platform full of coolies in red uniforms. Sabhrai and Beena looked for a familiar face, but could not recognize anyone. The orderly came from the servants' compartment and took charge of the luggage. They were counting their pieces when an Englishwoman approached them. She touched Beena on the arm and asked, 'Are you Sardar Buta Singh's daughter?'

'Yes.'

'I am Mrs Taylor. Good morning. And this I presume is your mother. Sat Sri Akal, Sardarini Sahiba. We have met before.'

Sabhrai joined her hands and answered the English-woman's greeting. It took the mother and daughter some time to realize that the Deputy Commissioner's wife had come to receive them. Sabhrai lost her composure and whispered agitatedly into her daughter's ear. Joyce Taylor saw the consternation on their faces. 'Don't be alarmed Sardarini Sahiba, all is well,' she said putting her hand on Sabhrai's shoulder. 'Your husband and son are in the best of health; you will see them soon. I had nothing to do this morning so I thought I'd come along to fetch you and spare you a long tonga ride.'

Beena translated this to her mother and they smiled gratefully at Mrs Taylor. Things must have changed for an English Deputy Commissioner's wife to take the trouble to receive the family of an Indian subordinate.

They were too bewildered to think that there might be other reasons. Beena gave the coolies more than twice their due to prevent them nagging and making a scene in front of the Englishwoman.

There was nothing at home to indicate a crisis. There were two policemen on duty, instead of one. They came to attention and saluted as the car went in. Nobody came out to receive them while they were unloading their luggage. That didn't surprise them. Buta Singh was likely to be at the courts; Sher Singh would be out somewhere and Champak in her room. But where was Dyer? He was always the first to greet members of the family returning home and had to be restrained from putting his paws on their shoulders and licking their faces. As soon as Mrs Taylor had said goodbye and left, Beena shouted for the dog. He came round the house, hopping on three legs; the fourth was in plaster. There was a gash on his nose on which flies were clustered. He whined as he came to his mistress and let out a long piteous howl. 'Hai, Dyer, what's happened to you? Who's hurt my little son?' Sabhrai fanned the flies off with her headpiece and put her arms round the dog. 'Didn't Sher take you to the doctor?'

Champak came out of the wire-gauze door. Her hair was scattered untidily on her face. Her eyes were red and swollen. She wore a plain white cotton sari without any make-up or jewelry — like a widow in mourning. Sabhrai's heart sank. Was her son dead? Hadn't the Englishwoman said he was in good health!

'What has . . . ?'

Champak clasped her mother-in-law round the waist and burst out crying. Sabhrai, who had never particularly cared for Champak, stroked her head. 'The True, The True, The Great Guru,' she chanted.

Beena could not stand it any more. 'What has happened? Why don't you tell?' she shrieked.

Buta Singh came out in the verandah. He, too, was shabbily dressed in a white shirt and pyjamas. His beard had not been pressed and he wore no turban. 'What is all this crying for?' he asked at the top of his voice. 'You behave as if he were dead. Perhaps that might have been better.'

'The True, The True. The Great Guru. What words are these? Where is my son, my Moon, my little Ruby. Where is he?' Tears streamed down Sabhrai's face. 'Why don't you tell me?'

Even her tears did not appease Buta Singh's temper. 'My nose has been cut; I can no longer show my face to anyone.'

'What has he done? Why don't you tell me where he is.'

'He's in jail. Where else can he be?'

'The Great Guru. The Great Guru. Who has been born to put my child in jail! What did he do?'

'Murder, what else! I can no longer show my face to anyone. All my life's work has been thrown into a well.'

'The True, The True
The Great Guru.'

They went into the sitting-room. After a few minutes, Sabhrai regained her composure and asked her husband to explain what had happened. Buta Singh did so in

a bitter voice, mincing no words. He ended on a note
of self-pity. 'All my years of loyal service thrown into
the well. . . . Just when I am due to retire and expect
to be rewarded, my son cuts my nose. I wouldn't
be surprised if the little land we have in reward for
services, were confiscated and I were given no pension.
I do not understand this complete lack of regard for
one's parents. And Champak must have known about
his goings on with these bad characters. I wouldn't be
surprised if that rascal Madan were one of them. To
whom can I show my face now?'

Champak began to sob once more. Sabhrai spoke
sharply: 'You are only concerned with yourself. Don't
you want to save your child's life?'

The snub had a salutary effect on Buta Singh's
temper. He relapsed into a sullen silence.

'What are we to do?' asked Beena at last.

'I don't know. I've gone mad,' replied her father.

'We shall have a non-stop reading of the Granth for
two days and nights. The Guru will be our guide,' said
Sabhrai quietly.

'Yes, yes,' commented Beena impatiently, 'we will do
that, but we must do something about getting Sherji out
of jail. Have you been to see him?' she asked her father.

'No. I don't want to see him.'

Champak's sobs became louder. Sabhrai put her
arms round her. Buta Singh felt guilty. 'If the Deputy
Commissioner had not been so kind to me, the police
would have beaten him straight. Even now, he has
promised that if Sher tells them all about the crime, he
will grant him the King's pardon.'

'Will he have to give the names of his accomplices?' asked Sabhrai.

'The police already know about them; they know everything. These other chaps were probably the ones to implicate Sher. It is only by the Deputy Commissioner's kindness that Sher can avail himself of the King's pardon. The others would give anything to have the offer made to them.'

'Will he have to become an informer?' asked Beena.

Buta Singh got angry again. 'These are stupid words. I am telling you that the police don't need an informer; they know everything. They are only willing to give Sher an excuse to save his life because the Deputy Commissioner is keen to help him.'

'Why haven't you told Sher of this offer?' asked Sabhrai.

Buta Singh felt cornered. 'I've been out of my senses. If it hadn't been for the Taylors, I don't know what would have happened to me! What more can a man do than offer your son's life back to you?'

'You must see Sherji,' said Beena, 'and tell him about Mr Taylor's offer.'

'We will first do the non-stop reading of the Granth,' said Sabhrai firmly. 'The Guru will guide us. We will do what He commands.'

Being the only son, Sher Singh had been pampered in his childhood and allowed to have his own way in his adolescence. Despite this, the two things he hankered after were affection and esteem. The one he sought through popularity amongst friends; the other through leadership. The applause that came from his family and his colleagues was offset by his early marriage. Champak, despite her expressions of admiration, gave him an uneasy feeling of being a failure. To impress her became an obsession. The form it took was to hold out visions of a successful political career by which he would take her to dizzy heights of eminence along with him. The more his physical inadequacy gnawed his insides, the more daring he became in his political activity. From fiery speeches, he went on to uniforms and discipline; from those to belief in force: the worship of tough men and love for symbols of strength, like swords crossed over a shield. These, with the possession of guns, pistols, cartridges, and the handsomely masculine Alsatian as a companion, completed his martial padding. Living with these symbols of strength and among people who vaguely expected him to succeed, Sher Singh came to believe in his own future and his power. He did not realize that strength was not a natural development of his own personality but nurtured behind the protection provided by his father's position as a senior magistrate and a respected citizen. He was like a hothouse plant blossoming in a greenhouse. The abuse, beating, and arrest were like putting that plant out in a violent hailstorm. His bluster and self-confidence withered in the icy cold atmosphere of the police station.

Sher Singh had never been beaten before in his life. Being kicked in the groin and hit in the face had been a shattering experience. He touched the depths of humiliation and anger. He had always feared and hated

Anglo-Indians. They did the Englishman's dirty work, spoke his language in their own ugly Hobson–Jobson, full of vulgar abuse, but had none of his cricketing spirit. They were the Hydes of the English Dr Jekyll. He had also envied and hated Punjabi Mussulmans. They were physically stronger and more virile than his type of Sikh. And on that fatal morning an Anglo-Indian sergeant had hit him in the face with the back of his hand and a Mussulman constable had told him to face his ordeal like a man. He had wept from fear; he had wept in anger; he had wept in hate. At the end of two days of weeping, his system was drained of anger and hate; only fear remained: the fear of another thrashing and the greater one of death by hanging.

After a few days, life in the police station became such a routine that it seemed to Sher Singh as if he had been there all his life. Every hour a brass gong was struck, it told the time and regulated the life of the station. At the stroke of six, the reveille was sounded and everyone had to get up. There was much sucking of keekar twigs, spitting, and gargling around the taps where policemen and prisoners took turns to bathe. An hour later they were given highly brewed tea and stale bread. Thereafter the courtyard rang with exercise and drill orders. Anglo-Indian sergeants drove in on their noisy motor cycles and took charge. Policemen went out in batches for traffic duty or investigation or to make arrests. Black Marias were brought in; prisoners were handcuffed, fettered, and taken to the law courts. They were brought back in the evening, locked up and fed. Anglo-Indians drove out more noisily than when they came. After the evening roll-call, there was another call of the bugle and the lights were switched off everywhere except in the reporting room. Then it was silent save for an occasional shriek or cry for mercy from the cells behind the courtyard where prisoners were interrogated. Through all this the brass gong marked the hours.

What Sher Singh dreaded most was a visit from his father. He had ruined the latter's career and he would now have no chance of getting an extension of service or a title in the next Honours list. The Government might even deprive him of his pension. Buta Singh was sure to denounce him and refuse to let him come back home — if ever he got away alive. Without Buta Singh there was no chance of reconciliation with the rest of the family. Sabhrai was the type of Indian woman who believed that her husband was a God and would do little more than plead for her son after the initial outburst was over. Champak would probably be sent away to her parents and not be heard of till he came out of jail — if that ever happened. It was an amazing thought that he had hardly missed her. His sister, Beena, did not really matter. The only one he really missed was his dog. Dyer's defense of his master had made a deep impression on his mind. He had often visualized his picture in uniform on large posters with his handsome Alsatian beside him. Now he visualized the same picture of himself as a sad disillusioned man with a distant philosophic look, loved by no one except his dog, who fixed his doting eyes on his master. He wished they would let Dyer share his cell.

Then there was the interrogation. Sher Singh knew his turn would come soon. The sergeant who had hit him said so every morning when he went round the cells: 'Well, Sardar, how are your plans for turning the British out of the country getting on? We must discuss them soon; perhaps I can help you, hm?'

How much did the police know?

Sher Singh tried to work that out hour after hour, day after day. It was obvious that he was the only one of the group they had arrested so far. Madan, who had got him in this mess, was back in Simla having a good time; the others were scattered in different places. Could one of them have been a spy? No, because then his arrest would have followed immediately after the murder. Unless one of the gang had also been arrested and had talked, the police could not possibly know anything about it.

How much should he tell to get away without a beating?

One afternoon a constable came to the cell, put two cane chairs against the wall, and said casually: 'The Sahibs want to talk to you.' The 'Sahibs' came slapping their putteed legs with their swagger sticks. They were the same two who had arrested him. Sher Singh got up from his chair — more out of fear than out of politeness. He did not greet them because he knew the greeting would not be answered. The sergeants sat down. One of them pulled Sher Singh's chair nearer him with his toes and put his feet on it. Sher Singh's only option was to squat on the floor or to keep standing. He kept standing. He was conscious of his arms hanging at his sides as if he were at attention.

'Well, Sardar, are you still plotting to get the British out?' He turned to his companion. 'Great leader this chap, mun. You wouldn't know looking at him, would you?'

The other nodded his head slowly, scrutinizing Sher Singh from head to foot. 'One never knows with these niggers.'

'One doesn't, does one!'

'Not unless one sticks a greased pole up their bums.'

They had their eyes fixed on him; they scratched their chins as if contemplating the course of violence. Sher Singh could do nothing except look down at his hands or at their feet.

'Is this chap also involved in the killing of that fat Sikh lambardar?'

'No mun! He's after bigger game. He wants to shoot the Guv or the Viceroy. Don't you? Speak, you big leader of the revolution! Don't you?'

Sher Singh felt the blood drain out of his system. Were they going to beat him? Why didn't they ask him a specific question and give him a chance to answer?

'Oi,' shouted one of them to the constable outside, 'ask the sub-inspector to *juldi karo*. We can't waste the whole afternoon with this fellow.'

The constable ran across the courtyard. The subinspector came with a sheaf of yellow files tucked under his arm. They got into a huddle. Sher Singh watched them carefully as they whispered into each other's ear. The older of the two sergeants pushed aside the file with disdain: 'Wot you wasting your time for on this chap if the other fellows have already given us all the names?'

'I don't know, Sahib,' answered the sub-inspector feigning surprise. 'Mr Taylor, Deputy Commissioner, say he Sardar Buta Singh's son, give him chance to be informer and save his life.'

'So that's it! You hear, mister? The DeeCee wants to give you a chance to save your bloody neck from hanging because of your old Bap. We have all the information we want from your pals. It's a watertight case. You confirm what they have said and we might consider granting you pardon. Otherwise you hang with the rest of the buggers.'

Sher Singh found his voice with great difficulty: 'What did they say?'

'The bugger wants to know what the others have said? Clever fellow isn't he? Don't try tricks with us, old chap. We've known too many like you.'

The Indian sub-inspector was more polite — obviously wanting to curry favour with Buta Singh. 'Sardar Sahib,' he said in Punjabi, 'as the Sahibs have told you, we have all the information we need from your associates. This is a very serious case; you can be sentenced to death for conspiracy to wage war against the King Emperor. Mr Taylor wants to reward the loyal services of your respected father and has ordered us to give you the chance to be a Crown witness. If your statement confirms what the other conspirators have said and is truthful about the crimes you have committed, the Government may decide to grant you pardon. Do you understand?

'Yes.'

Three pairs of eyes were fixed on him.

'Could I consult a lawyer?'

'Rape your sister!' exploded one of the sergeants. 'We want to give you a chance to save your neck and you want to bring lawyers here! Give him the rod properly greased.'

The Indian sub-inspector again took charge of the situation with a mixture of servility and firmness. 'Sardar Sher Singh, you have not appreciated our point. We know everything already and really have no need of your statement. It is only for your own good. If Taylor Sahib insists on sparing your life because of Sardar Buta Singh, we can make you talk; you know that, don't you?'

Sher Singh made no answer to the threat.

Three pairs of eyes continued to transfix him. He did not know what to say. But he knew that if they used any violence he would tell all he knew without considering the rights or wrongs of making the confession. He made one last attempt to postpone the decision. 'Could I at least see my father?'

'Now he wants to see his Bap. What's wrong with this fellow?'

'Perhaps he will want to see his Ma too,' added the other.

'You don't believe what we say?' asked the Indian sub-inspector angrily. 'It is because your father has been rubbing his nose at Mr Taylor's threshold every day that you are being given this opportunity!'

'It is very kind of you but I would like to speak to my father before making any statement.' For the first time Sher Singh spoke firmly, and that because an

Indian subordinate had dared to talk disparagingly of his father.

The three officers went back into a huddle and then rose up together. The one with his feet on the chair kicked it towards Sher Singh. 'O.K. You see your bloody Bap. We'll talk to you later.'

'And if you want our advice on how to kick the British out of India, don't hesitate to ask.'

They roared with laughter and left.

The non-stop reading of the Granth did not bring any peace in Buta Singh's home. What was worse, the Guru did not indicate the line of action as Sabhrai had promised. And soon after the ceremonial reading was over, Buta Singh resumed his sulking and self-pity. He refused to see Sher Singh in the lock-up, and would not let anyone else see him. He began to insinuate that Champak must have known of her husband's activities and had done nothing to stop him. When Champak's parents heard of it, they came over and took her back home. At last Sabhrai's patience came to an end. One morning she boldly announced her intention to see her son. Buta Singh was adamant. The crisis was averted by the arrival of the officer in charge of the police station. He told them that Sher Singh had expressed the desire to see his father before making a statement and that Mr Taylor had specially requested Buta Singh to comply with his son's wishes.

Buta Singh refused to comply. He thought that, in the circumstances, the refusal to obey Taylor would more than ever prove his loyalty to the Government and disapproval of his disloyal son. The responsibility fell automatically on Sabhrai. She accepted it readily, not because she had any advice to give her son on the statement he was to make, but because her heart ached to see her son and to clasp him to her bosom. She asked her husband to tell her what she was to say to Sher Singh about the confession.

Buta Singh explained the legal situation to her again. She asked: 'If the police already know the names of his associates why do they want them all over again from Sher?' He explained, as he said, for the twentieth time, because they wanted to give him a chance to get away. Why, she went on, were they so keen on letting him get away? For the hundredth time, answered her husband, because Mr Taylor was so kind and friendly to a family which had a long record of loyalty. Why, persisted Sabhrai, if the police really knew the names of Sher's associates hadn't they arrested any of them? Oh really, Buta Singh couldn't be bothered to go over things again and again. Sabhrai had developed a stubborn indifference to rudeness and irritation and asked her husband point-blank: 'What will happen if he refuses to make a confession?'

'What will happen? As far as I am concerned, my service, pension, and the land granted by the Government all go. But that is a small matter; in addition, the boy will be hanged.'

Sabhrai shut her eyes: 'The True, The True. The Great Guru, the Great Guru.'

She turned to her daughter: 'Have you any advice for your brother?'

'I only want him back,' she replied full of emotion. 'I don't care what he says or does, but he must come home now.'

Buta Singh felt that he should not let the matter be postponed indefinitely. 'Will you go tomorrow morning? I have to tell the sub-inspector.'

'What is the hurry? We have waited so many days. We should think about it a little more,' answered Sabhrai.

Buta Singh launched into another tirade. When he finished telling her how little she appreciated the gravity of the situation, how stubborn and stupid she had become of late, Sabhrai got up. 'I will talk to the inspector myself,' she said.

The sub-inspector stood up and saluted Sabhrai.

'Have you come from the police station where my son is kept?'

'Yes, Mataji, your son is in our care.'

'Tell your senior officer I will come to the police station four days from now. I will come, not my husband. I would also like to bring my son's dog with me. He has missed his master very much.'

'Very good, Mataji. I will tell the Inspector Sahib. Is there anything you want to send to your son or any message you want me to give him?'

Sabhrai thought for a while. 'If you wait for a moment, I will give you something for him.' She went into the house and came back with a small prayer book wrapped in velvet. 'Give this to my little Ruby and tell him to say his prayers regularly. Tell him that the Guru is with him in body and in spirit. Sat Sri Akal.'

The sub-inspector was a Muslim. Nevertheless he put the Sikh prayer book reverently on his forehead and then kissed it. 'Mataji, I will give it to him myself. Allah will protect your son from harm.'

For the next three days Sabhrai shut herself away from the world. Her sanctuary was not the gurudwara but her own bedroom. She sat in her armchair with her legs tucked beneath her and murmured her prayers. Her only companion was Dyer. She had never taken much notice of the dog but since her son's arrest she had tried to give him the affection Sher Singh had given. Dyer sat in front of his mistress with his chin stretched on the floor and his eyes dolefully fixed on her. After each prayer she would speak to him: 'Dyer, son, will you come with me to see Sher?' Dyer would prick up his ears at his master's name and cock his head inquiringly from side to side. 'Nobody takes you out for walks these days?' Like all dogs, Dyer knew the word 'walk.' He would get up with a whine and come to his mistress wagging his big tail. 'That's all right, son. Mama will take you out when you are well. And when my Moon comes home, we will all go for walks together, won't we?' And Dyer would again be full of questions cocking his head from left to right, right to left. Sometimes he would get too excited, put his paws in his mistress' lap, and lick her face. She would push him away gently, for this she did not like. She would wipe her face with her headpiece, wash her hands in the bathroom, and start praying again. An hour later the whole thing would be repeated: 'Dyer, son, will you come with me to see my Shera?'

The evening before the interview, she had her dinner with her husband and daughter and told them she was going to spend the night at the temple in the city. They did not ask her any questions. She wrapped herself in her Kashmir shawl, for it had become bitterly cold, and went away on a tonga.

When Sabhrai took off her slippers outside the main gate, the man in charge of shoes was already packing up. 'Brother, keep my shoes for the night; I will take them in the morning.' He gave her a ticket, put out his hurricane lantern, and locked the shoe-shed.

Not many people stay in the temple after the evening service is over. Visitors from other towns retire to the quarters provided for them; beggars are driven away by armed guards who patrol the sacred premises. Only those stricken with sorrow spend the midnight hours in different corners crying and praying for peace. These no one disturbs.

Sabhrai washed her hands and feet in the cistern at the entrance and went down the marble stairs gripping the silver railing on the side. The waters of the sacred pool and the milk-white of the marble walls glistened in the moonlight. The gilded dome of the shrine had a ghostly pallor. Sabhrai bowed towards the shrine. She walked along the side-walk and up the narrow passage, which ran level with the water, to the central place of worship. The room was dimly-lit by a blue electric bulb; the diamonds and rubies in the ceiling twinkled like stars on a dark night. In the centre of the floor the sacred Granth lay wrapped on a low cot. In the corners of the room were huddled figures of men and women, some asleep, some in prayer. Sabhrai made her obeisance and went out. She found a spot from where she could see the dome of the temple and the reflection of the moon and the stars in the dark waters of the sacred pool. She sat down on the hard and cold marble floor. An icy wind blew over the water, through the trellised fence, into her bones. But it was absolutely still and peaceful. The city was asleep; only the gentle clop clop of ripples on marble and the boom of the tower clock striking the hours disturbed the heavy silence.

Sabhrai did not know what prayer one recited during the night; so she went through all she knew by heart. When she had finished, the clock struck two. But the tumult in her mind was not stilled. They were going to hang her son if he did not mention the names of the other conspirators. Hang her little Shera whom she had borne and fed by her own breasts. She began to sob. She stifled her sobs and tried to meditate. How could she meditate with Shera crying for help: 'Mother, they will hang me and I am only twenty-one.' Tears coursed down her cheeks, hot and unceasing. She wiped them with the hem of her shirt and blew her nose. She felt her son's presence between her arms, and more tears flooded down. Why did she feel alone in this awful predicament? Her husband had no doubts; he wanted Shera to confess. So, obviously, did her daughter and daughter-in-law. Sher mattered as much to them as he did to her. Did they really believe that the police knew everything or were they doping their consciences with the thought? And what did Shera himself want to do? Surely it was really for him to decide rather than for her! And if she were the only one with doubts, couldn't she be mistaken?

So the tumult continued and the tears continued to course down her cheeks. Her grey head was full of dew and her limbs stiff with cold and damp. Why did the

Guru not guide her in her hour of need? Had she lost faith? She recalled the time when she had come to this very temple to take part in the cleaning of the sacred pool. The water had been pumped out and the enormous carp that ate out of people's hands had been put away in another tank. Millions of Sikhs had volunteered to carry on their heads the slime which had accumulated for over a hundred years. People said that the hawk of the last Guru would come to see the cleaning. Non-believers had laughed their vulgar laughter, shrugged their shoulders, and said: 'What can you do to people like that?' But the hawk had come. With her own eyes she had seen it swoop down from the heavens, scattering the thousands of pigeons that nested in the temple precincts. It had perched on the pinnacle of the golden dome, preened its lustrous white plumage, and looked down on the throng waist deep in slime and mire. The people had wept and prayed. Over and over again men had hurled the Guru's challenging cry: 'Ye who seek salvation, shout;' and the crowd had roared back: 'God is Truth.' People with faith had seen; those without faith neither saw nor believed that others had seen. Sabhrai also recalled the terrible days when the Sikhs wanted to take over their shrines from the clutches of corrupt priests and the police had decided to help the priests against the people. They had killed and tortured passive resisters. But for each one who was killed, beaten, or imprisoned, another fifty had come. Word had gone round that whenever a band of passive resisters prayed with faith, the Guru himself would appear in their midst and all the lathi blows the police showered on them would fall on him and not on them. That was exactly how it had happened. Frail men and women, who had not known the lash of a harsh tongue, had volunteered and taken merciless beatings without wincing. The police had tired and the priests had panicked. The faith of the Sikhs had triumphed. Was her faith shaking? She tried to dismiss all other thoughts and bring the picture of the last warrior Guru to her mind. He came as he was in the colour print on her mantelpiece: a handsome bearded cavalier in a turban, riding his roan stallion across a stream. On his right hand was perched his white falcon with its wings outspread. *There* was a man. He had lost all his four sons and refused to give in to injustice. She was to lose only one. How had the Guru faced the loss of his children? She began to recite his stirring lines:

'Eternal God, who art our shield
The dagger, knife, the sword we wield
To us protector there is given
The timeless, deathless Lord of Heaven . . . '

It went on in short staccato lines infusing warm blood into her chilled veins and making her forehead hot with anger. She was a Sikh; so was her son. Why did she ever have any doubts?

By the time the prayer ended, the grey light of dawn had dimmed the lesser stars — only the morning star shone a pure, silvery white. At last there was peace in her soul. She got up and went to the women's enclosure to bathe. The water was bitter cold and she shuddered as she went down the steps. She bobbed up and down naming members of her family with each dip, with five extra ones for her Shera. She had brought no towel and dried herself in the breeze. She got back into her clothes, wrapped the warm shawl about her shoulders, and went to the inner shrine where the morning prayer was about to begin.

The priest unwrapped the Granth and read the passage for the day.

'Lord thou art my refuge
I have found Thee and my doubts are dispelled.

I spoke not, but Ye knew my sorrow
And made me to meditate on Thy holy name.
Now I have no sorrow; I am at one with Thee
You took me by my arm
And led me out of Maya's winding maze
You set me free of the trap of attachment.

Spake the Guru: Thy fetters are fallen
Thou who wert estranged
Are united to Thy Lord.'

Sabhrai made her obeisance to the Granth and went out. At the entrance to the temple she scraped a palmful of dust that had come off the feet of pilgrims and tied it up in a knot in her headpiece. She took her slippers from the shoe-stand and went home.

The silence at the breakfast table was broken by the sound of a car drawing up in the porch. Mundoo came in to say that the Deputy Commissioner had sent his car to take Sabhrai to the police station. Buta Singh was very moved: 'What fine people these Taylors are! They have taken the trouble to find out and sent their car. Almost as if Sher were their own son.'

'The Guru will reward them for their kindness,' said Sabhrai. 'Those who are with you in your sorrow are your real friends. God bless them.'

The entire household, including the servants and orderlies, came to see Sabhrai off on her mission. Dyer, who had missed a car ride ever since the jeep had been taken away, cocked his unbelieving ears when his mistress asked him to come along. He gave a bark of joy and hopped on to the seat beside her. They drove off to the police station.

The Deputy Commissioner's car with its Union Jack and chauffeur in police uniform was well known to the staff of the police station. The sentries saluted as it went through the gates and the Anglo-Indian sergeants sprang to attention. Taylor's personal bodyguard stepped out of the front seat and opened the door. Dyer hopped out, followed by Sardarini Buta Singh.

The sergeants recognized the dog. They also realized that the native woman was Buta Singh's wife. The chauffeur enlightened them. They slunk away to the reporting room and let the Indian staff take over. The Muslim sub-inspector conducted Sabhrai to her son's cell.

Dyer was the first to greet his young master. He rushed at him, barking deliriously. He went round in circles, whining, pawing, and licking, and would not let Sabhrai get near her son. Sher Singh patted the dog on the head and pushed him aside gently. Mother and son clasped each other in a tight embrace. Sher Singh's pent up emotions burst their bounds and he began to cry loudly in his mother's arms. Sabhrai hid his unmanly tears by holding him to her bosom. She kissed his forehead again and again. They rocked in close embrace with the dog leaping about the cell, yapping and barking joyously.

'Could you leave us alone, sub-inspector Sahib?' asked Sabhrai addressing the officer.

'Certainly Mataji,' he replied, drying his eyes. 'Stay here as long as you like. Can I bring you some tea or something to eat?'

'No, son, just leave me here for a few minutes. I won't be long.'

The sub-inspector went out and ordered the inquisitive group of constables back to their barracks.

Mother and son sat down on the charpoy. Dyer put his head in his master's lap.

'How pale you are! Do they give you enough to eat?'

'They give me all I want; I don't feel hungry. I could not even eat the food you sent me.'

'I did not send you anything.'

'Oh? The Deputy Commissioner's orderly brought it every day. I thought it was from home; it was Indian.'

'God bless him and his wife. Son, your father would not let me send you anything.'

'Is he very angry with me?'

'He had to be angry. You have poured water over all his ambitions.'

'What does he want me to do? The police tell me he wants me to make a statement naming the boys who were with me.'

'Yes. He thinks that is the only thing that will save you.'

'Have you all thought the matter over?'

'We have talked of nothing else. Everyone says that if the police already know about the others, there is no harm in making a statement. And Taylor Sahib is showing you a special favour in letting you be the only one to get away.'

After a long pause Sher Singh asked: 'Has Champak said anything?'

'What can she say except to want you back! Her eyes are inflamed with too much weeping. She would accept any course which would bring you back home as soon as possible. What is your own opinion?'

'I . . . ' said Sher Singh hesitantly, 'I have no opinion. I will do exactly what you people tell me to do. If it is true they know all about the affair, there seems no point in hiding anything any more.'

Sabhrai shut her eyes and rocked to and fro. After a while she asked, 'Son! Have they been beating you?'

Sher Singh looked down at his feet. The memory of the first thrashing came back to him. 'No, but they beat everyone who comes here. I can hear their cries every night.'

Sabhrai shut her eyes again and chanted as she rocked: 'The Great Guru! The True . . . Are you afraid?'

'Who is not afraid of a beating? Only those who get it know. It is easy to be brave at the expense of other people.' He stroked Dyer's head and tickled him between his front legs. 'Then are you all agreed that I should make a statement? What do you advise me?'

'I am an illiterate native woman, what advice can I give in these matters, son? I only ask the Guru to guide you. What He says is my advice.'

Sher Singh gave her time to tell him what the Guru had to say on the subject. Sabhrai simply closed her eyes and resumed rocking herself and chanting, 'The True, The True, The Great Guru.' Tears began running down her cheeks. Sher Singh put his hand on her knees: 'Mother, what do you want me to do?'

She dried her tears and blew her nose. 'Son, I spent last night at the Golden Temple asking the Guru for guidance. I do not know whether I got it right. In any case His orders were for me; not for you.'

'What did He say, Mother? Why don't you tell me?'

'He said that my son had done wrong. But if he named the people who were with him he would be doing a greater wrong. He was no longer to be regarded as a Sikh and I was not to see his face again.'

She undid the knot in her headpiece in which she had tied the dust collected at the temple and pasted it on her son's forehead with her palm. 'May the Guru be with you in body and in spirit.'

Chapter XI

'Dear Taylor Memsahib. I am an uneducated Punjabi woman who cannot write nice words of thanks in English. Ask one of your clerks to read this to you. God bless you for what you have done. You wanted to share the grief of a mother whose child has been stricken. There is no greater act of kindness in the world. May the Guru's blessings be on you, your Sahib, and on your children. May you have many sons. May God ever keep your household full of plenty and keep sorrow and suffering away from your door.'

Sabhrai folded the paper with her shaking hands. Her head shook and she had difficulty in licking and sealing the envelope. She asked Shunno to give it to the Deputy Commissioner's chauffeur, who had driven her back from the police station, and then light a fire in her bedroom. By the time Shunno came back with old newspapers and firewood, Sabhrai was in bed with her quilt wrapped about her. Despite her will power, her teeth began to rattle and she began to shiver violently.

'Bibiji, you have fever,' said Shunno in alarm. 'You must have caught a chill.'

Sabhrai wanted to tell her to get on with her work, but no words would come out of her mouth. She shivered and shook; her forehead was hot, her body cold. Shunno quickly lit a fire. She came to her mistress and began to press her. The fit of shivering was soon over.

Sabhrai relaxed in her warm bed and fell fast asleep in the heated room.

Neither her husband nor her daughter got a chance to ask her about her interview with Sher Singh. She had gone straight from the car to her room. An hour later, Shunno came to tell them that she was asleep. They knew that she had been away all night and needed rest. If she had had anything really important to tell them, she would have done so before retiring. Obviously, thought Buta Singh, everything had gone according to plan and his son's release would now be a matter of time, an unpleasant time, with other arrests, and a public trial where Sher Singh, being the Crown witness, would be branded as a traitor. It would finish Sher's political career — but only for a time, for public memory was notoriously short. In any case it would save the boy's life. It would also save Buta Singh's face vis-a-vis Taylor who had trusted and relied on him and had been so good to his family in the worst crisis in his life. Buta Singh felt that at long last the nightmare of the past month was coming to an end. He was full of gratitude to Taylor and to God; even to Sabhrai — his illiterate, superstitious, half-companion of the past thirty years.

Sabhrai did not stir all afternoon. Beena tiptoed in and out of the darkened, stuffy room several times to see her. By evening she grew somewhat nervous and came to her mother's bedside. Sabhrai seemed to be in deep slumber. Beena watched her quilt for some time before she noticed the reassuring heave of her breath. She looked at her watch. Eight hours of continuous sleep was long enough. If Sabhrai stayed in bed longer, she would not be able to sleep at night; and she had not eaten all day. Beena called her softly. There was no sign of waking. She put her hand on her mother's forehead. It burnt with fever. Beena ran out to her father and told him. Buta Singh hurried in. They whispered to her, then called out loudly. She did not answer. They felt her pulse beat rapidly. Buta Singh sent his orderly to fetch a doctor.

The doctor took her temperature and examined her chest and back with his stethoscope. He asked a few questions and then told the family that Sabhrai had pneumonia. Her temperature was over 104° and she was in a state of delirium. But pneumonia was no longer something to be scared of, he assured them. The new American drug had got the better of it. He prescribed a medicine and gave detailed instructions about the nursing. He would call again in the morning.

Buta Singh and Beena took turns at watching over Sabhrai, and Shunno pressed her mistress' feet intermittently all through the night.

Next morning Buta Singh scanned the paper more carefully than he had done for a long time. There were no arrests of terrorists reported. Perhaps it was too early for the police to act or the boys had absconded. He felt as if he had been given one more day of respectability with the citizens. Would he be able to explain away his son's action? If his name appeared in the next Honours list (which would be published in another ten days), no one would ever accept his explanations. They would say that he had forced his son to betray his colleagues so that he could get his O.B.E. or C.I.E., or one of the other titles that the British had invented for the Indians. What would it matter in the end! He would retire to his village with his pension and property intact. His family would be safe. He would be able to get his son a good job; Taylor would surely continue to help him.

In the crisis, the Englishman seemed to have become Buta Singh's only hope. It would be Christmas in three days. Perhaps he should make the Taylors some gesture of gratitude for what they had done. He knew they were very particular about accepting gifts from subordinates. His case was different; he was a friend as well. Besides, the circumstances warranted a symbolic expression of thanks. Christmas was a good opportunity to do so. In any case he would send it from his wife to Mrs Taylor.

After the doctor had come and gone, Buta Singh asked his orderly to go to the bazaar and buy three dozen of the best Malta oranges with blood-red centres. He busied himself in composing a letter to go with the gift.

Respected Mrs Taylor,

Pray accept this humble gift of oranges for Christmas Day. They are the first pick of the year from our garden. I hope you will like them. To you and your noble husband, our most respected Deputy Commissioner, my husband and children owe their all. Madam will do us an honour by receiving this very little gift on

the auspicious occasion of the birthday of the World
Saviour, Lord Jesus Christ.

Your humble servant,
Sabhrai
(Sardarini Buta Singh)
wife of
Sardar Buta Singh, B.A. (Hons),
Magistrate First Class.

Buta Singh read the letter over several times. Did it
sound too servile? No, he decided, nothing sounds too
obsequious to the recipient. The only important thing
was that the gift should not be returned because a snub
in these circumstances would be hard to take. Also,
other people should not get to know about it and make
fun of him.

The basket of oranges and the letter were sent off
three days before Christmas. To Buta Singh's great
relief, it was not returned. Mrs Taylor accepted the gift
and, in accordance with Indian custom, left two oranges
and a five-rupee note as tip for the orderly. She told the
orderly to inform his mistress that she would come over
personally to thank the Sardarini.

Mrs Taylor came to call next morning. Buta Singh
had already told his daughter about the oranges. 'I said
they came from our garden because it sounds better,' he
explained blandly. 'I sent them from your mother. Mrs
Taylor has been specially good to her.'

'How extremely kind of you to send us the first pick
from your garden,' said Mrs Taylor as she stepped out
of the car and held out her hand.

'Oh nothing, Mrs Taylor. A very humble gift. It was most kind of you to accept.'

'And this is your daughter? We met at the station. How are you? Where is the Sardarini Sahiba? I must thank her for the wonderful oranges. I'll try my Hindustani.'

'She is very ill,' answered Beena. 'She has been in a state of delirium for the last two days.' Buta Singh realized that his daughter was contradicting his story of the oranges being sent by Sabhrai. He broke in quickly, 'No, nothing, it is just a little cold and fever. The doctor said it would be controlled by the new American drug. It costs me Rs 35 each day. But I say, "Money does not matter." Of course you can see her.' He opened the door to usher her in.

'I was a nurse before I married John,' explained Mrs Taylor. 'Perhaps I can be of some help.'

Buta Singh went on, 'You have done enough of helping. We will not forget it all our lives.'

Sabhrai's room was warm and dark. A fire smoldered in the chimney. The windows were shut and there was an oppressive odour of mint and eucalyptus. Under the table lamp beside her bed were an assortment of bottles of medicine, a thermometer, and a tumbler of water. There was also a picture of the first Guru in a silver frame, and a rosary. Beside the bed on the floor was a basin full of margosa leaves for her to be sick in. Shunno drew her veil across her face as her master came in and went on rubbing the soles of her mistress' feet.

Joyce Taylor was surprised that in an educated Indian home there should be so much disregard of the elementary rules of hygiene. Her nursing past got the better of her recently acquired status as the wife of the Deputy Commissioner. 'Why have you got the room so hot and stuffy?'

'You see, madam, she has caught a cold and draughts are not good for her,' explained Buta Singh.

'Rubbish! Open the doors and windows at once. She needs fresh air. Have you kept a temperature chart?'

Joyce Taylor opened the windows herself and took the temperature chart which lay under the tumbler of water. She examined it carefully. Then she put her hand under the quilt and felt Sabhrai's pulse.

Mrs Taylor put her cold hand on Sabhrai's hot forehead and gently pushed back her eyelids. Sabhrai kept her eyes open but there was no look of recognition in them.

'How are you, Sardarini?'

Sabhrai's lips quivered; she was trying to say something.

'Taylor's Memsahib has come to call on you. Don't you recognize her?' asked Buta Singh loudly in Punjabi.

There was another quiver of her lips. Then tears welled in her eyes and rolled off into her ears. Joyce Taylor wiped Sabhrai's tears with her handkerchief and gently pressed her hand on her eyes. 'Go to sleep like a good girl. You'll soon be well.' She asked Buta Singh about the doctor and scrutinized the prescription he had made out.

'Very expensive medicine this new thing,' said Buta Singh.

'Next time you send for the doctor, let me know. I would like to have a word with him,' she ordered. She gave a friendly pat on Sabhrai's cheek and got up. 'You mustn't allow any visitors for some days. There must be no excitement at all. She is very ill.'

Among happily married people there grows up a private language of accent, emphasis, and gesture which makes privacy between them almost impossible. If they have shared a common past, they get to know each other's reactions to particular situations and have an instinctive knowledge of each other's attitude to any set of new circumstances. Sometimes, long forgotten tunes come up in their minds and without any reason at all they find themselves humming the same notes at the same time. Then there are ways of behaviour which indicate to no one but themselves what the other has in mind. Even at the dinner table the way the wife will pass the bread or, later, the way she will walk up to her room will tell the husband that she wants to be slept with that night. It is not so simple when she wants favours other than sexual. Nevertheless the husband will become aware of something brewing in her mind long before it is put in words.

There was nothing subtle about Joyce Taylor's fidgets the evening after she had returned from the Buta Singh home. It continued throughout dinner and she remained close to her husband afterwards. This was contrary to the normal practice of giving him an hour with his files before rejoining him for coffee.

'Something on your mind, dear?' Taylor asked at last.

'Yes and no. I mean there is something but I don't know exactly what it is.'

'That doesn't get us very far. What have you been doing with yourself all day?'

'The same as any other day — apart from calling on old Buta Singh and his family. Curious lot, aren't they?'

'How did it go?'

'Not too bad. I don't understand the Old Walrus with his obsequious "respected Memsahib" and "our noble Deputy Commissioner." '

'Don't be too hard on the old stick; he's been brought up like that. The English are his Mai-Bap, Father-Mother when they are about; when they are not, he is more himself. But he is all right. Does his job honestly and has certainly done more for the war effort than any other officer in the district.'

'What I cannot understand is if he really feels that way about the British Raj, that he should have a son mixed up with terrorists.'

'Well! In a way you have the history of Indo-British relationships represented by Buta Singh's family tree. His grandfather fought against us in the Sikh wars; his father served us loyally. He has continued to do so with certain reservations. His son is impatient to get rid of us. Poor Buta Singh is split between the past and the future; that is why he appears so muddled in the present. He is not as much of a humbug as he appears to be.'

'One knows where one stands with the younger generation of Indians. They certainly do not want to have anything to do with us.'

'I am not so certain of that either,' answered Taylor. 'The boy in the police lock-up is in as much of a muddle as his father.'

'What do you mean? He wants India for the Indians; he is willing to kill the English if he can't get rid of them in any other way.'

'It isn't as clear as that. You heard about the Alsatian dog he has — the one which attacked one of the police officers who arrested him and which Sardarini took to the police station! Well, he named him Dyer, quite obviously because it was the most hated name he could think of: General Dyer fired on a crowd in this very city and killed several hundred men and women. In giving a dog that name, he expressed his loathing for the General. Now apparently he loves the dog more than his own relations.'

'I don't know if that indicates much,' laughed Joyce.

'No, except that it is all a bit muddled.'

Taylor began to show signs of impatience. 'Let's have coffee. I can do my work later on; there isn't very much to do.'

She ordered the coffee and the two came into the study. He lit his pipe. 'How is the family taking the boy's arrest?'

'I couldn't find out. The Walrus did all the talking; I couldn't get a clue from him. John, how does the case against the boy stand?'

'So far there is no evidence at all. The police haven't made up their minds what to do with him. They have means of making people talk when they want to. They never fail.'

'You mean torture.'

'You can call it that. It may be nothing more than a threat or an inconvenience. With educated city dwellers like Sher Singh they should have no difficulty.'

The bearer brought in the coffee. They drank it in silence. Joyce still showed no signs of leaving. When she noticed her husband impatiently emptying his pipe, she asked him in a nervous, high-pitched voice: 'John, you can't keep that boy in prison indefinitely till he confesses to a crime he may never have committed. That's the sort of thing we are fighting against in this war.'

Taylor filled his pipe and lit it before answering. 'A man is missing; it can be presumed that he is dead. If someone had told me about his disappearance a little earlier, I would have put the police on the right track. He had been seeing me regularly.'

'What makes you think Buta Singh's son killed him?'

'It is only a guess. He had seen some boys including Sher Singh at target practice; he brought me the fired bullets. They also tried to blow up a little bridge on the canal. He told me about that too.'

'Yes, yes,' she cried impatiently, 'but how did they know he was telling you these things?'

'Buta Singh's son was certainly aware of it; I had it conveyed to him that I knew. I hoped it would stop his goings on.'

'It is possible one of the others killed him without Sher Singh having anything to do with it.'

'It is possible but highly improbable.'

Joyce Taylor had no more arguments but was still reluctant to give up. 'How long do you deprive a man of his liberty because of probability of guilt?'

Taylor looked a little surprised at her vehemence. 'Not for long; if there isn't any further evidence. You seem very wrought up today. What is the matter?' He ran his fingers through her hair. She let her head drop on his shoulder.

'John, will you promise me something?'

'What is it, dear?'

'You won't be cross with me for interfering in your business?'

'I promise not to be cross, but I am likely to say "No." '

After a long pause she continued: 'The Walrus' wife — the Sardarini — is ill, very ill.'

'Oh!' exclaimed Taylor, a little surprised. 'This is the first I have heard about her illness. What is the matter with her?'

'The doctor has diagnosed it as double pneumonia. Apparently before interviewing her son she spent the night praying at the Golden Temple. She must have got the chill there.'

Taylor was not a religious man, but this sort of devotion moved him. 'I am very sorry to hear that. She has the dignity of an ancient people behind her. Without knowing her I have respect for her. If you like, I can ask the English Army doctor to see her.'

'I do not think she has the will to live. Unless she gets back that will, no doctor will be able to help her.'

Taylor continued stroking her hair.

'John, why can't we give her a Christmas present which will mean something to her? Really mean something.'

Taylor got up, carrying his wife in his arms as if she were a child. He kissed her and put her on her feet. 'They don't believe in Christmas; they are not Christians. Come along now. Time for bed.'

The Muslim sub-inspector entered the cell with a conspiratorial smile on his face. 'Congratulations, Sardar Sher Singh. A hundred, hundred congratulations.'

'What about?' asked Sher Singh feigning ignorance. He knew in prison there could only be one reason to congratulate anyone.

'If you give us some sweets, I will tell you.'

'Even so?'

The sub-inspector dramatically held out a piece of yellow paper. 'An order for your release. Tomorrow morning you will be discharged. Mr Taylor's orders are that your respected parents should not be told but that you should be taken home as a surprise for the Big Day. Tomorrow is Christmas, you know!'

'Christmas for the Christians,' said Sher Singh disdainfully. 'Tell me, what happened about the case? Am I being released on bail?'

'No, no, Sardar Sahib! Discharged! Finished! Holiday! There was no evidence against you.'

'I thought you had all the evidence for some case or other from the boys who had confessed.

'Oh, you are still yesterday's child, Sardar Sher Singh! You will get to know the ways of the Punjab police when you grow up. No one has been arrested so there are no confessions. You have nothing to worry about. Go home and have a good time. Some day when you are a big man, a minister or something, think of poor sub-inspector Wali Dad who gave you the good news.'

'That is very kind of you.'

Sher Singh pondered. Next day was Christmas. There would be no newspapers. 'I don't suppose it would be possible for you to delay my release by a day.'

The sub-inspector looked puzzled. 'Don't you want to go home? It is the Deputy Commissioner's order. If it is disobeyed, I'll have my plug taken out. It is not only because it is the Big Day tomorrow but also because your respected mother is in indifferent health.'

'Oh! No one told me about that.' Sher Singh really didn't believe it. Probably Taylor was trying to be a boy scout and an Oriental monarch in one — releasing a prisoner on Christmas Day to save the life of a dying mother. 'Would you do me a favour? Could you take a message to a friend of mine. He is Mr Wazir Chand's son, Madan. He is my best friend.'

'Mr Madan, the famous cricketer? With great pleasure. I will deliver it personally. I know his respected father, Mr Wazir Chand, Magistrate.'

Sher Singh took up a piece of buff coloured paper from a large pad and wrote:

Dear Madan,
You will be glad to hear that I am being released tomorrow. Please convey this information to all my friends in the University (but not to my parents for whom I want it to be a pleasant surprise).

The police did their worst to get information from me but they failed. I am proud to have been able to serve my God and my country. We should exploit this little service I have done to our best advantage. Greetings to all the comrades in arms.

Long live the Revolution.

Your brother,
Sher.

He put the letter in an envelope and sealed it. This is private, sub-inspector Sahib. I shall be grateful if the inspector does not read it before it is forwarded.'

'What will you say when you are a great man? Wali Dad did me a little service,' said the sub-inspector. He shook Sher Singh with both hands and put the letter in his pocket.

Sher Singh was flushed with excitement. At long last it had come. An imprisonment and a heroic stand against torture by the police. What more could anyone ask for? He would be the hero of the city for the next few days. If he kept up the citizens' interest and faith in him, a political career was his for the asking. What about his father? The Government could not penalize him for something it had been unable to prove against his son! He would make it up to him by his success. And his father had almost certainly more than made it up with Taylor. All was well. Sher Singh knew his star was in the ascendant once more. He hardly thought of his mother's illness. In fact, he did not believe there was any truth in it. It must be another canard let loose by his father to get round Taylor.

Madan did not fail his friend. He spent the whole of Christmas Eve going round to all the college hostels and telling the boys to turn up at the police station at the crack of dawn. He informed the Nationalist Party office and persuaded them to hire a brass band and get an open car to take Sher Singh in procession.

He got hold of press photographers and newspaper correspondents, all of whom had been obliged to him for exclusive interviews and pictures of sporting events. In publicizing Sher Singh they were on a safe wicket. Father, a senior magistrate — son, a student leader on the road to fame and power.

From the early hours of the morning crowds of students carrying garlands of marigolds and roses began to collect outside the police station. By eight o'clock, the crowd had swelled to three or four thousand. An open car decorated with buntings and flowers drew up and took its place behind the brass band made up of retired Sikh soldiers. When the gate of the police station was opened there were thunderous cries of 'Long live the Revolution' and 'Long live Sher Singh.' There were no white sergeants on duty on Christmas Day, and the Indian police officers were not unduly perturbed at an unlawful assembly at their doorstep. All said and done, it was to honour the son of a magistrate.

Sher Singh was escorted out by a couple of subinspectors. Camera bulbs flashed. The band leader ordered his men to attention. The drum beat a loud tattoo and then opened with the slow bars of 'God Save the King.' There was an uproar. The band leader had his baton snatched out of his hand. The anthem whimpered to a standstill amid roars of laughter. The crestfallen band leader started again. This time with 'It's a long, long way to Tipperary.'

Sher Singh shook hands with his police escort and was immediately submerged in embraces and garlands. Madan led him to the car through a crowd cheering and yelling wildly. He stood beside Sher Singh in the open car, waved his hand and shouted, 'Sher Singh.' The crowd roared back, 'Long live.' Sher Singh raised both hands asking for silence. Everyone shushed everyone else. The band stopped — still a long, long way from Tipperary.

'Comrades,' said Sher Singh in a voice charged with emotion, 'I will cherish the honour you have done me today for the rest of my life. I am proud that I was called upon to do a small duty to my country and I did it.' The crowd interrupted him with loud cheers. He raised his hands, demanding attention. 'I have been a guest of the King Emperor.' The crowd roared with laughter. 'You all know how well the King Emperor — may peace be upon him — looks after his guests.'. . . The crowd roared again. Sher Singh worked himself into a fury. He thumped his garland-laden chest. 'But they could not break the spirit of this son of India and God willing they never will.' Madan hurled his voice across the sea of human heads, 'Sher Singh' — the sea thundered back 'Long live.' Sher Singh joined his hands and bowed his head in humble acknowledgement. He was deeply moved by the affection of the crowd and by his own words. There were tears in his eyes.

The band struck up a slow march and the procession began to move. Sher Singh sat in the rear acknowledging the cheers and bowing to people who kept loading him with garlands and hurling rose petals at him.

On Christmas morning, Buta Singh and his daughter were having breakfast in Sabhrai's bedroom. Mrs

Taylor's warning that she was to be left strictly alone had been ignored. It was an old custom to be by the bedside of a sick person, and so they were — all the twenty-four hours — eating, sleeping, and gossiping. Sabhrai had remained in a state of delirium with the fever never falling below 104°. She opened her eyes sometimes and tried to speak, but only an inaudible whisper escaped her lips.

Buta Singh looked up from his plate and wiped the egg off his moustache with his napkin. 'Sounds like a wedding procession. They have started early.' Beena sat still. She heard the shouting of slogans. 'Couldn't be a wedding party; sounds more like a political procession.' The music and the shouting came nearer and nearer till it was inside the house. They got up and hurried out of the room. The band was playing in their porch. The garden, the driveway, and road were jammed with boys chanting 'Long live the Revolution.' As Buta Singh appeared on the scene the chanting changed to 'Long live Buta Singh. Long live Sher Singh. ' A dozen young men rushed forward to congratulate the magistrate. It was then he noticed his son loaded with garlands. Father and son fell into each other's arms. All differences of opinion, all rancour which had poisoned their relationship over the past months were submerged in the applause of triumph.

It was Sabhrai's ninth day in bed. On the ninth day the fever usually subsides and the patient is on the mend — unless, of course, there is a relapse. In which case, the process starts all over again. Nobody could say that the family had not done their best in looking after her. They never left her bedside for a moment. Her husband and daughter took turns to watch over her all through the night. During the day, there were other relations or servants always present. Shunno showed great endurance in keeping the house going and also being with the mistress at all hours; pressing her tired limbs, talking to her when she mumbled in her delirium, comforting her with words in baby language and with prayer. The doctor's instructions about the medicine and diet were also strictly carried out. As books of medicine prescribed, Sabhrai sweated profusely all night and in the morning her temperature was down by four degrees. She was obviously turning the corner.

She was awakened from her half delirious sleep by Beena embracing her and shouting in her ears that Sher Singh was back home. She heard the band and the slogans and the people talking excitedly. She saw many strange faces in her room till it was full of bright eyes and glistening teeth. She vaguely guessed what could have happened. Or was it another dream which would end in the nightmare of awakening?

Then her son appeared. His sister had reloaded him with garlands. He came and fell on her and smothered her with tears, kisses, and crushed flowers. His sister gently pushed him away; Mrs Taylor had said 'No excitement.' The physical touch of her son convinced Sabhrai that her son was free. She could not reason out why he was free. She had herself urged him on the way to death but merciful God had sent him back to her. Her lips quivered but no words came: only a long-drawn moan and then a flood of tears.

When the doctor came an hour later, Sabhrai was in a state of complete collapse. In the excitement that prevailed in the house no one realized that this was the crucial ninth day. The doctor examined the chart and discovered that she had had a relapse. But even he could not bring himself to being angry with as important a man as Buta Singh and on a day when there was so much rejoicing. Hadn't his only son been delivered from the jaws of death? He told the family that the son's coming had been too much for the patient and the fever would continue for another period. He assured them that Sher Singh's release would act like a tonic and she would pull through.

Five days later, Sabhrai got another dose of the sort of tonic the doctor had spoken of. On New Year's Eve, the correspondent of *The Tribune* turned up with garlands. This time they were for Buta Singh. He had been given the C.I.E. in the New Year's Honours list. Buta Singh refused to believe it. 'Not until I see it in print!' he insisted. An hour later it was in print in the special supplement published for the Honours list. By then Buta Singh's colleagues had also learnt of it. All the district's officers, clerks right down to the orderlies, and peons, turned up with garlands of flowers and gold thread. Those who knew the family invaded the house right into Sabhrai's bedroom to congratulate and garland her. It went on till late into New Year's Eve. Next morning it was the turn of the citizens who read of the honour conferred in the paper. So for more than twenty-four hours, the house was full of laughter, gaiety, and flowers. Even Sabhrai in her dazed state knew that God was back in His heaven because all was well with her family.

Sabhrai had not known many illnesses in her carefully regulated life and had considerable powers of resistance. Nevertheless more than a fortnight of high fever, which had touched 105°, came down and shot up again, had wasted her body and begun to tell on her heart. This was not noticed by the doctor. When the second period of fever came to an end, the family was more careful. In any case the period of excitement was over.

For two days Sabhrai had no fever; she was exhausted and looked deathly pale. She lay all day long staring at the ceiling above her and slowly telling the beads of her rosary. If she wanted anything she would slowly raise her hand for Shunno and whisper instructions in her ear. On the third day she seemed well on the way to recovery and was allowed to sit up in bed propped up with pillows.

The fourth day started well. She was in better form than ever. The family were having their breakfast in her bedroom. Her husband was airing his views on politics. 'This man Hitler must be an amazing character. He has raised the German people from defeat to such greatness. If India could produce a man like him, all would be well.'

Sher Singh took that sort of remark personally. The crisis produces the man,' he said pompously. 'India can only be ruled by strong men. This democratic business of votes for everyone, elections, assemblies, committees, is nonsense. I don't believe in it.' After

Sher Singh's short detention his pronouncements on politics had acquired sanctity.

Buta Singh swallowed a mouthful of curry. A stringy bit of vegetable stuck to his walrus moustache and began to dance up and down as he poured out platitudes with great earnestness. 'Absolutely right! What does a vote mean to illiterate semi-savage people! It may be all right in England, but not in India. What is the point of creating a jungle of committees and rules so that no one can see the way out? In our own administration they do the same. It doesn't take me in. I don't take any notice of committees. No red tape for me,' he said sitting back. The stringy piece of curry also sat back on his moustache. It looked funny but Buta Singh was talking so seriously that no one could draw his attention to it. 'If I had allowed myself to be fooled by files and rules of procedure I wouldn't have got where I have. It takes a shrewd man to see through them.'

A faint smile came on Sabhrai's pale face. She raised her hand with her rosary dangling between her fingers. Shunno got up and put her ear close to her mistress' mouth; then put her hands on her mouth and went into an irrepressible giggle. The family looked round. After two months of sighing, sorrowing, and sickness, Sabhrai had cracked a joke.

'What is it?' asked Beena.

Shunno could not speak; she was convulsed with laughter. The smile still played on Sabhrai's pallid face. Beena came close to her and she whispered the same words into her daughter's ear. Beena also burst out laughing.

'Tell us the joke too,' said Buta Singh, smiling eagerly. Beena held her laughter. 'Mama says there is a bulbul on the bough.'

Everyone including Buta Singh began to laugh. He brushed his moustache with his napkin and asked: 'Has it flown?'

Sabhrai nodded her head slowly still smiling.

'Thank God you are smiling today,' said Beena. She put her arms round her mother and kissed her on her cheeks and forehead.

Serious political discussion was over and everyone was happy. The joke was repeated to the doctor and other visitors who came. They dispersed to go to their work — to the law courts and the college.

More people die between nine and eleven in the morning than at any other time of the day or night. Body temperature falls to its lowest degree in the early hours and after a short struggle the heart gives in.

But death was far from Sabhrai's mind on the morning she died. She lay propped up on her pillow looking out of the window. The ixora creeper grew outside and was in full bloom with clusters of scarlet flowers peeping in beside the frame. A pair of magpie robins were apparently contemplating matrimony. She could not see the hen, but the cock flew up to the window-sill to serenade his sweetheart. Like a ballet dancer he ran across the sill in quick, short steps and came to a sudden halt. He jerked his wings behind him as a man tucks his thumbs in his waistcoat pocket. His tail went up, his chest swelled. He raised his head to the flowers and a full-throated song burst out of his tiny beak in sheer ecstasy. He pirouetted, ran back, and repeated the performance as if to an encore from his audience. Sabhrai knew that God certainly was in His heaven and all was right with the world.

There were a few things which bothered her mind. She had not understood why Sher Singh had been released. Had he ignored her advice and confessed? She did not feel strong enough to question him; she would do so when she was better. The first thing to do was to send him to fetch Champak from her parents. And now this calamity was over and Beena had taken her degree, it was time they got down to finding her a husband.

Sabhrai was immersed in these thoughts when the ormolu clock wound itself and after a preliminary *Krrr* struck the half hour. She looked round. There it was on the mantelpiece with its ivory face with faded gold spots. She had brought it with her in her dowry and it had kept the hours ever since. Only the clear metallic tinkle had gone. Sabhrai put her pillows flat and lay down. She felt very tired. Half an hour later, the ormolu clock again wound itself and after a long *Krrr* struck ten as if its nose were clogged with a heavy cold — *thig, thig, thig*. . . .

Sabhrai felt her feet go icy cold. She called out to Shunno as loud as she could. The maidservant hurried from the kitchen to her mistress' bedside. 'Send for my family,' whispered Sabhrai. 'My time has come.'

'The True, The True. Don't say such things, Beybey! Let the time come to our enemies.'

'Don't talk. Send for my family. My time is drawing near.'

Shunno rushed out of the house to the sentry and asked him to get the Sardar and other members of the family together. Neither she nor the sentry thought of the doctor. What use are doctors when one's time is up?

Shunno came back to the room. Even she could see that Sabhrai was not wrong. She began to press her mistress' feet chanting in loud sing-song: 'The True, The True. The Great Guru.'

Sabhrai shook her head. 'Read me the passage for the month. I was ill and nobody read it out to me.'

Shunno fumbled with the pages of the prayer book, found the month of Magh, and began to read loudly:

The Lord hath entered my being;
I make pilgrimage within myself and am purified.
I met Him
He found me good
And let me lose myself in Him.

Beloved! If Thou findest me fair
My pilgrimage is made,
My ablution done.
More than the sacred waters of the Ganga
Of the Yamuna and Tribeni mingled
at the Sangam;
More than the seven seas.
More than all these, charity, almsgiving, and
    prayer,
Is the knowledge of eternity that is the Lord.

Spake the Guru:
He that hath worshipped the great giver of life
Hath done more than bathe in the sixty and eight
    places of pilgrimage.

'Shall I read anything else?' asked Shunno coming closer to her mistress.

Sabhrai shook her head again. 'When is the first of Phagan?'

'I don't know. Many days yet.'

'Don't forget to clean the gurudwara and make the prasad. Wake up everyone in time and ask my Sardarji to read the prayer.'

Shunno began to sob. 'Beybey, why do you talk like this? You will read it yourself. We will sit and listen.'

Sabhrai ignored her sobs. She put her hand on her servant's shoulder. 'Now read the morning prayer to me.'

Shunno drew a chair beside her mistress' pillow. She never sat on a chair in the house but that was the only way she could get close to her. She picked up the prayer book and began to recite. Sabhrai lay back on her pillow and shut her eyes. She folded her hands across her navel and began telling the beads of her rosary.

Buta Singh was the first to arrive. 'Have you sent for the doctor?' he asked Shunno in an agitated tone. Sabhrai opened her eyes and spoke to her husband. 'I don't need a doctor,' she whispered. 'Let me go to my Guru with your blessings.'

Buta Singh began to sniff. A few minutes later Beena turned up. She saw the pallor on her mother's face and heard her father sobbing in his handkerchief. Sabhrai opened her eyes again and put her hands on her daughter's head.

'May the Guru keep you from evil.'

'Mummy, don't talk like this. In the name of the Guru, don't,' she sobbed.

The tears gave way to a gloomy silence. Buta Singh and Beena sat on Sabhrai's bed and pressed her arms and feet. Sabhrai fell asleep utterly exhausted. Sher Singh was the last to arrive. Sabhrai woke up as soon as he came in — just as if she had been waiting for him all the time. She smiled and beckoned him to come close to her. She whispered in his ear: 'I shall not hear the nightingales, my son. May the Guru give you long life.'

Sher Singh was more emotional than the others and began to cry loudly. His father and sister broke down again.

'What is all this noise?' asked Sabhrai audibly. 'You want me to go with the noise of crying in my ears! Say the morning prayer — all together. And do not stop till it is over.' They suppressed their crying and began to chant together:

There is One God.
He is the supreme Truth.
He, the Creator,
Is without fear and without hate
He, the omnipresent,
Pervades the universe.
He is not born,
Nor does He die to be reborn again.
By His grace shalt thou worship Him. . . .

Sabhrai joined her family in the recitation. She seemed to be at complete peace with the world. An unearthly radiance glowed in her pale face. A few verses before the epilogue her voice became faint and then her lips stopped moving.

Chapter XII

In India an old person's death is a matter of rejoicing: a young person's one of sorrow. In the case of the former, they decorate the bier with paper flags and buntings and often hire a band to lead the funeral procession. Married women put vermilion in the parting of their hair and wear their bridal jewelry. Mothers ask their children to walk beneath the stretcher on which the corpse is carried so that they may have as long a life as that of the deceased. During the seven or ten days prescribed for mourning, there is much ceremonial but little sorrow. On the death of a young man, woman, or child, grief refuses to be confined by custom and expresses itself with savage abandon. Relations and friends of the bereaved indulge in orgies of crying, wailing, and beating of breasts till sorrow is drained of all tears.

Sabhrai was neither too old nor too young. By conventional methods of calculation, she had died before her time because she had left a daughter unmarried. So her going had to be condoled with the necessary concern expressed for Beena's future. Except for that, it was like the death of any other person who had had a fair innings though not a full one.

Four hours after her death she was carried to the cremation ground with practically half the city following in procession behind her flower-bedecked bier. The

Taylors and many other officials had sent wreaths. There amongst a dozen other pyres in different stages of burning — some fiercely ablaze, others barely glowing under a mound of ashes — they put together a pile of logs and placed her body on them. They uncovered her face for a few minutes for all to see. She slept with a smile still hovering on her face. They put more logs on her, sprinkled them with clarified butter and rose water. A last prayer was said to consign her body to the Great Guru who had earlier in the day claimed her soul. Sher Singh took round a burning faggot and set the pyre aflame.

Next day, he and his father went back to the cremation ground, sprinkled water on the ashes, and picked up whatever had escaped the all-consuming fire: knuckles, knee-caps, ankles, and other unrecognizable little bits of bone. They put them in a sack and took them home. The sack was placed under the cot on which the Granth lay. It had to stay there till Sher Singh could take time off to go to the Beas and scatter its contents in the river.

For the first two days no fire was lit in Buta Singh's house. The Wazir Chands brought food from their house and persuaded the family to eat. Everyone slept on the floor and most of the day was spent listening to the recitation of the Granth. Then relations turned up by the dozens and Champak and Sita had to organize their feeding and comfort; Beena was too distracted to be of any help. It was almost like a wedding — crowds of children shouting and playing about in the courtyard and a lot of coming and going of friends and relations. Men came wearing sad expressions on their faces: 'Very sorry to hear the news. How did it happen?' each one would ask. 'It was God's will. When the time is up, who can stop its coming?' would be Buta Singh's weary answer. They sat down on the carpet and were soon busy discussing business affairs till the next visitor arrived with the same sad face and the same question. 'Very sorry to hear the news. How did it happen?' 'It was God's will. When the time is up. . . . ' Then as was customary, Buta Singh himself asked them to leave and go back to their work.

The women were more expressive. They drew veils as they came in, sat down on the ground, clasped each other by the shoulder, and rocked to and fro in silent embrace for a minute or two. Then they broke into a whine which changed to loud lamentation or beating of breasts till someone stopped them. They blew their noses in the hems of their shirts, wiped their tears with the backs of their hands, sighed, and turned to subjects closer to their hearts: a minute account of Sabhrai's last hour (followed by more crying). And then, 'Did Auntie Sabhrai fix her daughter up anywhere? How old is the girl now?' This lasted ten days. Then the relatives and the visitors departed and the family was left to itself.

Came the first of Phagan.

In accordance with Sabhrai's wishes, Shunno swept the gurudwara, opened the Granth, and got the family together. None of them was looking forward to it because this was an occasion closely associated with Sabhrai and for the first time in the living memory of any one of them, she was missing — and yet mysteriously present. She seemed to pervade the gurudwara like the incense which rose spirally from the stick and then scattered lazily all over the room.

Buta Singh took Sabhrai's place in reading the Granth. He had resolved to keep his emotions under control. He read the verse on the month of Phagan without faltering.

> She whose heart is full of love
> Is ever in full bloom.
> She is in bliss because she hath no love of self.
> Only those that love Thee
> Conquer self-love.
> Come Thou and abide in me.

> Many a lovely garment did I wear
> But the Master willed not, and
> His palace doors were barred to me.
> When He beckoned, I went
> With garlands and strings of jewels and raiments
>   of finery.

Spake the Guru:

> A bride welcomed in the Master's mansion
> Hath found her true Lord and love.

Buta Singh decided to say a few words to his family. 'Sabhrai has really found her true Lord and love, we. . . . ' He put his head on the Granth and began to sob. The whole family broke down and wept quietly. He gave up the attempt. After a while he proceeded to read the passage for the day:

> My eyes are wet as if nectar had dropped with
>   the dew and washed them.
> My soul is athrill and full of gratitude

For the Guru rubbed the touchstone with my
    heart
And found it was burnished gold.

Buta Singh was now in control of his emotions and decided to make another attempt. 'I only wanted to say this. I hope and pray that all of us will live up to the ideals of truth Sabhrai stood for. She was like the gold the Guru speaks of. She has left us and the light has gone out of our home. We must try to find our way in life in the same way as she did: through the Guru's words.'

Chapter XIII

Buta Singh had learnt not to rely too much on his memory. He did not make notes on the subjects he had to discuss, but usually numbered them and had symbols which fixed them in his mind. If it was only one thing he had to bring up, it didn't need much memorizing — and of course he thought of God, because there was only one God. Two didn't offer much difficulty either; it was 'just two things I had to ask you,' as one said even if there were more things to ask. There was no symbol for two. For three, there was the Trinity of Brahma the Creator, Vishnu the Preserver, and Shiva the Destroyer. Four was always causing trouble, but the mere fact that it caused trouble was good enough to remind him that he must have had four points to discuss. For five there were the 'Five Beloved Ones' — the first batch of converts to the Sikh faith made by the last Guru. And beyond five it was too much to expect symbols to remind him of what they were; they had to be put down in his notebook.

Buta Singh went over the 'Five Beloved Ones' one by one. First in importance was to thank Taylor for the honour done him in the New Year's Honours list; he had given up hope of it altogether after his son's arrest. Two, was to thank Mrs Taylor — if he saw her — or tell Mr Taylor to convey to his wife his thanks for all the kindnesses shown to the family over the terrible months

they had gone through. Third, was the business of his
son, which he had not understood clearly. If his son had
revealed the truth — as he must have for Buta Singh to
get his title — why had there been no other arrests? And
why had he been released in such a dramatic manner?
He had not asked his son because that was not the sort
of thing one talked about — particularly when the son
was being made so much of for his heroic stand against
police torture. Taylor might drop a hint as to what had
really happened. Fourth in order of importance was
Sher Singh's future. Couldn't Taylor help him to get a
job in the Government of India and save the boy from
the vagaries of a political life? He was bound to know
people in Delhi and an Englishman's recommendation
was so much more effective than any Indian's. Indian
VIPs were always recommending people for jobs in the
strongest terms and therefore no one took them seriously.
A mildly worded letter from a junior English official
could do miracles. That was four. Five! What was the
fifth? Oh yes, the memorial to Sabhrai. He couldn't
afford very much, but he would donate Rs 4,000 to 5,000
and perhaps Mr Taylor could suggest a charity and later
on open or inaugurate it. Sabhrai had been such a good
wife. Illiterate, but with some sort of charm that attracted
sophisticated Europeans like Mrs Taylor. The thought
brought tears to Buta Singh's eyes. He adjusted his black
tie — he had bought one especially for his first call on the
Deputy Commissioner after Sabhrai's death — and left
the house going rapidly over The Five Beloved Ones.'

Taylor was friendlier than ever before. He came out
into the verandah to receive Buta Singh and took him

inside. There was his wife, too, with the appropriate expression on her face. 'I was so sorry to hear about the Sardarini; I really was. I couldn't have felt the loss of any relation of my own more keenly. She had that something about her which makes people think of their own mothers. She reminded me of mine.'

'Thank you; very kind of you, madam. What God wills happens.' This was the fifth subject on the list; she was upsetting the order. How could one switch from that to being honoured in the New Year's list! 'Madam and madam's husband have been most kind to me and my family. I cannot find words to express my heartfelt gratitude.'

Joyce Taylor made a one word comment: 'Rubbish.' Her husband softened it. 'Not at all, Buta Singh. The last few months must have been somewhat trying for you all.'

Trying! These British with their understatements! It was like going through hell. Buta Singh answered in the same tone, 'Yes, sir, very trying.' Joyce Taylor went out to order tea. Buta Singh got the chance to tick off the first of the 'Five Beloved.'

'Sir, I must thank you again for my title. It is a great honour.'

'I am glad it came through, Buta Singh. You have done so much for the war effort. I was not sure if the people at the top would appreciate it. I was afraid somebody might distort this business of your son's and hold it against you. People are apt to be like that.'

'For that I have to thank my late wife, sir. She was the one to give good counsel to my son. I was too angry and disappointed at his disloyal behaviour. He had washed out the loyal services of four generations. I was relieved that in the end he redeemed it.'

Taylor looked a little puzzled. The expression on the Indian's face convinced Taylor that Buta Singh did not know what had passed between his wife and son in the lock-up. Taylor decided not to tell him. 'Your wife must have been a great influence on the family,' he remarked.

'She was old-fashioned and would not learn English,' answered Buta Singh. 'You know, sir, I got her many teachers, but she absolutely failed to learn the language. She was a very religious woman — she prayed all the time.' This was again number five. His son came before her. 'She was very keen that Sher Singh should give up politics and take up a steady job. If he could be fixed up somewhere in the government of India, I would be very happy.'

Taylor knew what the other was driving at. 'Sure, Buta Singh, I shall be only too pleased to help. Not that I count for much in the government of India.'

'How can you say that, sir? One word from you and everything will be done.' Buta Singh was happy. He would bring up the subject again when he had found out what to apply for and to whom.

Mrs Taylor came in carrying the tea-tray. She poured out the tea and handed Buta Singh his cup. Buta Singh took a noisy sip and put away the tea. Now for the fifth. He pulled a long face to preface the subject. 'Mrs Taylor, I want to seek your very kind advice on an important matter. I wish to erect a memorial for my late wife — a small library or a ward in a hospital or some such thing. I would be most grateful if you could advise me.'

'How thoughtful of you, Sardar Sahib! I will be delighted to help. Since she was so religious perhaps she would have liked to have given something to a religious institution — like a temple. I believe having wells dug is also a very popular form of charity in this part of the world. You must have known her mind?'

'You are right; she was very religious.' Buta Singh pondered. He couldn't possibly get Mr or Mrs Taylor to do anything with the building of a new gurudwara or having a well dug in some village. The object of the charity would be lost. 'You see she was illiterate,' he repeated, 'if I had asked her, she would have said, "Anything you like." That is why I ask you.'

'If you like I can find out what is needed in the city; we are short of practically everything. I will certainly let you know.'

Buta Singh was very pleased. He had succeeded in drawing Mrs Taylor into his plans. Now he needed no appointments to come here nor would he have to sit with other magistrates in the verandah waiting his turn to see Taylor. The 'Five Beloved Ones' had been satisfactorily dealt with. He finished his tea and put aside his cup. 'I must not waste your precious time,' he said, getting up. 'I will come and pay my respects again to you, Mrs Taylor. Goodbye, sir.'

'Goodbye, Sardar Sahib. It is so nice to see you cheerful after such a long time.'

'Thank you, madam. As a famous English poet has said, "All's well that ends well." '